CHARMED

www.**randomhousechildrens**.co.uk

Also by Michelle Krys

HEXED

CHARMED

MICHELLE KRYS

CORGI BOOKS

CHARMED
A CORGI BOOK 978 0 552 57166 1

Published in Great Britain by Corgi,
an imprint of Random House Children's Publishers UK
A Penguin Random House Company

This edition published 2015

1 3 5 7 9 10 8 6 4 2

Text copyright © Michelle Krys, 2015

Penguin Random House is committed to a sustainable future
for our business, our readers and our planet. This book is made
from Forest Stewardship Council® certified paper.

Random House Children's Publishers UK,
61–63 Uxbridge Road, London W5 5SA

www.**randomhousechildrens**.co.uk
www.**totallyrandombooks**.co.uk
www.**randomhouse**.co.uk

Addresses for companies within The Random House Group Limited
can be found at: www.randomhouse.co.uk/offices.htm

THE RANDOM HOUSE GROUP Limited Reg. No. 954009

A CIP catalogue record for this book is available from the British Library.

Printed and bound by CPI Group (UK) Ltd, Croydon, CR0 4YY

For Ben and Logan

Prologue

"**Y**ou have one new message, left yesterday at nine-forty-five p.m."

Static plays through the speaker, and then . . .

"Hello, Indigo."

Leo.

I gasp.

"I'm here with your friend Paige, and you know, even though you and I have had our problems in the past, I can agree with you on this one thing: she is an absolute doll."

There are muffled moans in the background. Someone grunts, and the sound of china shattering pierces through the phone. When Leo speaks again, his cool confidence is gone, and his voice is cut with an edge of hostility. "I was really hoping you'd come by and join us, but since you're not answering your phone, I think we'll just have to come to you."

1

Two Weeks Later

In medieval times, people were tortured with head crushers and limb-stretching devices. More recently, my ex-friend Bianca Cavanaugh tortured the fifteen members of our cheerleading squad with her brutal drills. And now? My aunt Penny is torturing me. Forcing me to have "a nice family dinner" with her—the very person who betrayed me— while my best friend, Paige, is missing, possibly dead.

I think I'd prefer the limb stretcher.

Aunt Penny sits across the dining room table from me, sawing into her dry pork chop. Cutlery scrapes against china. The grandfather clock ticks away the seconds, and I stare at her through eyes narrowed to slits, clutching my fork so hard my hand trembles in my effort not to leap across the table and go zombie-apocalypse on her.

She sighs heavily. "Indie—"

"It's Indigo," I interrupt.

She tenses at the venom in my voice.

Good.

"Okay . . . Indigo," she corrects herself. "I know you're very mad at me right now, but as your legal guardian, I couldn't let you keep living at your boyfriend's house."

I bark a laugh. "You *really* think I'm mad about that?"

Okay, so I *am* mad about that—after what my aunt did to me, she's the last person who should be telling me what to do, legal guardian status or no. But her barging into Bishop's house and demanding I come home or she'll call the cops to haul me back doesn't even crack the top ten list of the reasons I hate her. (Yes, I said hate. And yes, I know it's a strong word.)

"Oh," she replies.

And then it's back to the soul-sucking silence. It used to be that whenever Aunt Penny and I got together, we'd talk for hours about everything from boys to nail polish to our favorite movies. There was never a moment of quiet, and if there was, it was never awkward. But right now a conversation with a gynecologist while in stirrups seems comfortable by comparison.

"So what *are* you mad about, then?" she finally asks.

The heat grows in my core quickly, swirling and spitting like a ball of lava. Before I know what's happened, it's surged up and spread down my arms, stinging my fingertips like I've just come inside from the cold.

My magic.

I lay my fork down and draw my hands into my lap.

Aunt Penny knows *exactly* what I'm mad about. But as completely frustrating as her fake ignorance is, unleashing magic right now will just make everything worse. And so I close my eyes and take measured breaths until the heat sucks back into my core.

"You know who had to tell me?" I raise my eyebrows, challenging her to answer. "The Priory—one of the sorcerers who kidnapped Mom was the one to tell me my own aunt is a witch."

For a second it seems like Penny's going to cry, but then she closes her eyes, and when she opens them again, she levels me with a look more mom than aunt. "Listen, Indie, you don't know everything. Yes, I'm a witch."

My stomach does a little flip at hearing her admit the truth, but I try not to let it show on my face.

"But I can't use my magic," she adds.

I blink at her, trying to make sense of her words. In the sixteen days I've spent living at Bishop's house, I must have run through every possible reason, every possible scenario that could have led to my aunt's failure to help me when she knew my life was in danger. Every single one of them resulted in me cheerfully beating her to death. But this? This, I didn't think of.

She gets up and starts pacing behind her chair, twining her hands together. "See, a long time ago, when I was maybe a year older than you are now, I was well on my way to being a very, very powerful witch. I'd advanced so quickly with your grandma's training that I'd caught the Family's attention."

"You?" I blurt out.

"Yes, me," she says.

I can't hide my surprise. You'd have to be pretty damn great at magic to catch the attention of the leaders of witches and warlocks everywhere, and the only thing I've known Aunt Penny to be damn great at is body shots and being known by her first name at every club in Los Angeles County.

"They wanted me to work for them," she says. "Which was, like, this huge honor."

Honor, my ass. If the Family hadn't created fake copies of *The Witch Hunter's Bible* to divert the Priory's attention from the location of the real Bible—which contains a spell that allows a sorcerer to kill a witch without draining them of their powers—then Mom would be here right now, instead of six feet under. And Paige wouldn't be missing.

"I was the youngest witch ever to have an offer like that," she continues. "So I went to work for them. I started out doing small jobs, but I moved up quickly. And it was great for a while. I mean, there were some people who didn't like me, but Damien—he was the leader—he said it was natural, that they were just jealous of my talent. Truthfully, I think they were jealous that Damien treated me like his little pet."

"And then?" I prompt impatiently. Because I know how Aunt Penny's stories go, and they usually involve a lot of superfluous details and a lot of people having crushes on her. To think I used to love her stories.

"And then . . . I did something bad. Something very bad."

"Bad?" I repeat before I can stop myself. To say Aunt Penny isn't the most mature twenty-eight-year-old is like saying Lindsay Lohan has had a bit of trouble with the law. But Aunt Penny's always been the first one to brush off her problems. Like the time she was fired from a bistro for putting Tabasco sauce in an ex-boyfriend's drink—the tips were crappy anyway. If Aunt Penny thinks what she did was very bad, I'm willing to bet it's *impressively* bad.

Aunt Penny's face flushes, and she bites a corner of one manicured nail. "It was years ago, Ind. I was stupid, stupider than I am now. I wasn't really thinking. I mean, I knew I shouldn't have done it, but I was blinded. I just loved him so much, and—"

"Oh God," I say. "This is about a boy, isn't it?"

"It wasn't just any boy," she pleads. "I was in love with him! His name was Nate. God, he was so cute. The bluest blue eyes and the darkest hair. And he had these dimples."

I wave my hand impatiently.

"He was a sorcerer," she blurts out, then buries her face in her hands. "From the Priory."

"Oh, Penny." I mash my own palms into my eyes. "What were you thinking?" Hooking up with a member of the governing body of sorcerers everywhere? Sorcerers whose sole mission in life for centuries has been to maim and kill witches?

"I wasn't thinking, obviously. But you know how it is—I was in love! It could have worked out too if that wench Kendra hadn't followed me." She mutters swearwords under her breath, her brows drawn down over angry eyes.

I shake my head, my own anger boiling my blood. Right now, best-case scenario, Paige is somewhere scared for her life, and I'm sitting here listening to Aunt Penny's sexcapades.

"You know what?" I stand up so quickly the chair topples back. "This is too much. I really don't have time for this crap."

I storm up the stairs and slam my bedroom door so hard it's a miracle it doesn't come off the hinges. And then I fall facedown on my bed.

I won't cry.

I won't cry.

I will. Not. Cry.

My eyes sting with the threat of tears, so I think of everything that makes me mad—Mom's death; the fact that the Family used us as bait and didn't care if we all died; that Paige was kidnapped by Leo, the vilest sorcerer I can imagine, after our friendship had only just begun; that we killed Leo without knowing he'd kidnapped Paige, leaving us no way of finding her or even knowing if she's alive or dead somewhere. That I can't just be a normal sixteen-year-old girl whose biggest problem is a zit on prom night. Who answers *Seventeen* magazine quizzes to find out if my crush really likes me, and who drinks too much and regrets it the next day.

I don't want to cry—it's just so much easier to be mad.

But all my tricks don't work this time, and a tiny gasp escapes me.

So I'm going to cry.

As soon as I give myself permission, the ragged hole in my chest opens up, and I sob. I bury my face in my pillow to muffle the sound, but I'm sure I can be heard blocks away.

God, I'm so mad at her.

When Mom died, I felt like I'd been tossed into a raging sea in the middle of a storm, struggling to stay above water and losing strength by the second. But then Aunt Penny moved in, and between her and Paige, I felt like I'd been thrown a life preserver. Penny's the only family I have left with Mom gone, and to discover she lied to me, didn't help me when my life was on the line, made me feel like that life preserver had been violently ripped away.

By the time a few minutes have passed, my pillow is warm and damp, my eyes are hot and puffy, and my head pulses with the promise of a whopping headache.

I hear the door creak open, but I don't have the energy to get up and tell Aunt Penny to go away. She doesn't say a word, but I can feel her lingering in the doorway. Finally, her footsteps pad across the carpet and her weight sinks onto the end of my bed. A long minute passes in silence, save for my raspy breath.

I speak without turning to face her, finally asking the question that's been plaguing me since it all happened. "Why?"

I don't have to explain—she knows what I'm asking her. I've thought about this every day since that night at that swamp, and I've come to the conclusion that Aunt Penny might not have known about the trouble I was in before Mom died. But sometime between her death and the night of homecoming, Penny knew. Instead of helping me, she waved me out of the door in my crystal and taffeta gown, giving me some cryptic message that only by sheer luck I figured out was the key to saving our lives. I was chased by a fire-breathing dragon through the sewers of Los Angeles, starved, nearly drowned in a marsh in the middle of nowhere, and barely escaped being stabbed to death by the same sorcerers who killed my mom, all while I had a powerful witch living right under my nose. I want—no, I *need*—to know why she didn't help me. Even without using magic— why she didn't do anything at all. Call the cops, for God's sake. Do something!

She sucks in a shuddery breath as if holding back tears of her own.

"I think about it all the time," she says, her voice high and tight. "There's no good excuse. There isn't. There's nothing I can say that will make my actions okay."

It's not like Aunt Penny to admit she's wrong. And it's so surprising, I'm glad I'm not facing her so she can't see the tears that brim suddenly in my eyes.

"All I can do is tell you what went through my mind and hope"—she presses her hand against my calf tentatively, but when I tense, she draws it away—"hope you can understand, even in some small way, why I did what I did."

I say nothing.

"Getting together with Nate—that was considered treason by the Family. The last witch punished for treason was burned at the stake, and the one before was sent to the most god-awful place full of murderers—just a really bad place." She shudders. "So when the Family found out what I'd done I thought I was a goner. But I guess because Damien liked me so much he slapped me with an AMO instead."

I raise my eyebrows.

"An Anti-Magic Order," she clarifies.

She lifts the hem of her pants to reveal a thin silver bracelet around her ankle. A tiny round charm hangs off the chain. What looks like a family crest is stamped into the delicate metal.

"It's basically a magic tracker. If you use magic while you're wearing one of these, the Family will find out. I was ordered to wear one for the rest of my life, and Damien said if they discovered I'd used my magic he'd make me wish I was dead. And you don't understand—Damien, the Family—they're not nice people, Indie. If he threatens you, he *will* follow through." She lets go of her pant leg. "Anyway, that's why I didn't help you. But, Indie, you have no idea how hard it was for me to sit back when I knew something big was going on. I wanted to help. Really, I did. I was just so scared. I know now that's not good enough. I know I was wrong."

She lapses into silence. It's my turn to speak now, if I'm going to.

My brain fires a million miles a minute, trying to process all the new information. I don't know how to feel. All I know is that I'm still angry.

And so I say nothing. After a while she leaves.

When I'm sure she's gone, I roll onto my back and think about everything my aunt said. One minute I decide she couldn't have done anything to help without her magic, that she could have been burned alive if she'd tried, but the next I decide she's the most selfish person in Los Angeles—nay, the world—for valuing her life over mine. I'm so confused about how to feel that I become resentful of Aunt Penny all over again for making me use this much headspace on her when there's a bigger issue going on: Paige is missing.

I haven't admitted it to anyone—not even to myself—but I feel like I'm failing her. Statistics say if you don't find a missing person within forty-eight hours, they're likely dead.

It's been sixteen days.

Bishop and I have searched for her everywhere, done every spell imaginable. I've replayed the voice-mail message Leo left me over and over, trying to get a hint, listening for something I might have missed. But nothing. If I'd only known Paige had been taken hostage by Leo the night of homecoming instead of safely watching a marathon of *Jeopardy!* at Jessie's house, I never would have let him die. Not until we'd found her. And now we're reduced to questioning various lowlifes of Bishop's acquaintance for information, and though he won't say it, I know he's wondering if it's hopeless.

But I won't give up.

When that thought even dares to flicker into my mind, all I have to do is think of Paige—of her bangs falling over thick-rimmed leopard-print glasses, of the violin case hiked over her shoulders, of her unlaced Doc Martens and fishnets worn way before hipster clothes went mainstream, of her dashing across the street at two in the morning when I needed help, just to be a good friend—and I know I won't give up. I'm her only hope. It's too late for Mom, but not Paige. Not yet.

My phone vibrates on the end table, Bishop's name flashing across the screen. I remember I was supposed to call him.

"Bonding with your aunt yet?" he asks.

"Yeah, if that's what you want to call it." I wipe my nose with my sleeve, because no one's watching and I can.

"So it didn't go well then, huh? Are you upset?"

"I'll be fine," I answer unconvincingly. I start picking at a loose thread on my quilt.

"So I have a plan," he says. "It involves a violin and a fat man."

"I'm not in the mood for joking," I mutter.

"I'm serious. About the violin part, anyway. Can you get Paige's violin? Unless you'd rather we sneak into her bedroom, which is also doable."

"What?" I sit up, like it's going to help me understand his crazy talk a bit better.

"We're going to try a locating spell. Paige was always lugging that violin around, so I figured it'd be good for the personal-object part of the ceremony."

"A locating spell? But I thought you said we couldn't do one because we were missing the key ingredient—the magic mushroom or whatever."

"I did. And we were. I found it."

"You said it was impossible. If it was so easy, then why didn't you find it earlier?"

"Who said it was easy? I got a tip. And I had all this free time on my hands after my girlfriend moved out, so it was either follow that tip or turn to booze and strippers. It was a tough call but the tip won out."

I huff. "So where did you find the mushroom?"

"In this delightful little west-facing valley in Erlbach. We should really go there sometime. You'd love—"

"Erlbach?"

"Yeah. In Germany."

"You went to Germany," I say, incredulous.

"Yep."

"In the last couple of hours?"

"Yep."

"After I left your house?"

"Don't act so surprised," he says. "I'm getting offended. I am a practiced warlock, you know. So think you can get it? The violin."

My mind slips back to the morning after Paige went missing, when I'd knocked on her front door. I'd expected Mrs. Abernathy to be a mess of snot and tears, but instead our conversation went something like this:

> **Me:** OMG, is Paige here? Please, dear God, tell me she's here!
>
> **Mrs. Abernathy:** Would you like some tea? You seem like you could use a cup of tea.
>
> **Me:** I don't think you understand: I'm looking for your daughter. I think she's in grave danger.
>
> **Mrs. Abernathy:** I have mint and chamomile. Doesn't that sound nice?
>
> **Me:** She could be dead—her guts could be spilled out in some alley for rats to feast on.
>
> **Mrs. Abernathy:** Chamomile it is!

Okay, so that's not *exactly* how it went. But still. It was obvious she'd been brainwashed by someone, and she wasn't concerned Paige was gone.

"It's not at her house," I say.

"How can you be sure?" he asks.

"I looked around after Mrs. Abernathy told me about the music school."

During tea—that part actually happened—Mrs. Abernathy had broken the news to me that, due to a medical emergency with another student, Paige had been accepted late to the fancy-schmancy music school she'd applied to. Her mom didn't seem the least bit disturbed about the fact that she'd left in the middle of the night, on a weekend, midterm.

"Think Leo took it?" he asks. "You know, since she's supposed to be at this music school."

"Too much foresight for a grunt like him," I mutter.

"Hmm," Bishop says. "How 'bout her locker at school?"

"That's if she even has a locker anymore. She transferred, according to the school administrators. They might have emptied it already."

"Can you check?" he asks.

"You mean go to school?"

"I know. I hate to suggest such a torturous plan," Bishop chides.

I groan. It feels like centuries since I've been to school. "Well, I guess Aunt Penny's going to make me go anyway. She started talking about my grades slipping and me not getting into college like I actually care about that right now. God, she's impossible."

"Yeah, what a bitch," he says without any real heat behind it. "So you get the violin, and I'll get the other stuff ready. Pick you up after school?"

"Sure."

Then there's this awkward pause that's been happening a lot lately. We've been dating for less than a month, but sharing a bathroom and running for your lives together tends to make a couple close. A simple goodbye doesn't seem like enough. Finally, I mumble a goodnight and end the call.

I pull my body up to sitting and catch a glimpse of Paige's bedroom window glaring back at me accusingly through a break in my curtains. I cross over to my window.

All my life, Paige has lived so close I could reach out and touch her house if I wanted to, but instead I listened to Bianca when she'd said I couldn't afford to be friends with a loser. I wasted all those years pushing away the only real friend I'd ever had, and now she was gone.

The lampposts on Fuller Avenue flicker on, and I realize the sky has become the blue-gray color that comes just before full dark. My eyes are gritty and heavy with exhaustion. I know every minute counts, but I'm just so tired. I haven't been able to get in more than fitful naps since the night of homecoming—how could I, when Paige was out there somewhere, in danger?—but now it's almost impossible to stay awake.

I wake up sweat-soaked and gasping for air. I blink my eyes open into the damp pillow, the image of Mom from my nightmare—of her bound to a chair under the spotlight of a single bulb, a steady flow of thick blood oozing out around the knife buried in her temple—seared into my brain. My heart gives a painful twist. I do everything in my power not to think about Mom's gory death during waking hours, but it always finds me at night.

I wordlessly reach for Bishop, but all I find are cold sheets. It takes me a moment to realize I'm not at his house. And that something woke me.

The floorboards under the carpet creak behind me.

"I was sleeping," I say, irritated. Though I'm actually relieved to be woken up, whether or not it's for another sob session with Aunt Penny. My alarm clock flashes 1:26 a.m. in bright blue numbers; I probably could have slept all night. That's just unacceptable when Paige is missing.

Aunt Penny doesn't take the hint, though, and I need her to go away so I can sneak out. Growling, I roll over onto my back. "Can't this wait, I'm really—"

My words die in my throat. It's not Aunt Penny.

2

I scuttle up against the headboard, my heartbeat rapid-fire in my chest. The figure, much taller than my aunt, remains in the shadows, leaning against the wall opposite my bed.

Watching me.

"Who are you?" I demand.

It's silent a moment, and all I can hear is the sound of my heart thumping in my ears.

Then: laughter. Not a menacing snicker, but genuine, belly-clutching giggles.

Confusion gives way to indignation, and I gain enough sense to flick on my bedside lamp. Jezebel clamps a hand over her mouth to stifle her laughter, which only seems to get louder when I give her a venomous glare.

Jezebel's been MIA ever since the swamp debacle sixteen days ago. Not that I tried to find her or anything (I make it a point not to reach out to my boyfriend's hot exes, especially when they're as bitchy and self-centered as Jezebel). But apparently she hasn't been suffering too badly. Jezebel looks like she just stepped off a catwalk: a vision of high cheekbones, enviable curves, and shiny auburn hair falling in perfect curls over her shoulders. The hooker even makes jeans and a tank top look cutting edge.

I don't know what the hell she's doing in my room, but something tells me it isn't because she wants to paint my nails and have a pillow fight.

After a few minutes, she finally gets control of her laughter and straightens up.

"Done?" I ask.

She wipes tears from the corner of her eyes. "God, you should have seen your face."

"I'm glad you found that amusing. You do know the last time someone broke into my bedroom it was Frederick, and that he kidnapped and killed my mom?"

The smile drops off her face. "Right, forgot about that. Sorry."

I'm sure.

"What are you doing here anyway?" I demand.

"Just came to see how you're doing. You look like shit, by the way."

I cross my arms, hyperaware of my puffy, bloodshot eyes and snarl of curls. "I'm sorry I haven't had a chance to visit my stylist since my best friend went missing."

Jezebel shrugs.

"So where have you been?" I ask.

"None of your business."

"*Okay,* so what are you really doing here?"

"I'm offended, Indie." She ambles over to the computer desk next to my nightstand and falls into the little wooden chair. "But . . . since we're both here, there *is* something I wanted to talk about."

Ding, ding, ding!

Jezebel leans forward and rests her elbows on her knees, giving me an intense stare. "The Family, they really screwed us over, didn't they? It's not like they just created this fake Bible and sent it out into the world not knowing what deadly consequences could arise from it; they knew the Priory was gunning for it, knew you were being targeted, and they didn't help—they even agreed to help us on the night of homecoming and then didn't show up. They knew we'd die and they didn't care, just as long as their own Bible was safe."

"Yes, thanks for the reminder," I say dryly.

"The Family is supposed to lead us. Protect us. They're

supposed to uphold the law for witches and warlocks everywhere, but how can we trust them when they'd do this to their own people?"

"We can't," I agree.

"Exactly." She leans even farther forward, a fiery glint in her eyes. "That's why we have to get rid of them."

My heart falls into my stomach. "Get rid of them?"

"Exact our revenge," she says, and now her eyes look downright maniacal. "Let them know they can't do this anymore. Take away their power and give it to someone who would rule fairly."

I snort. "Like who, you?"

"No, not me." She dismisses me with a wave. "I don't know who, just not them. They're murderers, Ind. Don't you understand? It wasn't the Priory who killed your mom—it was the Family. It was because of them that the sorcerers were after you guys in the first place."

I think about it. She's right, in a way. "So what are you suggesting?"

A smile creeps onto her face, and I'm suddenly not so sure I want to know the answer to that.

"We use them as bait, just like they did with us. How many people were at your homecoming dance? A couple hundred?"

Dread pinches my nerves.

"A couple hundred people saw a dragon chase you through the ceiling of the Athenaeum." She pauses to let that sink in.

"And yet not *one* person has come forward to accuse you of witchcraft. Not one picture, not one cell-phone video has leaked to the Internet. How is that possible?"

I already know the answer. I just didn't want to acknowledge that I was the reason that hundreds of my classmates had their memories erased. I was once a victim of that myself, and I still feel sick to my stomach when I think about what might have happened to me before my memory was wiped. I wouldn't wish that feeling—one of such deep violation—on my worst enemy (i.e., on Bianca Cavanaugh).

"So what's that got to do with your plan?" I ask.

"It's the *key* to the plan," she answers cryptically. "We know the Family will come running if there's a chance the public could find out about witches. It's a risk to their very lives. Sorcerers can't kill a witch without draining themselves of their own powers—not without *The Witch Hunter's Bible*—but a human? A human could kill a witch. And look at what happened the last time the public thought witches existed. They can't risk a repeat of the Salem witch trials."

I have an idea where this is going, though I wish I didn't.

"All we have to do is stage something big—something that would get the Family to race over to clean up the mess and make sure there are no witnesses—then hit them with force when they're caught off guard." Jezebel leans back and drapes her arm over the chair back, satisfied. "I haven't thought of the perfect thing yet, but it'd have to be big. We could blow something up—"

"Blow something up?" I shriek.

"I know," Jezebel says. "That wouldn't really work. The public might think it was terrorist activity. It'd have to be something obviously paranormal."

I feel dangerously close to puking up my pork chop.

"It'd have to make the news too," she adds, lost in thought, her eyes focused on the middle distance. "Have to involve an L.A. landmark of some kind, something that people really care about. Maybe the Capitol Records building or the Staples Center. Oooh!" She straightens up excitedly. "LAX!"

"Jezebel," I say. "Are you crazy?"

Her smile melts into a scowl. "That's exactly what Bishop said."

"You talked to Bishop?" I ask before I realize how jealous I sound—correct that: am.

"He didn't tell you? Interesting."

So like Jezebel to latch on to my weakness like a vulture. The simmering heat in my core rises.

"I don't like the Family any more than you do," I say carefully, steering us back on topic, "but you're talking about putting innocent lives at risk. I wouldn't want any part of your plan even if I had the time to care about the Family. My best friend is missing, and all I care about right now is finding her."

"You're so small-minded," she spits, flicking her hair over her shoulder. "Think about someone other than yourself for once. This is for the good of our people, not just you."

"Oh please," I retort. "You can act like this is all for the greater good and blah blah blah, but it's obvious you just want to get back at the Family for bruising your little ego."

She stands up, her beautiful features twisted in anger. I kick off the blankets and stand too, though I wish I hadn't when I only come up to her chin (and I'm not short, not by a long shot).

"Can I get you a step stool?" she asks, giving a condescending laugh.

"Get out," I demand through gritted teeth.

It takes her a moment to realize I'm serious. I swear I actually see her eyes turn a darker shade of green. "You're going to regret this," she says, staring down her nose at me.

"Not as much as you're going to regret it if you don't get the hell out of my room," I counter.

She tosses her head and laughs again, and the heat of my magic surges up into my chest.

"You?" she says, pointing at me. "Are threatening *me*? You forget I've been a witch for *a lot* longer than you, honey. Not a smart move."

The heat stings my fingertips, growing hotter and hotter until it's almost unbearable. "Get out," I repeat.

"You're the crazy one," she says. "Look at you. What are you gonna do, huh? Attack me? I've seen your skills before, and trust me, they're not that impressive."

"Get. Out."

"Screw you," she says darkly. "You couldn't stop the

Priory when your own mother's life was at risk. What makes you think you can stop me if I wanted to hurt you now?"

I don't think before I act. All the anger overwhelms me, and I just want to hurt her. I hold out both my hands, and a blast of wind shoots from them, so powerful I can see the air currents. It rocks Jezebel back off her feet and she almost smashes into the window. Almost. She disappears before that can happen.

Vanishes into thin air.

3

I sit at the kitchen table, mechanically eating a bowl of
Cocoa Puffs even though I'm not remotely hungry. I feel
like a bad person eating a bowl of cereal when my best friend
is who knows where, suffering who knows what, and all because of me. But I've been getting brutal headaches lately,
and Bishop says it's probably from malnourishment. I'd ac-
cused him of being dramatic, but truthfully, he's probably
not far off the mark.

I can't stop thinking about what I did to Jezebel last
night. *Almost* did, I remind myself. I mean, sure, Jezebel's
a bitch and her plan was crazy with a capital *K*, but I really

wanted to hurt her. Who knows what I would have done if she hadn't made herself disappear?

"Don't look so pissy," Aunt Penny says, pulling out a chair and slumping down across from me. She's still in her fluffy pink bathrobe, and her blond hair is pulled up in a messy bun on top of her head.

"Trust me," she says, noticing the direction of my stare. "I don't want to be up this early either."

I look down into my cereal. If she thinks one little apology is all it takes for me to forgive her, then she's been watching a few too many Lifetime Originals.

Aunt Penny turns on the TV on the kitchen counter and flicks through the channels, pausing on the news.

"*. . . was last seen leaving school on Friday afternoon. Efforts to reach him via phone and social networking sites have been unsuccessful. His parents say this is out of character for Josh, and are asking the public to help search for the missing teen.*"

"Know him?" Aunt Penny asks, nodding at the TV.

On the bottom of the screen is a photo of a boy with bright blue eyes, scruffy red hair, and a smattering of freckles across his cheeks. He's wearing a baggy sweatshirt and scowling at the camera.

"Nope," I say, slurping up the last of my milk. I take my bowl over to the sink and give it a quick wash.

"I'm going to need you to work at the shop for a bit tonight," Aunt Penny says as I dry the bowl.

"What?" I whirl around, tea towel still in hand.

"I have a meeting with the bank at four. House stuff. It's really important or I wouldn't ask."

Must stay calm. Must not explode.

"It'll be for only a few hours at most," she adds.

I'm about to tell her where to shove her bank meeting when I realize that she's providing me with both the perfect place to perform the locating ceremony and a chunk of unsupervised time.

"Fine," I grumble. I chuck the tea towel into the sink for effect and grab my messenger bag.

"Come straight after school!" she calls to my back as I fly out of the front door into the bright morning sunshine.

I've never been particularly excited to go to school, despite managing straight As in all my classes (which are probably D's after the mounds of tests and assignments I missed in the sixteen days I've been absent), but today, the prospect is especially unappealing. There are a few reasons for this.

1) Paige is missing—duh.
2) I look like I should be at home hoarding newspapers and feeding my eighteen cats. Allow me to elaborate: my hair is an Afro on a good day. Without time to blow it out this

morning, it's an absolute nest of snarly blond curls and I wouldn't be surprised if an actual bird had made a home in there. I'm also still sporting dark shadows under my eyes that not even Aunt Penny's Hollywood makeup artistry could conceal, and I'm all too aware that the shirt I grabbed off the back of my chair has a jam stain, which I have to use the strap of my bag to conceal.

And lastly,

3) I have to face Bianca and the rest of the people who saw Bishop and me being chased by the dragon that Leo and his goons sent after us the night of homecoming. Despite all signs pointing to their memories of the incident having been wiped clean, I'm still nervous to see everyone for the first time.

And the worst part? I have to do it alone. I briefly tossed around the idea of begging Aunt Penny to consider home-schooling until I realized QT with my aunt would be more painful than school.

I park my Sunfire, then take a quick glance in the rear-view mirror. I shudder and make a mental note to avoid any reflective surfaces for the rest of the day.

The hallways are a din of voices, laughter, and the metallic sound of lockers slamming closed. A massive blue and silver banner strung across the hall proudly proclaims Fairfield as the winner of the annual homecoming game against Beverly Hills High—Go Renegades—and members of the football team engage in a wrestling match, which Mrs. Hornby tries to break up as a crowd calls out bets on the winner.

For a split second, it's comforting, the familiarity of the place. I start to feel like, hey, maybe the world *hasn't* tipped off its axis. But in that same split second I remember that— no—everything isn't normal, Paige isn't here, and then I'm angry with myself for deigning to think anything could be okay when it's so, so not.

At least no one's staring at me, I think as I maneuver through the halls toward my locker.

Someone grabs my arm and says, "Indie?" very hesitantly.

Thea, all four feet nine of her, stares up at me with eyes the shape of saucers as she realizes that, yes, in fact, it *is* Indie. She drops her hand from my arm as though looking like crap might be contagious.

Heat creeps up my neck and onto my cheeks. "Hi, Thea."

"What happened to you?" she asks.

I roll my eyes. Does the girl have no tact? I'm inclined to tell her that my chemo has been especially hard this month, just to make her feel bad for asking such a dumb question. Instead, I settle for the vague "I just haven't been sleeping well lately."

Thea gives a slow blink. "Oh. Well, where have you been?

You missed, like, a trillion cheer practices and you weren't at the mandatory meeting on Sunday. Did you drop out of the squad?"

"Well, nobody informed me about this mandatory cheer meeting on Sunday, so why would I have shown up?"

I guess I must have said that a little more tersely than I'd planned, because there's at least a handful of people staring at me now and whispering behind cupped hands. Goodbye, anonymity.

Thea shrinks visibly. "I dunno. . . ."

I heave a sigh—I'm taking out my anger on the wrong person. It's not Thea's fault I wasn't invited. "Anyway, no, I'm not going to be on the team anymore. I've realized cheerleading's not my thing."

"You mean, it's not a loser thing?"

I stiffen at the sound of Bianca's voice behind me.

Snickers bounce along the hallway, and I swear a freaking spotlight descends on me in all my ratty-haired glory. Of course it was too much to hope that she'd died of Ebola since I last saw her.

Heels clacking, Bianca walks around me. Her white-blond hair is clipped back from her face, the rest falling in gleaming strands somewhere between her shoulders and boobs (which, FYI, are on full display in her low-cut tank top).

She gives me a long up-and-down appraisal, and a grin pulls up her lips. Now more than ever I wish I knew how to conjure objects, just so I could make Valtrex tumble out of her pocket. I can't believe I ever thought this girl was my friend.

"I think you're conveniently forgetting I chose not to be friends with you, Bianca," I say.

"Right," she answers. "And it looks like you've been pretty torn up about it too."

"Ha-ha," I deadpan. "But actually, that's one decision I know I'll never regret. Unlike you, who will probably regret many things, like the incident in Ian's bathroom last spring, for example?"

Her face burns redder than if her mom had caught her reading *Fifty Shades of Grey*. I give her an innocent smile. I like to think I wouldn't stoop as low as Bianca and spread around all the dirt I have on her, but I'm not above threatening to do it, and often, if just to see her squirm the way she's made countless others do.

"Come on, guys, no fighting."

As if this morning couldn't get worse.

Devon sidles up, blond waves flopping around his tanned face and a backpack slung over one shoulder.

"Can't we all get along?" he adds.

I want to sock my cheating asshole of an ex. Bianca looks like she does too. But then her expression clears and she smiles a deranged sort of smile.

"You're right, sweetie." She hooks her hands around Devon's neck and pulls him in for a deep kiss. For a moment he looks embarrassed, but then he draws her in by the waist, shoving his tongue down her throat like he's trying to eat her face.

The wind is knocked out of me.

I know I shouldn't care. I have a much better boyfriend now, and I'm pretty sure all girl codes for dating your friend's ex are off if you're no longer friends . . . But still. Could they have moved on any faster?

Everyone's looking at me. I fight the urge to call a meeting at the bike racks at three o'clock.

"Well, the plot thickens," I say flatly, feigning nonchalance.

The bell rings, and I couldn't be more grateful. I step around the tangled bodies, the crowd giving me a wide berth as I pass like I'm some sort of leper.

I know it'd be easier if Paige were here. She'd laugh at all this. Tell me they were lemmings and who the hell cares what lemmings think. I feel a pang in my gut that she's not here with me now. That she might never be again.

I've been at school for all of six minutes and already I'm counting down until I can leave.

In homeroom, Mrs. Davies drones on about the yearbook committee's desperate call for members, while Bianca stage-whispers in the back of the class to a rapt crowd about the annual *HallowSCREAM!* party she's throwing the weekend before Halloween (she whispers especially loud so I'll know what I'm missing out on by not being invited). To make matters worse, I keep catching Paige's transfer-student friend Jessie Colburn staring at me. Even when I'm not looking at her, I can feel her eyes following me like the freaking *Mona Lisa*. I decide now's as good a time as any to get the violin.

I raise my hand.

Mrs. Davies pauses reluctantly. "Yes, Ms. Blackwood?"

"I need to use the bathroom."

"Do you ever," Bianca says, and the class erupts into laughter.

I cut her a glare.

"Bianca Cavanaugh," Mrs. Davies says, tsking, then turns to me. "Yes, go ahead, Indigo."

I snag one of the orange lanyard hall passes from her desk on my way out.

"Not too long!" Davies calls after me.

My shoes squeak loudly in the hall, the sound echoing off the army green lockers. It's empty now, but that could change at any moment. I make a beeline toward Paige's locker and say a silent thank-you for the MUSIC NERDS RULE! sticker she's got plastered across the front—I won't have to waste my time breaking into the wrong locker. I do a quick shoulder check to make sure a teacher isn't lurking in the hallway, and then take the combination lock into my hands.

I close my eyes and call out to the heat. It responds with a flash of warmth that spreads like fireworks up my body. I whisper the Latin word for "open."

"Aperi, aperi, aperi."

The lock clicks heavily in my hands, and a satisfied smile blooms across my face.

"What's going on?"

I gasp, spinning around to find Jessie with her arms crossed over her chest, an orange hall pass slung around her neck.

Dammit to hell.

"I—I was just . . ."

"That's Paige's locker," she says.

Heat courses to my cheeks. "I know that. I was . . . getting something for her."

She arches an eyebrow, challenging me. Could she have seen me do my little trick?

I push my shoulders back. "She gave me her combination."

She looks down at my hands, I guess to confirm I'm not hiding a hacksaw up my sleeve. "So then why'd you sneak out to do it?"

"Who says I snuck out? I had to use the bathroom, then I remembered the thing Paige wanted and dropped by here."

We engage in a staring contest for a few seconds, before Jessie gestures to the locker as if giving me permission to open it.

I pull the metal door open, and have to stop myself from crying out with relief when I see the black violin case propped up on a stack of books.

"There it is," I say, pulling out the case.

"She went to music school without her violin?" Jessie asks.

Crap.

"Yep. Funny, huh? She was in a really big hurry, and school was closed when she left. I'm giving it to Mrs. Abernathy so she can send it to Paige."

Jessie stares at me while I hike the case onto my back.

"Well," I say. "Love to chat, but I need to get back to class."

I paste on a smile, then make a quick escape down the hallway. I don't know how I'm going to explain the violin to Mrs. Davies, but in the grand scheme of my problems, it doesn't even rate.

4

The bell above the door jangles as I enter the Black Cat. I expected to be sad coming to Mom's beloved occult shop after so long away, but it's so much worse than that: walking inside strikes me like a baseball bat straight to the gut. If Aunt Penny wasn't ringing up some goth kid at the till, I might lunge at her.

The big oak bookcase that took up the entire back wall until the night *The Witch Hunter's Bible* was stolen and the bookcase destroyed has been replaced with a new, more modern dark wood shelf. It's still filled with the same explosion of occult books, but Aunt Penny has them all stacked perfectly instead of in the pattern Mom preferred, with some lying horizontally now and then "for variety." The same pentagrams hang from the low ceiling, the same old Turkish rug is spread across the hardwood floor, but the black cauldron that used to be on display in the center of the store is now in front of the window, and racks of bath salts have taken its place. The shop even smells different somehow.

I hate it.

While Aunt Penny counts out change, I shove the violin case behind a shelf before she sees it and starts asking questions I don't want to answer. When the customer leaves with his ceremonial dagger or whatever, I sulk over to the counter.

"Like what you've done with the place," I say. "Might have waited for Mom's body to cool before redecorating, though."

Aunt Penny chews the corners of her fingernails and looks around the store anxiously. "You hate it. I'll move it back. I just thought I'd try something new. The cauldron took up so much space in the middle of the room."

Mom always said that too. I say nothing, though, plopping heavily into the chair behind the till.

"Listen, thanks for doing this," Aunt Penny continues. "I really need to sort this house stuff out. It's been such a pain trying to get the mortgage moved over to my name. I mean, I don't exactly have the most solid credit history and—"

"Yep, no problem," I interrupt.

Aunt Penny visibly deflates. I feel a pang in my gut about

being such a jerk after she poured her heart out to me yesterday, and briefly consider apologizing, but she's already grabbing her purse.

The door jangles on her way out, and I'm alone in the shop. I pull out my cell and text Bishop.

> The wicked witch is gone.

"You don't say."

I shriek, practically leaping off the chair.

Bishop leans against the bookcase, his hands jammed in the pockets of his slim black pants and his lace-up army boots crossed casually at the ankles. He gives me a brazenly sexy smile that makes laugh lines sprout up around his eyes, and his dark hair falls in tangled waves around his chin, almost concealing the naked Betty Boop tattoo that snakes out from the collar of his faded leather jacket. My mouth goes dry at the sight of my boyfriend. The guy could wear footie pajamas and still look sexy.

"You scared me, you know." Which is *so* not convincing when I'm smiling like an idiot.

He pushes off the bookcase, laughing as he approaches.

"Couldn't help myself. Been thinking about you in your old cheerleading uniform all day. It was torture."

"God, you're such a perv," I mutter, but I'm smiling.

He hooks his fingers in the belt loops of my jeans and tugs me against his chest, so I have to crane my neck to see his face (being the six-three giant of a boy that he is). My heartbeat quickens at his nearness and the sight of his brown eyes winking with mischief.

He moves a hand from my jeans and tips my chin up. My stomach warms as his lips brush mine, and this time it has nothing to do with my magic. He pulls his fingers through my hair, sending a tingle down my spine. Then he cradles my head in his hands to take the kiss deeper. When his tongue finds mine, a moan involuntarily slips out of my mouth. My cheeks flame, and he chuckles against my lips.

Huffing, I push against his chest until there's a big space between us. "Laugh it up, asshole."

"Hey, come back here," he says, grinning.

It's tempting, but I'm sober enough now to realize that a snogfest with my boyfriend while my best friend is missing definitely qualifies me for some sort of Shitty Person award.

"I don't know how long we have before Aunt Penny gets back," I say, crossing to the door. "Get the curtains." I flip the dead bolt closed and flick off the neon Open sign while Bishop lowers the venetian blinds over the big picture window so that we're enveloped in darkness. A sense of déjà vu washes over me, and I remember the summonings we did to hear Mom's voice. I won't let myself do those anymore. It's too painful.

"You got the goods?" Bishop asks.

I pull the violin case from its hiding spot behind the shelf near the door. "Yep. And for the record, you sound like a drug dealer."

"What would you know about that?" he asks, a thick caterpillar eyebrow arched high.

"I've watched movies," I say, mock-offended. "So, what do I do with this?"

"Lay it down there," he says, indicating the center of the rug. Metal scrapes as he drags the cauldron from its display by the window and hauls it next to the violin. Then he disappears down a darkened aisle. He returns moments later with five fat candles bundled in his arms.

"Hope your aunt doesn't mind us borrowing," he says, grinning.

He sets the candles around the violin and cauldron. With a flick of his hand, the candles burst into flame, lighting the room with a soft orange glow. I realize that if I connected the dots, they'd form the shape of a pentagram.

Bishop pulls a crumpled piece of paper from his jacket pocket and brings it close to his face.

"Oh. I guess we should have gotten inside the circle before I lit them," he mumbles.

"Dear God, tell me those aren't instructions," I say.

"What? I've never done it before." He pockets the paper. "Okay, we need to get inside the circle and face west."

I take a careful step between two burning candles and stand next to Bishop as he pulls a little black pouch out of his pocket. He releases the tie cord and shakes the bag's contents into his hand. A mushroom with a fat stem and bulbous, black top with tiny freckles of white sits in his palm. My heart gives a hard beat.

Bishop makes a fist and crushes the mushroom, then shakes the crumbled black remnants into the cauldron, dusting off his hands when he's done. Then he pulls a medicine dropper from his breast pocket. Red liquid sloshes inside.

"What's that?"

"Blood of fox."

"You killed a fox?" I shriek.

"I bought it pre-vialed," he says. "Relax."

I don't bother to ask from where as he leans over the cauldron and carefully dispenses three drops inside. When the third drop hits, a huge puff of smoke erupts. Bishop reels back in a coughing fit. When the smoke settles, I see that the cauldron is full to the brim with thick, black bubbling liquid. Steam hovers around the edges of the pot, filling the shop with the metallic scent of blood and, strangely, cooked meat.

"Whoa," I breathe. "That's insane." I peer into the cauldron. "So what now? Eye of newt? Toe of frog?"

"Now we sit," Bishop says.

He settles onto the carpet. I sit cross-legged next to him, our knees bumping awkwardly in the candlelit room.

"Wanna make out first?" he says into my ear in a corny soap-actor voice. I give him a playful punch on the shoulder that almost knocks him over. "Right. Later, then. The goal of the ceremony is to invoke the energy of the person we're trying to locate. The personal item allows the magic to focus on the correct person."

"Did you get that from your cue card?" I ask.

"I thought we were being serious," he answers.

I motion that I'm zipping my lips.

"According to my cue card," he continues, "the witch or warlock should put their hands to the cauldron and summon all their magic inside it while chanting the spell. If done correctly, an image should appear inside the cauldron of the location of the missing person." He looks at me, going off script. "You could probably do it by yourself, but I figured you might need the boost since you're new. I hope you don't mind."

I smile at my boyfriend; he could be doing anything in the world right now, and he chooses to be with me, doing everything in his power to help me find my best friend. I interlock my fingers with his. He gives me a small smile, and we put our hands onto the cold metal of the cauldron.

"I feel like a real witch," I whisper.

Bishop hisses at me to be quiet, suddenly all business.

I call the heat. Maybe it's the candles—which Bishop says are like an energy drink for witches—but my magic bursts to life inside my stomach almost before it's a thought in my head, burning like a hot oven in my body, making me delirious. A thrill passes through my veins as the heat surges down to my fingertips. The sound of busy Melrose Avenue traffic becomes muted by the thumping heartbeat in my ears.

And then I close my eyes and concentrate, because moving my magic outside of my body has always been the trickiest part.

"*Inveniere Paige Abernathy,*" Bishop says, his voice loud in the quiet shop.

I join in.

"*Inveniere Paige Abernathy. Inveniere Paige Abernathy.*" Our voices sync, and beneath my hands I feel the cauldron vibrate slightly with our combined force. *It's working!*

Bishop shifts beside me. I open my eyes to find him kneeling over the cauldron. I follow his lead and peer inside.

Nothing but the swirling black sludge.

"What happened?" I ask. "It seemed like it was working."

Bishop pulls out his note and scans the directions. "We didn't miss anything." He shoves the paper back in his pocket and grabs hold of the sides of the cauldron again. "Come on," he says, nodding me into action.

We repeat the words. Just like last time, the cauldron hums to life under our touch. And just like last time, the spell doesn't work.

"I don't get it," Bishop says.

I slump back onto my butt, disappointment weighting my heart. "Maybe we did it wrong," I say listlessly. "Maybe that was a bunk mushroom."

"The mushroom was fine. We did it right." His tone leaves no room for argument, but still, he scans the directions again.

"Maybe it's the violin," he says. "Can you think of anything more personal to Paige?"

"This is her prized possession. There's nothing better in the world."

"Then I don't get it," he says. "It doesn't make sense." He continues to examine his note and mumble to himself, while I sit in silence, feeling dead inside. We're back to square one. The realization that we might not ever find Paige makes tears prick my eyes. I should never have gotten Paige involved. Never asked for her help. It was selfish. Unbelievably selfish and awful and—

"I know someone we can talk to," Bishop finally says.

———•———

I skip out of school after homeroom the next day. I've figured out that if I make it to roll call, then I won't trigger the automated message to my house that I've missed class. Sure, someone will eventually call home personally and Aunt Penny will catch on that I haven't really been going to school, but it buys me some time. And that's all I need right now.

As I slip outside I try not to think about the mountains of homework I'm behind on and the upcoming math test that I'm going to epically fail. I have to shield my eyes from the glaring morning sun to scan the school property for Bishop. From literally a mile away, across the huge expanse of lawn,

I spot his Mustang, pulled up to the curb. It's hard to miss, with the bright yellow racing stripe across the body of the cherry-red muscle car.

I make a dash across the lawn, lest someone notice I'm fleeing and try to stop me. Bishop guns the engine as I near. I make throat-cutting gestures at him, but that only makes him laugh. I swing open the door and fall into the bucket seat, ducking my head low while Bishop peels away.

He pumps a fist out the window. "See you in our dust, suckas!"

"Would you stop it? This is serious." I can't help but laugh as I sit up, though. Dude could make crocheting doilies fun.

"So where are we going?" I ask, looking out the window as we zip past the palm trees that line the road.

"Venice Beach."

I scrunch up my face.

"It's where the Black Market is," Bishop says. "A street market for magic."

"At the boardwalk?"

"Yep." He turns up the volume on the radio so that an eighties punk-rock song blasts through the speakers. He sings along absently while we merge into the bumper-to-bumper traffic on the freeway.

It's hotter than usual for so early in the morning, and the sun beats down through the windshield. By the time we get to Venice Beach and Bishop parks, my legs are stuck to the leather seats and it's actually painful to get out of the car.

But Venice Beach doesn't disappoint. The ocean is impossibly blue, and the beach stretches for miles, white-as-snow sand crammed with so many people that they look like ants converging on a three-day-old half-eaten cookie. The boardwalk itself is just as busy, swarming with people in various states of undress, skateboarders and cyclists darting through the foot traffic. Vibrant blue, green, and pink low-roofed shops and booths face the water, filling up every possible square inch of retail space. The guitar riffs and drumbeats of street performers filter down from the market, and seagulls caw and circle overhead, periodically diving low to snatch at food or crap on someone's head. The scent of deep-fried food and suntan lotion hangs heavy in the air.

"This way," Bishop says, hooking his arm through mine. We hike over to the boardwalk. Before long we're dodging Jesus prophets and skateboarders, weaving through a crowd gathered around a guy swallowing fire and another walking on six-foot-high stilts. An outsider might be convinced this is a magic market, but not me.

I stop. A few beats later, Bishop notices I'm not following him and turns around.

"What's wrong?" he asks.

"I don't see a magic market here." I don't worry that I said it out loud and people might have heard. It'd hardly make me the weirdest person here today.

"That's right," he says, grinning, so his eyes crinkle up

adorably at the corners. I get the distinct feeling I'm missing something. I look around, but the scene is the same as moments before.

Bishop comes up behind me and puts his hands on my shoulders. His chest presses into my back as he leans down to speak into my ear.

"What do you see?" he asks. His lips graze my skin and a flash of heat involuntarily shoots down into my stomach.

I clear my throat. "Uh, I see a man who probably shouldn't be wearing a Speedo." He says nothing, so I continue. "I see a lot of overpriced souvenirs, a lot of mindless commercialism . . . um, a lot of palm trees?"

"Close your eyes," he says. I huff and do as he says. "Now repeat after me. *Videre, videre, videre.*"

"*Videre, videre, videre,*" I repeat.

"Now look again. And this time, *really* look."

I open my eyes. An entire row of booths has sprung up across from the existing, familiar ones, creating a narrow street market.

If I thought this place was weird before . . .

A woman walks past me, her hair so long it drags like a veil on the littered pavement. Four little people dressed in period clothing chant around a bonfire in the street that sends curls of smoke and dust into the sky. A bald man wearing absolutely not a stitch of clothing presses long needles into his stomach like no one's watching—which they aren't—and a woman walks past with an owl perched on her shoulder, muttering to herself in a clipped accent. The smell of exotic spices and farm animals fills my nose.

"Come on," Bishop says. He leads me farther into the land of the freaks.

I take a closer look at the booths—one has what appears to be raccoons hung from the rafters by their tails. A sign outside reads SACRIFICES. Another booth sells bottles and fluted vases in various sizes and colors, another one carries creepy porcelain dolls, and I don't even want to know what the booth swathed in rich, black velvet with only a picture of a human skeleton on the outside sells. A rooster crows close by. I recoil as a flash of white feathers runs past chased by an irritated old woman in a beaded gown. If it weren't for the fat guy in the Speedo, who walks past a fortune-teller's booth without so much as a glance at the Morticia Addams look-alike calling to him, I'd swear we'd been transported to a market in the 1600s.

"No one can see this?" I ask, despite it being obvious. I myself couldn't see it just moments before.

"Just us magical folk," Bishop says. He keeps a brisk pace, and I hurry to keep close to his side.

"Cat bones!" a woman calls. "Ten for ten. Cheapest in town." She leans out from her booth as we pass. "Won't find cheaper anywhere. Ten for ten. Okay, ten for five. Cat bones. Ah, whatever." She gives up on us and slumps back onto her stool.

I try not to make eye contact with any of the vendors after that, lest they think I'm interested in their wares. I stick close to Bishop, stopping myself from clinging to his arm only because it's not the 1920s and feminism and whatnot.

He squints into the booths as we pass, mumbling.

"What are we looking for?" I ask.

"Irena," he answers. "She's a genius. If anyone knows anything about why the locating spell isn't working, it'd be her."

I shrug. I doubt Bishop's friend is going to be able to help, but I can tell he feels like he failed me with the spell, so for him, I go along with it.

A nagging feeling that someone is watching me begins to tickle at my brain. I try to ignore it, but it's too hard to resist casting a look around. My eyes catch on a woman three booths down. Her wrinkled skin is the palest I've ever seen on a living person, so fair I can see the blue river of veins beneath it. Her eyes are circled with dark shadows, as though she hasn't slept in a century, and her gray hair is thinning to the point I might call her balding.

And she's staring right at me.

A thousand people on the boardwalk, and she's staring straight at me. I suck in a little breath, my heart hammering in my chest.

Bishop notices the focus of my attention and draws a protective arm around me, pulling me against him as he walks steadily through the crowd. I crane my neck to watch the woman until we get too far away to see her clearly. A chill shudders through me.

"Finally," Bishop says.

He pulls me up to a tent draped in dark purple beaded silk. A sign out front reads simply IRENA'S. Bishop draws back the curtain, and I almost have a coronary right there.

Based on what I've seen of the Black Market so far, I expected Irena to be a creepy old woman, possibly fat and goitered. Instead, I find a drop-dead-gorgeous girl whose pale blue eyes contrast sharply with smooth skin the color of a Werther's Original. Her lips are red-stained and sensual, and a mane of shiny dark hair tumbles in thick waves over a chest busting out of her corset gown. She sits gracefully on a ruby-red cushion surrounded by candles, looking like an Egyptian princess. Of course this is Bishop's friend. *Of course.*

"Bishop!" she purrs, climbing to her feet. I give him the side eye. He shrugs and sends me a look that distinctly says "What? Don't blame me!" as she draws him into a warm hug. She seems to notice me for the first time over his shoulder, and dismisses me with a cool glance.

It's not exactly like I fell out of the ugly tree and hit every branch on the way down, but next to Irena I can't help feeling like my every flaw is on display—Afroed hair, practically no boobs, knobby knees. I have to wonder just what Bishop sees in me when he's got girls like Irena and Jezebel fawning all over him. I can feel my bottom lip jutting out farther by the second.

"I heard the news about the Priory," Irena says into his neck before finally releasing him from her clutches. "Everyone's been talking about it."

"Actually, that's why we're here," Bishop says.

"Oh?"

"I have reason to believe—" He stops and grabs my hand, interlocking our fingers. I feel a burst of happiness and can't help smiling as Irena looks down at our joined hands. I swear I can actually see her hormones snuff out.

"*We* have reason to believe our friend was kidnapped by the Priory before they were killed," Bishop finishes.

"That *is* a problem," she says disinterestedly. "So you want to find her?"

Duh. Genius, my ass.

"We've tried a locating spell and it didn't work."

"And you used a deeply personal possession?" she asks.

"Yes," Bishop answers.

"And you're sure it's personal?" she asks, falling heavily back onto her cushion, like the pretty-pretty-princess act was only for when Bishop was available. "Because that's important."

"Yes, I'm sure," I cut in, annoyed. Like I don't know my best friend.

"And you did the spell correctly?" she asks.

"Yes," Bishop says, matching my annoyed tone.

"Then there's only one place she could be." She locks eyes with me for the first time since we entered her tent. "And it's not on earth."

5

I can't breathe. Paige can't be dead. She can't be.

"What's her problem?" Irena asks, looking at me as though I'm an animal behaving in a strange yet fascinating way.

"She thinks you're saying her best friend is dead," Bishop answers before turning to me to interpret. "That's not what she meant."

My head spins so fast I can't form words.

Irena rolls her eyes. "Even if your friend were dead, you could summon her voice. If you can't summon her at all it means she's not on this earth, in this dimension."

I try to grasp her words, but it's like she's speaking another language. What I do register is this: Paige isn't dead. I suck in a breath, feeling my lungs expand enough that I can finally take in a good breath.

"She doesn't know about Los Demonios?" Irena asks Bishop.

"She only just had her two hundredth moon," he says defensively. "And lots has happened since then." He turns to me. "There's another dimension."

"Yeah, I got that," I say, just to remind everyone that I'm not, in fact, an invalid. "Los Demonios. And you think Paige could be there?"

"That can't be," Bishop responds. "Why would the Priory bring her there? They kidnapped her for leverage. What would be the point if they couldn't get her out after?"

Irena shrugs, playing with the ends of her hair. "I don't pretend to understand sorcerers."

"Wait a minute," I say, stepping around Bishop. "What's this about not getting her out?"

Irena looks at Bishop. I know instantly that whatever she's going to say next isn't going to be good.

"This other dimension—" she starts.

"Not just anyone can go there," Bishop interrupts. "In fact, most people would never want to go there."

"Why?" I ask, though I'm not sure I want to know. Nerves skitter in my stomach, making bile rise up my throat.

Bishop looks as though he's searching for the right words.

"It's a prison," Irena blurts. "Los Demonios is an alternate dimension of Los Angeles where the most evil and murderous witches and sorcerers are sent after they've been convicted for a crime."

A dimension filled with evil paranormals? And Paige is there? To think that just moments before I thought it was good news when Irena said she wasn't dead.

"Oh God, why?" I whine.

"Because they couldn't be sent to regular jail," Irena answers, with a dismissive flick of her hair, misinterpreting my lament as a question. "They'd just magic themselves free."

Bishop drags a stool over and sits me down, and I put my head between my knees the way Mr. Johnson made the kid do when he almost fainted after we'd dissected a pig in Biology last year. It doesn't help; my head spins so fast it makes me dizzy. It's because of me that Paige is in Los Demonios. Because she's my friend that she's in unspeakable amounts of danger. She must be losing her mind with fear.

"How do we get her out?" I finally ask.

They're both silent. The sounds of the boardwalk filter inside the tent.

"How do we get her out?" I yell.

"Indie," Bishop says, and the way he says it is like an apology. "Los Demonios isn't like prison here. There are no appeals, no time off for good behavior."

"What is that supposed to mean? She's not a criminal!"

Irena heaves an annoyed sigh. "The portal to LD goes only one way. Once you're in, you're in. And you're not getting out unless someone from the outside lets you out."

"We'll let her out, then!"

"Indie, only top-level Family members know where the portal is. Even my uncle has no idea where it could be, and he's been in the Family for two decades."

"So we'll talk to them. Once the Family realizes what happened . . ."

I trail off. I almost got slaughtered a couple of weeks ago because of the Family. Their sole concern in life is to protect *The Witch Hunter's Bible* so they can continue to dominate the paranormal world. They aren't going to suddenly grow hearts and give me access to a top-secret paranormal prison just because one human life is in danger.

"We'll find out where the portal is, then," I say.

"Good luck," Irena says. "People have been searching for that thing for centuries. You're not the first person to want to break someone out of the clink."

I let out a strangled moan, despair and frustration breaking me down. "You can't tell me there's no way!"

Bishop pulls me against him, and I dissolve into tears.

I flip down the rearview mirror. Yep, just like I thought. I look like crap warmed over. My eyes are red-rimmed and puffy, and pretty much any makeup I had on when I left the house this morning has been washed away, revealing a nose and cheeks that would make an alcoholic jealous.

Sighing, I flip the mirror up and grab my bag from the passenger seat. If I get upstairs quickly and quietly enough, Aunt Penny won't see my bedraggled appearance and start asking questions.

I climb the steps to the house, making as little noise as humanly—or witchly—possible. But when I open the door Aunt Penny is standing at the foot of the stairs, both hands squarely on her hips as she gives me the bored/exasperated expression that moms are famous for.

"Where have you been?" she asks.

Awesome.

"Did you practice that in front of the mirror?" I answer, stepping inside and pulling the door closed.

"Don't change the subject. I got a call from the school today. You skipped out after homeroom."

Damn. That was sooner than I expected. I mentally run through a few plausible excuses.

"I want the truth," she says, as if reading my mind.

I toss my bag onto the stairs and look Aunt Penny straight in the eye. "I was searching for Paige. You know, my best friend who went missing?"

She pinches the bridge of her nose.

"But no worries," I continue. "We found out where she is: Los Demonios. Ever heard of it?"

Her eyes widen.

"So as you can imagine, school isn't really a big priority

right now. Every second Paige is in Los Demonios, she's at risk."

"Los Demonios? Wow. I mean, wow. I can't believe it. That's just . . ." Aunt Penny shakes her head, at a loss for words.

My shoulders relax a fraction at her unexpected response. Maybe she's going to be reasonable about this after all. Maybe she can even help—she probably knows a lot about the place, having been a member of the Family in the past.

"So basically all afternoon we've been trying to come up with ways to infiltrate the place," I say. "Nothing so far, but we will come up with something. Any ideas?"

Aunt Penny looks up quickly. "Infiltrate?"

"Well, yeah," I answer, laughing dryly. "We're not going to just leave Paige in a place full of murderers."

"Indie," she says, taking a step closer. "No one who's gone into Los Demonios has ever come out."

A chill passes through me hearing those damning words again, but I pretend her comment hasn't ruffled me. "Maybe nobody's tried hard enough. I mean, of course nobody wants to go there under *normal* circumstances."

She closes the gap between us at such a clip I take a step back. She's right in my face, looking at me with a fiery intensity in her eyes that I've never seen before. It's a bit scary.

"You can't go there," she says, spittle flying out of her mouth. "You *won't* go there."

So much for the theory of Aunt Penny helping.

"I *can* go there," I answer, meeting her gaze. "And I will."

She throws her hands in the air and looks around, as if seeking support from the Mexican knickknacks littered across the living room. "You'll get yourself killed!" she yells. "You don't know this place. I do. The fact that you're even thinking about going there is insane. You'll die!"

And Paige is there. Rather than persuading me not to try, Aunt Penny's comments only bolster my resolve to do anything necessary to get to Los Demonios.

"I knew you wouldn't understand," I say. "You were happy to stand back when your own family was in danger."

It's a low blow, and her lip wobbles like a toddler about to cry. But I was done feeling sorry for her a long time ago.

"I'm out of here," I say, turning away before her tears have a chance to change my mind.

"Wait!" she calls to my back. I bound down the front steps toward my car, then peel out of the driveway.

———•——

I left the house with the mission of getting away from Aunt Penny, but it's not until I'm almost there that I realize I've been driving to Bishop's.

The lush green hills of Mount Washington pop up before my eyes, and soon I'm pulling up to Bishop's house. Correction: mansion. The Spanish-style home rises three stories high and stretches for what seems like an entire city block. Towering palm trees and lavish gardens spring up from every corner of the property, and lattices of ivy climb the white stucco walls and coil around the arched windows framed with ornate cast-iron grilles, all the way to the terra-cotta roof.

I park in front of the tacky naked-mermaid fountain in the driveway that shoots water out of its nipples (so obviously Bishop's contribution to the décor) and climb out of the car.

I don't even get a chance to knock on the heavy wooden door before it opens, and Bishop is there.

"What's up?" he asks, pulling the door wide so I can come in. Instead of his usual badass rocker clothing, he's sporting a pair of baggy plaid pajama pants and a white T-shirt so old it's see-through in places. His hair is adorably mussed up on top and flat on one side.

"Hey," I answer.

A rumbling sounds from behind him, and seconds later, his rottweiler, Lovey Lumpkins, barrels down the spiral staircase. Just weeks ago, I wanted to run when he approached, but now I don't even break my stare from Bishop as the dog's nails clatter on the marble floors.

"What?" he asks, noticing my stare.

"I've missed your holey pj's," I say. "You look sickeningly cute." I smile at him as I swat Lovey's nose out of my crotch. Only Bishop could pull me out of such a horrible mood—I knew I kept him around for a reason.

He grins. "Yeah, I was thinking about taking a nap, then you came along and ruined that idea."

I give him a playful shove in the shoulder and walk inside. He follows me through the foyer.

"So why are you here?" he asks. "Didn't you say you had to get home or else Aunt Penny would send a lynch mob after you or something?"

"We got in a fight." And like that, whatever good mood I had drains out of me and my anger comes crashing back full force. I toss my keys on the glass table, and the sound echoes off the high, wood-beam ceilings.

"Let me guess: Los Demonios," Bishop says.

"Yep. And get this, she actually wants me not to go." I pad into the kitchen—my favorite room in Bishop's house. It features the same wooden beams across the ceiling, smooth archways, and windows covered in cast-iron grilles as the rest of the house, but there are also stone walls, an ornate tile backsplash, dark-colored wood cabinets, and a low-hanging candle chandelier suspended over an island full of planters, and combined, the look is just so *warm* that I can't help gravitating here. I haul myself up onto one of the stools at the island.

Bishop follows me into the kitchen, with Lumpkins trotting in behind him.

"She said, '*You won't go there*,' " I say, mimicking Aunt Penny. "'*You'll get yourself killed*.' " I roll my eyes. "She just doesn't understand."

Bishop doesn't respond.

"I mean, like I'd just forget about my best friend. To suggest that I don't even try to get her out, I mean, that's just crazy!"

The refrigerator hums in the wake of my outburst.

I sit up straighter and look at Bishop—really look at him. He plays with the drawstrings of his pajama pants, pointedly avoiding eye contact. A sinking sensation washes over me.

"You don't . . . agree with her, do you?"

He doesn't immediately respond, and right away I know it's true. I hop off my stool, surprised that smoke isn't blowing out of my ears with the force of my angry huffing.

"You can't be serious," I say. "You too?"

He shakes his head, approaching me with his hands up in apology, but I back away from him.

"Does nobody care that she's in danger?" I shout. Lumpkins sits up and lets out a little yelp. Bishop pets him behind the ears and murmurs, "It's okay," until the rottweiler sinks back to the ground.

"That's not it," Bishop says, turning his attention back to me. "No one is happy this happened to Paige. It's just that we care about you and we don't want to see the same thing happen to you."

I bark a humorless laugh. "So everyone figures we should just cut our losses and move on." Bishop opens his mouth to speak, but I interrupt him before he can get a word out. "No, that's it, isn't it? You just want to go back to a normal life. Paige being in Los Demonios must be convenient. 'Hey! Would have liked to continue spending my every waking second searching for this girl I don't really know, but sorry, she's in this other dimension, so no can do. Wanna make out?' "

"Indie," he says, shaking his head.

"Don't 'Indie' me," I say. "You're not even two years older than me, so you can stop treating me like a child. Everyone treats me like a child, and I'm done with that."

He strides up to me with a challenge flashing in his dark eyes. "So you think if you die too that'll make this whole thing better?" he demands.

"Who says I'd die?"

"Just look at history, Indie. No one who's gone into Los Demonios—"

"Has ever come out," I finish for him. "God, did you and Aunt Penny read the same textbook or something? Yes, it's not going to be easy. But just because something is hard doesn't mean you shouldn't try."

"Indie." He grabs my wrists and pulls me to him.

"No!" I shout so loud that Lumpkins lets out another bark. "This can't be fixed with a make-out sesh, okay?"

Hurt flashes across his face and he lets go of my wrists. I feel a quick stab in my gut—God, what is with me lately?—but I turn my back to him so he doesn't see the tears that spring to my eyes.

And then, for the second time in a day, I storm out of a house while pleas to stop follow me out the door.

6

The engine idles. Through the bug-splattered windshield, I watch the sun sink into the ocean, casting the sky into the oranges and pinks of sunset.

The boardwalk is practically a ghost town. The crowds have disappeared, leaving just a few dozen people scattered across the huge expanse of beach. A woman closes the shutters on her booth, while another sweeps the stairs in front of her shop. A few people stand in line at a pizza parlor, but otherwise the place is empty.

I don't know what I thought I'd accomplish by coming here, but I'm sure that whatever it is won't happen with me sitting in the car.

I turn off the engine and step out. Without the sun stinging my shoulders, the breeze coming off the water sends goose bumps racing up my bare arms. I wish I'd brought a sweater. I make a mental note to remember that next time I run away from home.

I trudge through the sand toward the boardwalk. A single seagull circles overhead, silent. The Black Market is gone. Except it's not really gone, just hidden from view.

"*Videre.*"

I say it only once, and as I blink, the market appears.

The place is suddenly teeming with activity. It's so crowded my eyes can't catch on one single thing to notice instead of another. Where the boardwalk was alive with tourists this morning, twilight seems to have brought out all the witches and warlocks. The market gave me the creeps before, but with the sun setting and Bishop not a comforting presence by my side, a spider of dread climbs my spine.

Irena wasn't exactly friendly when we chatted last, but I can't deny she knows more than I do about witchcraft. *Most people* know more than I do about witchcraft. But maybe she'll be more forthcoming without Bishop there making her go into heat.

I weave through the crowd, trying not to wince or shriek when someone bumps my shoulder or loudly calls to a friend behind me.

I'm almost at Irena's tent when a strange sensation comes

over me, and I'm overcome with the feeling of being watched. My breath catches as I recall the woman from this morning.

I spin around wildly. Sure enough, there she is, staring at me from her darkened booth. A breeze blows wisps of thinning hair across her face. Her penetrating gaze almost makes me cry out, and I realize my hand has involuntarily come up to my heart.

The woman crooks a bent and knobby finger in the air. Instinct tells me to run far and fast from this creepy lady, but for some reason I don't. She settles her hand back into her lap and waits, like she's sure I'm going to come closer.

And I do.

Alarm bells sound in my head the nearer I get to the witch, but my feet keep moving, almost of their own volition, like an undercurrent is pulling me toward her across a sea of people. I start to wonder if she's doing some sort of spell, and my heart beats so fast I think it's finally going to crap out from all the stress I've put it under lately. By the time I'm standing in front of her booth, I'm so sure she's going to kill me that I'm wondering why my life isn't flashing before my eyes.

"Hello, Indie," she says. I don't know what shocks me more: that she knows my name, or that she has the clear voice of a woman much younger than the minimum seventy I'd pegged her as.

Up close, I see that the sallow, sagging skin, lifeless eyes, and thinning hair have lent an aged appearance to what is probably a woman no older than thirty. What could have happened to a person to make her look like this? Also: how do I avoid it, and is it contagious?

"H-h-how do you know my name?" I stammer.

"You need help," she replies. It's a statement, not a question. I can't even reply before she says, "Come in," then climbs off her stool and disappears behind the curtain into the dark recesses of the shop.

A moment passes. I look behind me; the boardwalk is a zoo, but no one's paying attention to me. I could leave right now and be home in half an hour, snuggled up under my big, warm duvet.

Instead, I reach inside the booth and unhook the latch for the swinging door.

Candles bathe the small room in flickering orange light. At the back sits a worktable scattered with pots and pickle jars filled with colorful liquids and questionable foodstuffs. The dark walls are cluttered with crooked shelves and clocks of every shape and size. A large chipped sink sits to the right, stained with what I hope is red paint and not something else, and across the cobblestone floor from it is a stone hearth. Perfect for cooking children and ex-cheerleaders.

The woman is gone. There's a door set into the back wall. *What the hell,* I decide. I cross over to it in two long strides, grasping the cold knob in my hand.

I open it.

The candles from inside the booth cast just enough light that I can see the faint outline of a staircase twisting down into a black hole. Following her is a Bad Idea. But the woman knew I needed help. The promise that maybe, just maybe, she knows how I can save Paige drives me to take a melting taper candle from the shelf and hold it out in front of me like a weapon as I descend the stairs. *This is how horror movies begin*, I think.

The temperature immediately drops as I go down, and the scent of damp earth fills my nose. As my eyes adjust to the dark, the room begins to take shape—"room" being a massive overstatement. The place looks more like a cave. The candlelight casts shadows across the rocky walls and glints off the stalactites hanging from the low ceiling. Shadowy passageways snake off from the main room, twisting in different directions. There must be tunnels running under the entire boardwalk.

The warm wax of the candle molds to the shape of my hand as I walk.

"What is it you want?"

I leap at the sound of the witch's voice and whirl around, trying to locate her. I gasp when the whites of her eyes light up a darkened corner to my left. What the hell is she doing, just standing there in the dark?

There's a quiet *pop*, and then the small flicker of a flame appears in the witch's cupped hands. She reaches up to light a lantern overhead. The flame spits as it comes to life, illuminating a long worktable in the middle of the space strewn with even more bottles and jars. The witch takes a mortar and pestle and begins grinding what looks like black rock.

I wait for her to say something, but she doesn't. I realize I haven't answered her question.

"My friend," I start nervously. "She's been kidnapped."

The witch doesn't react, just continues crushing the rock with surprising strength considering her arthritic-looking hands.

"We think she's in Los Demonios," I add.

I expect her to jump down my throat at the mention of the place, but she just says, "What makes you think that?" as though I were commenting on the weather. I instantly like her more.

"We did a locating spell. It should have worked, but we picked up nothing."

"And you want to get her out," she replies.

I nod.

"I know of a way," she says.

My heart skips a beat. "You—you do?"

"It will cost you three thousand dollars." She lays the pestle down and pats the worktable until she finds a funnel, which she uses to feed the ground black crystals through the narrow opening of a bottle-green jar.

Three thousand dollars. I don't have three *hundred* dollars, let alone ten times that.

"I don't have that much money," I say.

"Well, then you're not going," she says, mimicking my voice.

I bite my lip, scouring my brain for a way to make this happen. In a flash, I remember the lockbox Mom kept on the top shelf of her bedroom closet. My college fund. Anytime I used to bug Mom about keeping so much money in the house, she'd bring up the Depression and how everyone who put their money in a bank lost everything, while the smart people who kept their money under their mattresses prospered. I'd tried to tell her that a robber was a *bit* more likely than another Depression, but Mom was steadfast in her ways. There's got to be close to fifteen thousand dollars in there.

Mom would *lose her mind* if she knew I'd taken money out of the fund she'd worked so hard to save. For a brief moment I consider trying to find another way to come up with the cash, but then I think, *Oh, who am I kidding?* Mom's dead. And anyway, she would have been okay with it if she knew what I was using it for. Not to mention I'm almost halfway through the school year and I haven't even glanced at an SAT prep book.

So I'll do it, I decide. Borrow the money.

The thought crosses my mind then that maybe this lady is swindling me. What does a witch needs money for? Bishop has a mansion funded entirely in money he magicked into existence. Surely she could do the same.

"Why not just conjure money?" I ask.

"I can't." She doesn't elaborate.

Has the Family punished her too, I wonder? Is that why she looks so prematurely old? I want to ask but decide that it may be taboo.

"Are you sure it will work?" I ask.

She glances up for the first time since I came down here, and then goes back to her work. I guess that's a yes.

The enormity of it hits me. I found a way. A real way to get to Paige. If only Bishop were here to see how much I'd accomplished on my own, all without his help.

Jerk.

"I'll do it," I say.

She gives a terse nod at my big announcement.

I shift my weight to my other foot. "Aren't you going to warn me about how dangerous this is? How I probably won't come back, and yada yada yada?"

"Do you want me to?" she asks.

I think about it, then shrug. "No, I guess not."

She lays her pestle down again and uses the funnel to add more ground rock to the jar. "Come back when you have the money."

"I want to do it now. Can't I pay you later?"

"No."

"Why not? I'm honest. I'll get you the money."

I realize right away the answer to my own question: because I might not come back.

I chew the inside of my cheek. I want to do it now. I'm worried that if I leave, rational thought might take over and I'll be too scared to return.

An idea strikes.

"I'll give you my car," I say, fishing my keys out of my pocket. I hold them out in front of me; the metal glints in the candlelight. "As collateral. If I don't come back, you can keep it."

Her hands pause. I jump on her hesitation.

"It's a good car. Parked right in the lot. A green Sunfire. A little old, but definitely worth more than three grand."

She considers for a moment. Finally, she holds out her hand, and I let out a breath I hadn't realized I'd been holding.

She snags the keys. Suddenly she's all business.

"This spell will send you to Los Demonios for a short time only. The exact amount of time is unknown and changes with each attempt. You will arrive at an unknown location. The location changes with each attempt. You will have pain in your head, which can vary from mild to excruciating. I am not responsible for anything that may happen to you on your visit. You will not be refunded if you find your experience unsatisfactory."

My stomach churns.

Her little speech has me seriously questioning my decision, and I might even have backed out if she weren't leading me firmly by the shoulder through a dark, narrow tunnel so small we have to crouch to fit through, all the while holding the swinging lantern out in front of her.

Where is she taking me?

I wish Bishop were here. As soon as I have the thought, I remember the way he took Aunt Penny's side, and my anger comes flooding back. I don't need Bishop's help. I got by sixteen years just fine without a man in my life. I'm sure I can get through another day.

Just when my back is starting to get sore from crouching down at an unnatural angle, the tunnel mercifully opens up into another room. It's round, smaller than the last, with five black entrances carved into the rock walls. It's furnished with only a wooden chair that has cutouts of roosters on its back. I wonder whose grandma she robbed for it.

"Sit," she demands.

She takes my candle, then gestures to the chair as she looks around for someplace to hang the lantern.

I cross to the chair and sit, my hands gripping the arm-rests. She crouches back into the hole we came through and disappears.

I'm alone in a cave. This day hasn't turned out at all the way I'd imagined.

I wait for what feels like forever. A drip sounds somewhere in the distance, but otherwise it's completely silent.

After a while, I hear a shuffling sound in one of the tunnels behind me—not the one we entered through. My body shifts into panic mode and I picture a cave monster ripping me to shreds, but then the witch emerges. She has her apron full of supplies, which she dumps unceremoniously onto the ground. As she tinkers, I peek over and spot a dirty chalice, a rusty dagger, and a rabbit's foot, to name only a few things. Just what does she plan on doing with all this?

"Give me your hand," she says suddenly, gripping the rusty dagger in her palm.

I white-knuckle the armrests.

"Give me your hand," she repeats impatiently.

"What are you going to do with that?" I ask.

"Cut you."

Well. Don't beat around the bush or anything.

"That thing looks like it has hepatitis," I say, eyeing the dirty blade.

She doesn't respond.

"Haven't you got a cleaner one? Or some bleach to disinfect it at least?"

She glares at me, what's left of her patience rapidly evaporating.

I take a breath of courage and thrust out my arm. She catches it around the wrist, and I recoil at the surprising coldness of her hand. She poises the blade horizontally, just below the crook of my elbow. I look away before the metal makes contact with my skin, trying not to focus on the lifetime of treatments I might require after this ceremony is done. I gasp as the blade slices into me, then bite down hard on my lip as heat spreads across my arm. I can't help looking as the first pricks of pain burst from my arm, where bright red blood spills from a three-inch gash at an alarming rate. I was not expecting her to cut me that bad.

My instinct is to curl my arm against my body and try to stanch the blood flow, but the witch holds the dirty chalice—which now contains the rabbit's foot, the black-rock crystals she was crushing earlier, and what appears to be a peacock feather—right under the wound, filling it with my blood.

In just moments, the crystals are completely dissolved and the brown fur of the rabbit's foot is nearly fully covered in my blood, but still the witch holds my arm over the cup, staring into it with an unblinking gaze.

A damp sweat breaks out on my forehead. My head spins, though I'm not sure if it's due to the blood loss, my revulsion, or a combination of the two.

After my last complaints, I'd decided to shut up and just go with it, but the way the witch is staring into the cup, I'm starting to get worried that she nodded off to her special place.

"Isn't that enough?" I ask.

Instead of her usual nonresponse response, she deigns to speak. "No."

"Well, how much do you need?"

"Enough to open your mind."

"That's cryptic." I realize I'm hyperventilating. I bite

down on my lip again. *It's okay. This will get me to Paige. I need to do this. It's for a good cause.*

"The portal to Los Demonios lies in all of our minds," she continues in a rare display of chattiness. I guess she feels bad for draining my lifeblood as well as my bank account. "But few people can access it. Only when your mind is in a fragile state can you see it. Even then most need help passing through."

"How . . ." Black spots dance in front of my eyes when I try to speak. I focus on the words, wetting my lips. "How do you open the—"

And then everything goes black.

7

I blink my eyes open and find myself lying flat on my back, two tall buildings rising up on either side of me into a sky thick with smoke. The air crackles with electricity; the scent of something sharp and dry fills my nose.

Where am I?

Hot pain radiates down my arm.

In a flash, I remember the witch. The ceremony. My blood in a cup.

I look down. Sticky streaks of red have dried all down my forearm, and fresh blood still oozes from a nasty gash below the crook of my elbow. Vomit rises up my throat, and I have to look away before I hurl.

I'm in Los Demonios.

Holy. Crap.

How long have I been lying here? How much blood have I lost?

I roll over and flatten my palms against the gravelly sidewalk, letting out a little grunt as I struggle to my feet. I cradle my arm against my body and, after a wave of nausea passes, take cautious steps toward the street.

It takes me a moment to realize where I am. Gone are the charming boutique shops, hipster bars, and outdoor terraces pushed up against luxury high-rise apartments, the towering palm trees and massive billboards stacked one on top of another, fighting for every inch of available retail space, but I'd recognize the wide, twisting street, with its Hollywood Hills backdrop, anywhere: Sunset Boulevard. Only it looks more like a war zone than the iconic street I know.

Fires blaze on nearly every rooftop not yet blown clean off, cracking and spitting as they send huge tunnels of smoke into the sky. Some of the buildings are nothing but a heap of bricks, while others look like they've recently been used for target practice, small holes peppering their char-blackened facades. Most of the billboards have holes ripped through them, save for one of Jennifer Aniston, who smiles at me as she holds a bottle of water.

Something red flashes across the sky. I duck low just as an explosion sounds, so violently it rockets me off my feet. I land on my ass, a barb of pain shooting up my back. A shop across the street erupts in a huge ball of fire. Screams come from inside, and a victorious battle cry sounds above all the other noise.

My blood curdles.

There are people in that building. And someone is trying to blow them up. And seemingly enjoying it.

What have I gotten myself into?

I consider my options:

1) Run. I could probably make the Olympic team what with all the adrenaline pumping through my veins, but I don't know which direction is safe, and with my luck I would run straight into enemy hands.

2) Fly. Considering the fireballs, this option doesn't seem appealing, not to mention that I'm hidden right now and flying would definitely put me on a few radars.

3) Hide somewhere while the battle rages on and hope no one finds me and I don't get blown to smithereens.

Not exactly the best options.

There's a flicker of movement in the sky, and then a pair of boots crunch onto the roof of a car parked next to the curb across the street. I gasp as a man stretches up to his full height, his back to me as he scans the street. I scurry against the building, my heart a jackhammer.

The man ducks just as a ball of flame whizzes past him. It smacks into the side of the building across the alley from me. My ears ring as a shower of stucco shards sprinkles down on my head. I'm too shocked to scream.

The man on the car drops to one knee and extends his hand up. A bolt of lightning shoots from his palm, rending the sky as it strikes a shop across the street. The building lets out a low groan before it crumbles, sending a huge puff of dust and smoke into the sky. More screams pierce the air. I just catch the man's smile before he springs back into the sky.

Option #3 seems considerably less sucky all of a sudden.

Adrenaline courses through my body so intensely I no longer notice the pain in my arm as I dash back through the alley. Where is a large garbage bin when you need one? I sprint to the back of the building and sweep a glance down either side of the lane.

Empty.

Voices bellow from the street. I quickly turn the corner before anyone sees me.

The ornate cast-iron back door of the building swings open in the breeze.

I'm gripped with indecision. There could be baddies in that building. But when footsteps crunch in the alley I just came from, I can't rush through the door fast enough.

I enter a large room that looks like it used to be the lobby of a boutique hotel for trendy Hollywood types. The flowered wallpaper is ripped halfway down the wall so that a yellowed corner curls back on itself; I can see mold growing on the drywall beneath. The reception desk and the banister leading to the second floor are made of rich carved wood, and a crystal chandelier hangs crookedly from a single remaining chain over an antique carpet caked with boot prints and dust and random garbage, like the place has been used recently for squatting.

A closet behind the receptionist's desk beckons to me. I cross over to it and whip the door open, nearly shrieking when a pair of green eyes set in a dirty face stare out at me. I leap back from the girl in the closet.

"Get out of here, this is my spot," she spits, before pulling the door closed. I swallow, but my heart doesn't move from its spot in my throat. I hadn't expected to see another teenager in this place, let alone one in a freaking closet.

"Get out of here!" the girl hisses between the door slats. "You're going to get me caught."

I step backward, nearly tripping over a stack of yellowed phone books, then spin around. A silhouette moves past the back door. I need to hurry. I scan the lobby and spot a door with a small pane of frosted glass. I dash to it, and nearly cry with relief when it's not locked: a set of stairs winds down into the dark basement.

My pulse races as I step inside and let the door quietly

click closed behind me, plunging me into darkness. I think about the girl in the closet and wonder if the basement will hold more fun surprises. I hesitate, but then a set of male voices echoes through the lobby and a bolt of fear goes through me. I want to run, but I force myself to tiptoe down the stairs.

My feet finally hit the floor. The scent of musty cardboard and gasoline fills the chilly air. After a moment, my eyes adjust to the dark, and the silhouette of storage crates and boxes set against a brick wall comes into view. I dash over and shove aside a stack of boxes, then climb behind them. I sink to my butt and wrap my arms tightly around my drawn-up knees. My whole body shakes, but not from the cold.

Someone screams.

The girl's voice is so loud it's like she's right in front of me instead of a whole floor up. There's the sound of a struggle, and then, just as quickly as it began, it's over and the eerie quiet is back.

The girl in the closet—something awful has happened to her. And if she hadn't been hiding there when I came in, that awful thing would have happened to me.

The door at the top of the stairs creaks open. I slap my hand over my mouth, stilling my breath even as my heart races. A shaft of light slants onto the basement floor. I shrink into the wall, trying to make myself invisible in the dark. Boots clomp down the stairs, then across the concrete. Through the space between the boxes I see someone pass by just feet from me, cracking his knuckles loudly. He stops. I hold my breath until my lungs feel like they're going to explode. A silent tear trails down my cheek. This is it. This is how it ends.

Then the footsteps begin to retreat.

I don't want to breathe, don't trust myself to breathe until he's clear of this room, but when his boots stomp up the stairs, my face grows so hot that my cheeks prickle with lack of oxygen, nausea overwhelming me until the need to exhale is too much. The air puffs out of my mouth in one huge rush.

The footsteps pause.

Shit, shit, double shit.

In a flash, a man's face appears above the boxes. His mouth pulls into a grin when he sees me. The guy looks wild, feral, and ready to rip me apart with his bare hands.

I scream.

8

With one sweep of his forearm the guy shoves the heavy boxes aside and then yanks me up by my wrist.

"Let go!" I pull and twist against his grip, but his fingers clamp my arm like a vise. I dig my heels into the floor as he marches steadily across the basement, but he doesn't so much as glance back at the girl he's dragging behind him.

I drop to the ground, so it's like my captor is a mom dragging a screaming toddler through a grocery store. He grunts and takes a few labored steps with my dead weight in tow before swinging me easily over his shoulder so that I'm upside down. Blood rushes to my head, my face mashed into his dirty canvas jacket.

My stomach warms with the promise of magic. I call it down to my fingertips only to come to the realization that moving objects and flying aren't going to help me out of this particular situation. I try to summon the wind power I used on Jezebel in my room, but no matter how hard I concentrate, my body doesn't react.

Panic takes over, and I give up on magic, straining instead to grab on to the banister as he carries me up the stairs. All I get for my effort is some serious palm burn. When we reach the top of the stairs, I try to latch on to the doorframe, but my fingers can't catch purchase. The lobby carpet flashes beneath me, and then we burst into the pale outside light.

"Help! Somebody help me!" I scream.

"Quiet," he orders, a hint of a Spanish accent coming through.

"Screw you!" I shout back.

"Have it your way."

I open my mouth to scream again, but this time, no sound comes out. I scream at the top of my lungs. I scream until my face is red and hot and I can't scream anymore. But the only sound is the distant crackle of the fires. Icy fear shoots down my spine.

I beat and pound against his back even though I know it's a waste of effort, until he unceremoniously drops me into the back of a van. The wind is knocked out of me when I land on my injured arm, my mouth yawning open in a silent scream.

"You're hurt," he says.

He reaches for me, but I scuttle back on the dirty carpet, cradling my arm against my body.

Someone kicks me.

"Watch it!"

I gasp. The girl from the closet cowers next to a sweaty blond guy who looks no more than fifteen. They've both got their hands tied behind their back.

My captor grabs the fleshy part of my good arm and pulls me out of the van. I get my first good look at him in the dim light of dusk.

He's got close-cropped dark hair, blue eyes, and straight, white teeth that stand out against his darkly tanned skin. He's average height, but beneath his jacket, his shoulders are broad with muscle. He could be eighteen or twenty-eight. I don't know.

He shrugs out of his jacket, and in one swift motion reaches back and pulls his shirt over his head, revealing a stomach absolutely ripped with muscle. A trail of hair leads from his belly button to the boxer briefs that peek out over his pants.

My God.

It takes me a half second to snap out of it and realize it's not such a great thing when an angry prison inmate takes off his shirt in front of you.

I frantically search for an escape route, only to feel fabric wrap around my injured arm. He's . . . binding the shirt over my wound.

I—I don't get it.

I look up at him for an answer.

"I don't want you bleeding all over my van," he says gruffly.

"Yeah, right, Cruz." I glance over to see a guy in a trucker hat coming around the corner with a cocky strut.

"You just wanted to show off for the chick." This comes from a dark-skinned guy in a blood-splattered tank top who jogs up the alley.

"Laugh it up, *pendejos*," Cruz answers, without so much as a glance over his shoulder. "I bagged three. That's a re-cord. How many did you get?"

Silence.

"Exactly," he says. He pushes me back into the van, then slides the door closed. A moment later, he's climbing into the driver's seat. He turns the key in the ignition, and the engine rumbles. Latin club music fills the van.

The guy in the hat pokes his head inside the open passenger window.

"Need some help with your catches?" He glances back at me, his eyes roving over my body. I become acutely aware of my layered tank tops and jean cutoffs that show a lot more tanned skin than is strictly necessary in a jail setting.

"I think I can handle a few humans," Cruz answers.

Humans? If Los Demonios is a prison for the paranormal, then why would he think I'm a human?

I open my mouth to tell him as much, but no sound comes out. I kick the back of his seat in frustration.

"Do I need to tie you up too?" Cruz asks, putting the van in drive. He peels out of the alley. "I would have thought you'd relax a bit since I helped you and all."

A vein the size of a highway pops out in my forehead. *Help me?* I mouth. *You're freaking kidnapping me!*

He chuckles at my silent rage. "Relax, *mamacita*."

That blows me over the edge. I struggle to my feet and stagger to the driver's seat.

"What are you doing?" he asks, glancing away from the road to look over his shoulder at me. I lunge for his neck. The van swerves, throwing me off-balance. I slam against the door hard and slump to the floor. Pain splits my arm. The other two kids watch me with a mixture of fear and shock.

Cruz sags into his seat as he gets the van back under control. "Serves you right," he mumbles before turning up the music.

I could attack him again, but the simple truth of the matter is I'm no match for him. Panic and desperation overwhelm me, and I feel a sob build in my chest that I work hard to choke down. I need to think. I need to be smart.

Small fires flash by in the growing dark, but before long the view changes to the silhouette of a mountain range.

Where is he taking us? If I had an idea, that could inform my decision. I almost laugh. My decision. Like I have a plan. Like I'm not being kidnapped.

The same song restarts for the third time, but Cruz taps his hands on the steering wheel as though it's the first time. It makes me want to scratch my eyes out.

"Can we hear something else already?" I scream.

I touch my throat, surprised to find I actually said the words out loud.

"I love this song," he says.

"So did I," I retort. "The first five hundred times."

"Any requests?" he says.

I huff, which only makes him chuckle.

"Do you find this funny?" I ask.

"What?"

"Kidnapping girls. That's funny to you?"

"There's a boy in here too."

I exhale.

"And to answer your question, no, I don't find it funny. But it's a job, and I have to do it."

"Who makes you do it?" I ask.

"You'll meet him soon."

I can't hide the shiver that passes through me. "Why do you do it, then? If you don't like it, why don't you just quit? Tell your shitty boss to find someone else to do his 'nappings."

The girl gives me a kick in the thigh.

"That's not the way it works," he answers.

"Why not?"

"Because . . . that's just not the way it works. You got here, what? An hour ago? You don't know squat."

"Maybe I've been here a year," I say defiantly.

"You haven't."

"Okay, how about this?" I say. "Maybe you do this because you're a spineless asshole."

"Shut up," the boy in the back warns me.

"You're going to get us killed," the girl hisses.

Cruz's jaw tenses in the rearview mirror.

"Is it because you're scared to speak up?" I continue. "Or do you secretly enjoy taking young kids against their will?"

When he doesn't answer, I know I've hit a nerve.

"That's it, isn't it?" I laugh.

He slams on the brakes. Tires squeal against the pavement as we rocket forward into the seats. He jerks the parking brake on and rounds the front of the van before I can even rearrange myself.

"Now look what you did," the girl says.

Cruz whips the door open, then flourishes an arm toward the road. I look out, past his shirtless chest. We've stopped in the middle of a residential street. Massive Gothic mansions rise up against the dark sky like the jagged fangs of some predatory animal. Wind whistles, and a coyote howls nearby.

"Go on!" he barks. "Don't be shy, girl. Get out."

I inch forward, then hop out of the van.

"Any of you want to get out too?" he asks, poking his head inside the van. The girl and boy blink back at him, stunned. He slams the door closed.

My heart bangs a steady beat.

He locks eyes with me and pauses in mock shock. "What? This is what you wanted, right?"

"It is. Thank you," I spit. But I can't help the edge of fear that enters my voice. I wish I could turn back time four seconds just so I wouldn't have to see the satisfied smile on his face.

I bite my lip to keep it from trembling. Cruz's eyes fall to my mouth.

"*Mierda,*" he mutters, wiping his chin with his thumb.

"What?" I ask.

He sighs. "Listen. I'm going to give you some advice because I think you sorely need it, though I'm not sure how much it's going to help. The only people that matter here are the Chief and Zeke. The Valley, East L.A., downtown, and Hollywood are the Chief's turf—sorcerer turf—and trust me, the Chief is *not* someone you want to run into. Beverly Hills, the west side, and the beaches down to Redondo Beach are where Zeke's people hang out. You don't want to run into them either."

I nod, committing his words to memory. "So where is safe?"

His face cracks into the barest of mocking smiles, and I get my answer.

"Okay, one last question," I say. "I'm looking for a friend. Her name is Paige Abernathy. She's got shoulder-length brown hair and bangs, and she'd probably be wearing leopard-print glasses. Any thoughts on where I might find her?"

He stares at me, but this time like he feels sorry for me. "Look, I don't know anything about this Paige, but I do know this: you don't have any friends. The minute you stepped into this place, you were on your own."

Cruz takes a step back and turns, when high-pitched laughter rises from the darkness behind the houses. He pauses, shoulders tensing as if ready for battle.

"What was that?" I ask, backing up toward the van. Everything is still and quiet. A breeze shushes through the trees.

And then: the laughter sounds from right behind the van. I shriek and spin around. With a *whoosh*, something passes by on my left, but whatever was there is gone in a flash. I back up against Cruz, my breath coming in gasps.

"Thanks a lot," he mutters.

"What the hell did I do?"

"Made me stop the van right in rebel territory, that's what."

"Rebels?"

"Zeke's people. Witches and warlocks," he answers, scanning for movement in the dark.

A cackle rises up from behind the houses again.

Witches.

"What do they want?" I ask.

"Right now? To kill us."

"Duh," I say. "But why? Just because we stumbled into their territory by accident?"

Cruz smacks his forehead, like I couldn't possibly have said anything more naive. "You don't just 'stumble into' someone's territory," he says, doing air quotes. "In jail, your turf is religion. It's the only thing keeping witches and sorcerers from blowing each other to shit."

"So witches hate sorcerers here too?"

His eyebrows draw up suddenly, and I realize I've slipped up big-time. I've let him know that I knew about the magic underworld before I came here. Before he told me. I open and close my mouth, searching for a way to backtrack. I almost admit that I'm a witch, but a realization stops me short: Cruz is a sorcerer. And he's probably taking me to some sort of sorcerer headquarters—the most likely place in all of Los Demonios for Paige to be held. Ever since Cruz captured me, I've been trying to escape, when he could be taking me straight to my best friend.

Idiot.

He's still looking at me with suspicious eyes.

Something moves against the sky, saving me from having

to continue this conversation. A shape flashes in front of the crescent moon. And I swear I see a wing.

The dragon that chased me at homecoming pops into my mind, and white-hot fear rips through my body.

"What. The hell. Was that?"

"Mierda," Cruz mutters.

"You keep saying that. What does that mean?"

"And I can't even fly with the three of you," he adds, ignoring my question. "This is awesome. Just great."

The shape swoops down, landing with a thud on the patchy grass in the yard across from us.

I gasp. Shrieks rise from the captives in the van.

The thing looks like a cross between a monkey and a bat. Its bony, fur-covered body hunches over in the grass, a long tail curling up between glossy, leathery wings. It watches us with beady red eyes, smiling with a mouthful of too many sharp teeth.

"Get in the van," Cruz orders.

He doesn't have to tell me twice.

I dive inside the van, sliding the door closed just as the thing leaps toward us. I jump back from the door and land in the girl's lap. She shoves me off, sobbing so loudly it's practically all I can hear.

Cruz holds out his hand. Flame bursts from his palm, but Bat Boy takes flight before it can hit. I don't see where the creature has gone until its paws slam against Cruz's back and pin him to the ground. Panic overwhelms me—if Cruz dies, we're all dead—but in a flash, he disappears. The bat is still sniffing confusedly at the spot where its dinner had been when Cruz materializes behind it. Blood trickles out of the claw holes in his broad shoulders, and sweat has pooled in the hollow of his back. He holds a long knife over his head, its blade glistening in the moonlight as he prepares to strike the bat's wing.

Smart, I think. He wants to take away its ability to fly.

Cruz brings the knife down swiftly, but not before the bat whips around. The knife stabs into the ground, making a dull sound I can hear clearly even through the glass. Bat Boy hisses, baring its teeth, eyes flashing a murderous red. It lunges at Cruz, claws reaching to wrap around his throat. They fall back in a tumble of bodies. A loud *snap* splits the air, followed by an unearthly wail. I have to look away, cringing at the thought of what could have made that sound.

"I just want to go home," the boy next to me cries, his hands clasped in prayer.

"I love you, Mom," the girl cries as messy tears pour down her face.

My chest knots up. I don't know what was going to happen to these people wherever it was Cruz was taking us, but I do know that if they die right now, it will be because of me.

I have to do something.

I scramble to the door.

"What are you doing?" the girl screeches. "Don't go out there!"

I hop out of the van. My landing sends up a puff of dirt, but neither Cruz nor Bat Boy seem to notice. Cruz twists out from under Bat Boy's grip. He heaves for air, his face a mask of rage, his rippled chest smeared with dirt and gleaming with sweat.

Now's the time.

I sprint across the road, my head down against the biting night wind. When I reach the other side, I whirl around and cup my hands around my mouth.

"Hey!" I yell.

Bat Boy's head snaps up. The creature has grabbed hold of Cruz again, and hoists his body over its head, as if ready to smash him.

"Over here! Catch me if you can!"

It drops Cruz so fast I swear I hear bones crack; then springs into the air.

I spin around, but I don't make it a step before a clawed talon digs into the back of my shirt.

This wasn't one of my best ideas.

"Help!"

My body folds over like a rag doll as I'm pulled into the sky. The ground shrinks below me at an alarming rate until the van and Cruz lying unconscious in front of it are just a couple of black specks on the road.

Bat Boy drops me suddenly. I don't have time to brace for the fall before I land on the sticky black shingles of a roof. A wet nose sniffs at my ears, fur itching up against my cheek. I shriek and roll away.

"You got one. Excellent."

I look up at the sound of a voice. There's a woman on the roof.

Bat Boy curls back its lips, baring razor teeth.

"That's enough," the woman says, her unstyled black Mohawk blowing in the breeze. She pushes off the spire she's been leaning against and walks over. As she nears, I notice a cowbell nose piercing, spiked collar necklace, and heaps of dark eye makeup that make her look like she just blew her life savings at Hot Topic.

"There are still more down there," she says, flicking a dismissive hand at Bat Boy.

It ignores her, bending its fanged mouth toward me like it just can't stop itself from getting one little taste. Its hot breath makes me gag.

"Go on, before he wakes up." She gives the bat a swift kick in the side. It hisses, but the woman doesn't flinch, and it finally takes flight.

I look frantically after the bat as it retreats.

"Hey." A boot lands in my side, knocking my breath out of me. I curl into myself, tasting something metallic in my mouth: blood.

"Who are you?" the woman asks.

I can't even find breath to speak. The kids in the van. What's going to happen to them?

The woman bends down and takes my chin in her hands, snapping my head up so that I have to face her. "Did they tell you why they kidnapped you? Give you any idea what they're using you for? Why all the humans?"

I cough up a mouthful of blood.

"Spit it out!" she yells, shaking my head.

A splitting pain shoots into my temples. I gasp, instinctively grabbing my head. I squeeze my eyes shut against a sudden rush of tears. I've never felt a more intense pain in my life. I wonder if I'm having a stroke. I can feel the woman standing over me, hear her words floating around my head, but the more I try to grasp onto them, the further and further away they get. I vaguely feel another boot in my side before everything goes black.

9

I have the nightmare again—the one with Mom tied to the chair. This time a tiger paces around her. It makes a low rumble that causes the fur on its chest to vibrate. Mom draws back into her chair, shaking with fear as tears pour down her cheeks. She whimpers into the rag stuffed in her mouth. The tiger reaches out a paw and claws at her face. Three long slashes cut down her cheek.

I scream.

"So you survived."

The words pull me back to reality, and the nightmare fades to black. I flutter my eyes open. My head pulses against cold stone, exhaustion pulling at my body so intensely I can't move an inch. The witch from the boardwalk stands over me. Her hair hangs down over her bony face as she watches me with a measure of disinterest mixed with annoyance.

I'm back at the Black Market. I never would have believed I'd be so happy to see the creepy witch, or to be in her basement lair.

For a split second I feel satisfied. I traveled to Los Demonios and made it back safely—haters can suck it!

And then I remember that the point wasn't just to survive—it was to save Paige. And my euphoria evaporates.

The woman shuffles out of the room. I try to sit up, but it's just too hard, and I sink back onto the stone floor.

"Where are you going?" I ask, then let out a raspy cough that tastes of blood.

Clanks echo from deeper in the cave.

Los Demonios. I can't believe I survived that place. Everyone said it was dangerous, but in the span of an hour or so, I almost got killed on three separate occasions, if you don't count the freaky goth woman on the roof. She wasn't exactly friendly, but I can't say for sure she wanted to kill me. More like she wanted to beat answers out of me.

Her words reverberate through my head.

"Did they tell you why they kidnapped you? Give you any idea what they're using you for? Why all the humans?"

What does it all mean?

The witch comes back with a goblet of pink fluid and some

mystery capsules, which she sets down in front of me before moving back to continue watching. I could lie here forever, but the promise of potential painkillers is making me salivate. I flatten the palm of my uninjured arm against the floor and force my body up. It feels like my head is weighted with lead, and my movements are sluggish, like I'm coming out of anesthesia.

Cruz's dirty T-shirt is still wrapped around the crook of my right arm, making it hard to bend, so I pick up the goblet with my left hand and bring it close to my face, taking a whiff of the pink fluid. I cough at the unexpected acrid scent.

"It'll make the pains go away," the witch says, reading my mind.

I eye the capsules. Taking unmarked pills from a stranger seems like something I probably shouldn't do, but surely if she wanted to kill me she could have done it when she was slicing me up with a rusty dagger.

Still coughing, I pop the capsules in my mouth, throwing back half the liquid in one gulp. I almost spit it out, but force it down my throat. And then I sit there, panting, until the urge to vomit finally passes.

"Get up," the witch says, then disappears back into the tunnels again.

I realize the pain and the sluggishness are gone.

I get up and follow the witch upstairs.

The cab rolls to a stop. It's four a.m., yet all the lights are on inside my house. Anxiety grips my chest. Aunt Penny's probably been up all night worrying about me. Maybe she even called the cops.

"I got places to be, lady," the cabbie complains.

I consider asking him to drive right past the house, maybe drop me off at the park so I can sleep under the slide or something. Even going up against Bat Boy again seems appealing compared with going inside right now.

But I'll have to face Aunt Penny sometime. And so I fork over the cab fare, take a deep breath, and climb out of the taxi.

She's on the front steps before he even pulls away.

Marvelous.

"Where the hell were you?" she screams, storming down the driveway. "And where the hell is your car?"

Aunt Penny's eyes fall to the bloodied T-shirt wrapped around my arm. She circles me, taking in my disheveled appearance, and I can tell from her intake of breath the moment she discovers the ragged hole in the back of my T-shirt from where Bat Boy sank its claws into me.

"Oh my God, what happened?"

"I got mugged," I say. Though I practiced it a dozen times in the cab, it still comes out with the ring of a lie.

"Bull. What really happened?"

She moves to touch my arm, but I pull it back.

"I got mugged," I repeat.

"Where?"

"The movies."

"You went to the movies?" she asks incredulously.

I nod.

"So you called the cops, then?" She crosses her arms over her chest, challenging me to lie.

I hold her stare.

"You got mugged and beat up and your car was what, stolen? And you never called the cops? Where were you really? Who did this to you?"

I exhale, pinching the bridge of my nose. "Can you just . . . not? I'm so tired. I just want to get cleaned up and go to bed."

She shakes her head. "I'm so sorry to inconvenience you with—"

The outside lights next door flick on. Mrs. Abernathy appears on the porch.

"Everything okay?" she asks.

"Fine!" Aunt Penny calls cheerily. "Just typical teenager stuff. Thanks for asking!" She turns to me. "Inside," she growls out of the side of her mouth.

I groan as I follow her into the house. As soon as the front door clicks closed behind us, she swings on me.

"Do you have any idea how worried I was? Do you even know what time it is?"

"It's around the time you usually roll in from the clubs," I say, and immediately regret it.

Her face twists into a mask of anger. "Used to, Indie. I don't go out anymore because I have responsibilities now."

"Sorry to ruin all your fun."

She points her finger inches from my nose. "Don't. Just don't. You don't get to make this about me right now."

I bite my lip to keep from saying anything else. I've never seen Aunt Penny this mad, and I do feel sort of guilty for making her worry.

Her hand hangs in the air a moment longer before she lets her arm drop to her side. She turns so that her back is to me, but not before I see the brightness in her eyes. Her shoulders shake with silent tears.

"Aunt Penny," I say, hesitantly touching her shoulder.

"I thought you were dead," she sobs.

My gut twists. She lost her sister and she thought she'd lost me—she must have been out of her mind with panic.

"I'm fine," I say. "Totally safe. I'm . . . sorry I made you worry. But I'll get my car back, okay?"

"I don't care about the stupid car!"

I gasp at her outburst.

I'd half expected her to soften with the apology, but she swings around on me again, her face ugly with anger. I take a step back. Aunt Penny may look like your typical L.A.-type bar star, what with the blond hair and manicure, but she can really go from zero to ghetto in sixty seconds.

"This isn't going to happen again," she says. Not a question. A statement.

"Okay, I'll try to be more—"

"No," she interrupts. "This *won't* happen again. You won't run off like this. You'll go to school and actually *stay* at school. You'll get good grades and you'll go to college. And if you don't? If you don't follow my rules exactly as I've laid them out? You'll go to witch boarding school."

I bark a laugh.

"I'm dead serious," she says. She holds her body so still that if she weren't standing up I'd wonder if she was breathing.

"Is that even a thing?" I ask. "Witch boarding school? Did you just make that up?"

"Don't you wish," she answers. "It's a thing. And it's where you'll be going if you don't follow my rules."

"But Paige—"

"But nothing," she interrupts. "I've spoken with the Family. They've agreed to help search for Paige. This isn't your problem anymore. You're a teenager, and it's time you started acting like one."

"This is all really funny coming from you," I say. "You just 'grew up,' when? A few weeks ago? And the Family— you *really* think they're going to help us? They don't give a rat's ass about us. Don't you remember what happened last time?"

"It's not your problem anymore," she repeats.

I want to argue. I want to shake her until sense comes back, or some semblance of the old Aunt Penny. But I can tell by the fiery look in her eyes that she won't be argued with right now. And though I have serious doubts that a witch boarding school actually exists, I can't say for sure that it doesn't. And the last thing I need right now is to get sent away from Los Angeles. I need to get back to the boardwalk and the witch. I need to get back to Los Demonios to look for Paige.

I *don't* need Aunt Penny on my back.

"Fine," I sigh. "I'll follow your stupid rules."

———◆———

I'm shoving my textbooks into my locker the next morning when Bishop calls my name. I should have guessed by the girlie exclamations and the rise in pheromones in the air that he was near.

I hike my messenger bag up on my shoulder and swing around. And there he is, leaning up against the opposite bank of lockers. And he doesn't look happy.

I *did* consider calling or texting him when I got in last night, but I just couldn't bring myself to do it. My anger at him for taking Aunt Penny's side may have dissipated a bit in the face of near death in Los Demonios, but it took only a few minutes of being back home and remembering the terrors of that place, knowing that Paige is still there, for it to come flooding back again, stronger than ever.

I probably should have called.

Sighing, I shoulder my bag. The concentrated stare of the female population of Fairfield High follows me as I join my boyfriend, but I pretend not to notice the attention.

"Where were you?" he asks, his tone low and dangerous.

"Sorry, I should have called—"

"Where were you?" he repeats. His eyes lock on mine, dark and unblinking. I've never seen Bishop this angry.

I square my shoulders, trying to disguise my nerves. "My dad's been gone since I was three, and I don't need a replacement, thanks."

My words crack his shell. His shoulders deflate a fraction, and he looks out at the busy hallway.

Guilt tears at my insides. What's gotten into me? I know what I did was wrong. I touch his arm, and he flinches. Laughter echoes through the hallway, and my cheeks burn.

"Just . . . just tell me you didn't do something stupid." He looks at me again with an intensity that makes my breath hitch.

I briefly consider telling him everything about Los Demonios, but something about the threatening look in his eyes tells me that confessing to him would be a very bad idea. Which brings me to plan B: throw him off the trail. *Stat.*

"Look, Bishop. I'm sorry. I was just so mad. Aunt Penny just finished saying there was nothing I could do about Paige, then I went to you and expected you to be on my side but you just said the same thing and"—I shrug—"I guess I just lost it. I needed to get away for a bit." It's not technically a lie. "But I realize now that I made you both worry, and I won't take off like that again without letting someone know."

He doesn't respond. A twist of dark hair falls around his jaw; his lips are so tense I have the urge to part them with a kiss. He's so close to me, yet the space between us feels like a chasm.

"Look," I whisper. "If you're going to break up with me, could you at least make it quick? Everyone's looking."

He laughs then, low and quiet. The sound startles me.

"You think I'm going to break up with you?" he asks.

"You're . . . not?"

"Indie," he says, hooking his fingers through the belt loops of my jean skirt and tugging me closer. He gives a half smile—not his characteristic grin, but not his new scowl either, so I'll take it. "I would never break up with you."

Relief floods my body, and I swear I can feel actual endorphins racing through my veins. "You might regret saying that later," I reply.

He tucks my hair behind my ear, grinning genuinely as he leans in to kiss me.

"All right, break it up, you two!"

I startle at Mr. Lloyd's voice. He stands in front of us,

wedging us apart with his palms. "More booky booky, less kissy kissy, *comprende*?"

Bishop laughs, and Mr. Lloyd shoots him a glare.

"Are you even a student here?" he asks.

Crap.

"See you after school?" Bishop says as he walks backward away from me.

"Sure," I say. He gives me a two-fingered salute, and then he slips into the crowd.

One thing I haven't missed about school is Mrs. Davies's boring lectures. After I slept like the dead for just a few hours last night, her monologue on some after-school SAT prep course has me fighting the urge to head-desk.

It doesn't get better in math class. My exhaustion, combined with the fact I haven't cracked a textbook in ages, makes the test questions look like they're written in an alien language. I get about halfway through before giving up and taking a nap on my desk.

I almost leap out of my skin when the intercom buzzes. Mrs. Malone's voice comes over the speaker.

"Good morning. Would all students and teachers please file down to the gymnasium for a mandatory assembly? Thank you."

"I guess the test will have to be rescheduled," Mr. Lloyd says.

Joy. I can fail tomorrow instead.

Whoops rise from the class. In the back of the room, Bianca loudly discusses skipping out for Starbucks. It's probably the first great idea she's ever had. I'm already imagining what kinds of research I can do with my free time when Mr. Lloyd claps his hands.

"Did everyone hear Mrs. Malone? This is a mandatory assembly. Anyone not present will be reported to the office and dealt with appropriately. I will be taking attendance in the gym."

All twenty-five kids let out a groan.

The gym is already three-quarters full and booming with the murmurs of students by the time our class arrives. I file into one of the hastily erected rows of orange chairs and scan the crowded room for a sign of what this is all about. I notice a few uniformed police officers chatting by the side of the raised stage, and my back stiffens.

Five minutes later, Mrs. Malone crosses the stage as briskly as one can in a leather miniskirt too tight to allow full range of leg motion. She stops in front of a microphone, then taps it twice, sending interference through the speakers, which makes everyone groan.

"Quiet, please," she says. "Thank you all for joining me. I've asked you here this morning for a very important issue.

A tragedy has befallen one of our own." She pauses. "Mrs. Hornby's daughter has gone missing."

Shock slams into me as the gym falls completely silent.

Mrs. Hornby is the coach of the girl's soccer team, and ever since Ms. Jenkins died (or rather, was killed by Leo), she's been filling in as the cheerleading coach. All I know about her is that she loves soccer with a passion and has been nicknamed Horny, on account of her unfortunate last name. I didn't even know she had a daughter.

Mrs. Malone allows a moment for the shock of her statement to wear off before continuing.

"Samantha Hornby, a junior at John Marshall High, hasn't been seen since yesterday morning." Mrs. Malone covers the microphone with her hand and speaks to a janitor. In a moment, a picture flashes across the drop-down screen behind her. The girl in the picture smiles brightly at the camera, her brown hair pulled into a glossy ponytail at the top of her head.

"Samantha was last seen by her parents at ten to eight yesterday, when she left for school with a friend. She was wearing a black T-shirt and jeans. All efforts to contact her via phone and social networking have failed. Her family says this is very unusual for Samantha and they're very concerned for her welfare. Please, everyone take a close look at this photo. If you have any information that could help in the search for Samantha, anything at all, please come forward to speak to one of the officers, who will gladly take your report."

I stare at the picture. Something niggles at the back of my mind, but it's like I'm trying to grab hold of rubbery fish: every time I think I've got a handle on it, it wiggles out of my grasp.

I remember the news report Aunt Penny was watching the other morning about the redheaded boy. That makes two teens gone missing in the course of a few days.

Chairs squeak against tile as the gym empties out, but I don't move, just keep staring at the picture. There's hardly anyone left in the room when I finally figure it out.

Wipe away the smile, pull down the ponytail, and smear dirt across her cheeks—and that girl becomes the one in the back of the van in Los Demonios.

10

It doesn't make sense. What the hell could Mrs. Hornby's daughter be doing in an alternate-dimension prison?

The lack of sleep and the guilt must finally be catching up with me, I decide. It can't really be her. I'm superimposing her face on the girl I saw because I can't stop thinking about what might have happened to her after I left her in that van, Cruz unconscious or worse, and with Bat Boy on the loose.

Yes. That's it. It's not her. I say it so many times that I almost convince myself it's true.

Back in math class, I wait for Mr. Lloyd to turn his back before digging in my purse for my phone. I cradle it in my lap under the desk and open the web browser, sneaking glances down to type in the search bar whenever the opportunity strikes. I've gotten as far as "Samantha H" when Mr. Lloyd suddenly stops his impromptu lecture on the importance of good math grades for getting into a decent college and not failing at life.

"Yes, Bianca," he says.

"Sorry to interrupt, Mr. Lloyd. I'm trying to pay attention, because college is, like, super, super important to me, but I'm just really distracted by Indigo on her phone."

I stiffen, blood rushing to my face. The classroom calls out "Oooh" in unison as Mr. Lloyd's shoes slap down the aisle. He holds out his hand, under my nose. Exhaling, I hand over my cell.

"You can pick it up at the end of the day," he says.

"What?" I shriek.

He ignores my outburst. As he retreats to the front of the class, I twist around to send eye daggers at Bianca. She gives me a huge, satisfied smile. I can't help myself. I turn to face the blackboard, calling my magic; it answers quickly, the heat stinging my fingertips. I think of Bianca's desk and repeat the incantation to move objects inside my head.

Sequere me imperio movere.

A loud crash sounds behind me, followed by a roar of laughter. I twist around to see Bianca splayed out on the floor under her tipped-over desk.

"Get this thing off of me!" she screeches.

Devon jumps up to right the desk.

"Who pushed me?" she yells, scrambling up and struggling to rearrange her impossibly small skirt.

"Pushed you?" Devon asks. "Don't blame me because you fell."

I laugh, but quickly turn it into a cough.

"All right, that's enough, people," Mr. Lloyd says. "Miss Cavanaugh—take your seat. And try to stay in it, please."

Repressed snickers bounce through the room. Bianca snaps her head around, as if she's trying to burn every laughing kid's face into her memory so she can remember to ruin their lives later. And then she notices me. Her eyes narrow, and I know she's trying to figure out how I could have caused her fall from three rows over. I give her a smug smile before I spin around to face the blackboard again.

Well, that was fun. But I make a note to myself not to lose my temper like that again. Being loose with my magic could get me in some *serious* trouble.

The rest of the morning passes by like sludge. When the lunch bell rings, I practically sprint to the library.

The library at Fairfield High is enough to cause clinical depression. The outdated shag carpet, cheap plywood bookcases, and Commodore 64 computers make the place look like it has been royally screwed over in the budget department since 1970.

Mrs. Sutton glances up from her computer at the reference desk when I enter but quickly goes back to doing whatever it is librarians do. I cross over to one of the computer stations and drop my bag on the floor.

My fingers shake as I bring up Google, then type "Samantha Hornby" into the search bar. The police report comes up as the first option. I click on it and skim the paragraphs looking for details not already mentioned at the assembly.

She went missing yesterday. She left for school with a friend, but never showed up to class. I read the rest of the report but learn nothing new. I click out of the page and open up her Instagram, zooming in on her most recent pic. It's the same picture from the assembly, but up close, Samantha looks even more like the girl I saw in Los Demonios.

My heart beats hard. I click on another picture, then another and another—star soccer athlete, devoted friend, smiling and happy in every photo. I keep looking, hoping to crush my theory, but the longer I search, the clearer it becomes that I'm right: Samantha and the girl in the van are the same person.

My mind speeds in a dozen different directions. What was this seemingly well-bred human doing in a place like that? I don't know what it all means.

A thought strikes: maybe Samantha is a witch. Hell, maybe she's a sorcerer. Why not? It's unlikely that I'm the only teen witch in Los Angeles County, even if the thought makes me feel a tad less special.

But then Goth Woman's words on the roof stream through

my head again. *"Did they tell you why they kidnapped you? Give you any idea what they're using you for? Why all the humans?"*

Okay, so Samantha's probably a human, I decide.

I turn over the rest of the woman's words again, trying to pick some meaning out of them. So someone is kidnapping humans. . . . Could it be that someone is collecting them from the outside and dumping them into Los Demonios?

My breath hitches, a sense of foreboding falling heavy on my shoulders.

It can't be.

I click out of Instagram and return to Google. My fingers hesitate over the keyboard. I don't even know what to type. Finally, I punch in *sorcerer spells + humans*.

Twenty-six thousand results pop up. My throat feels hot and dry as I click on the first link. It opens to a web page that looks like a homemade LiveJournal. I skim the passage, barely breathing.

"Interesting reading material."

I yelp and spin around to find Jessie standing right behind me, her books pressed against her chest. I click out of the web page, but it's too late. My cheeks flame.

"It's research," I spit out. "For school. For an English paper."

"It's okay," she says.

I open my mouth to say something, but she shakes her head. "You don't have to be embarrassed around me. Paige told me all about your mom's occult shop. I think it's cool."

I swallow, my heart continuing its frantic beating despite her words. "You, you do?"

"It's interesting."

She slides out a chair at a nearby table and drops her bag onto her lap, then pulls out a sandwich. She carefully unwraps the cellophane and takes a big bite.

"Want to sit?" she asks, through a mouth full of food. "I could use the company."

"I–I'm sorry. I have to go." I grab my bag and dash out of the library before I can see the hurt on her face.

I don't know what's going on, but I do know that it's not just Paige's life in danger anymore. I need to get back to Los Demonios. I *don't* need to make new friends. Besides, not much good has come from letting anyone get close to me so far.

———

I knew exactly where to look for the Ancient Spells book. Mom kept an autographed copy on display in the dining-room china cabinet ever since the author came to the shop to do a signing a few years back (she didn't seem to think it was funny that a "warlock" was doing book signings). I almost cried with relief to find the book still there. Thank God, or I'd have to jack a copy from the Black Cat and risk Aunt Penny finding out. Or worse: take out a witchcraft book from the library.

I flip onto my stomach and flatten the cover on my bed, scanning passages for something that might help me inside Los Demonios.

Now that I have a good idea where Paige is being held, it's incredibly tempting to speed down to the boardwalk and return to LD as soon as possible, but if my experience in that place has taught me anything it's that I'm way out of my league. I may have survived, but only just. I can't take credit for it and I definitely can't expect to have the same luck if I go back with the same sad skill set as before. I need to be able to defend myself. I need a few more tricks in my magic bag besides flying and moving objects.

There's a knock on my bedroom door. I find Bishop smirking at me from the doorframe. He's got his hair tied back in a ponytail, with a few strands pulled loose around the colorful tattoos on his neck. His leather jacket is draped over his arm, and he gives me a smile that crinkles his eyes, like nothing at all happened between us today.

"Can I come in?"

I return his smile. "Of course."

"Where's your car?" he asks, ambling inside. "It's not in the driveway."

I drop my eyes to the book. "Oh, uh, in the shop. Oil change."

"You know I could have done that for you."

Note to self: get back down to the boardwalk and buy back my car ASAP.

"I'll remember that for next time."

"Door stays open," Aunt Penny says, walking past.

My cheeks flush, but Bishop doesn't seem the least bit bothered. He plops down heavily on the bed and picks up the book, turning it over to look at the gold-embossed cover.

"Man, math has really changed since I finished high school," he says.

I grin at him.

"Seriously, though—I thought you were studying for your retest. What's all this about?"

I shrug as he flips through the pages, like I don't know exactly what it is and exactly why I invited him here. "Just some old book I found in the china cabinet," I say.

" 'Battle Tactics,' " he says, reading the chapter title. "Some nice light reading." He tosses the book onto the floor and leans over suddenly to bite my neck.

"Bishop!" I complain, though I can't help giggling at the flash of pleasure it sends through me.

"What?" he asks into my neck.

"Aunt Penny."

"She went downstairs," he says, grazing his lips along my jaw. "Kiss me. I missed you."

I can't resist the desperation in his voice, and climb into his lap. He takes my head in his hands and transfixes me with a look that sends a thrill through my body, the tiny space between us thrumming with electricity. His lips find mine, hot and urgent and full of apology. A trail of tingles follows Bishop's hands as they roam down my sides. When his fingers dig into my hips, it's like a match is struck inside me. I kiss him harder, slipping my hands under his thin T-shirt, up over the planes of his warm, hard chest. He lets out a little groan and pulls my hips harder against his. Some semblance of sense comes flooding back.

"Bishop." I push at his chest, panting for air. "I was doing something, you know."

"More interesting than this?" he says, his voice husky. He nips at my earlobe, which is so not fair because he knows what that does to me. I almost give in and magic the door shut. But instead I climb off his lap, fighting the dizziness his kiss brought on.

"Yes. No. I mean, I was practicing my magic."

He seems to sense the change in me and sits up straighter. "Something wrong?"

"No." I pace over to the computer desk, then spin around to face him. "Well, yeah, actually, there is."

His brow creases with concern.

"It's just . . . I hate not being able to protect myself."

"Oh," he says. "What brought this on?"

I shake my head. "Nothing, really. I've just been thinking."

He crosses the room in two long strides, drawing his arm around my shoulders. I can't help melting into his touch, resting my head against his warm shoulder.

"Indie, you don't have to worry about that anymore."

"Yeah? Well, *The Witch Hunter's Bible* is still out there somewhere," I say.

"Which isn't a big deal because the Priory is decimated, remember?" He tucks my hair behind my ear. "No one's going to come after you. Everything's okay now."

Anger flashes hot in my stomach, and I almost ruin my whole plan by yelling that everything is not okay—Paige is still missing.

"I know that," I say instead. "But I just feel uncomfortable. Like, what if they come back. What if their numbers swell, or what if some lone sorcerer wants revenge on the witch who killed his people? I think . . . well, I think I'd just feel better if I knew how to defend myself." I glance up at him. The way he looks at me is like I'm the most important thing in his world.

"This is really bothering you, isn't it?" he says.

I bury my face in his chest. Guilt twists my stomach for manipulating him. This is Bishop—the guy who's been there for me through thick and thin, through losing Mom and losing Paige, who held me all those nights while I cried myself to sleep. I must be seriously deranged to abuse his trust like this.

I consider ending the act right now—spilling everything about my trip to Los Demonios and the real reason that I want his help. Maybe hearing my theory will tip the balance in my favor? But terror that he'll refuse to help me after he knows what I plan to do with my new skills, or worse, that he'll tell Aunt Penny, who will ship me off to witch boarding school, keeps my lips firmly sealed.

"Okay," he says. "We'll practice."

I let myself smile then, guilt giving way to excitement.

"We can even start right now. What do you want to learn first?"

"How about throwing fireballs?" I answer too quickly.

Bishop gapes at me, and blood rushes to my face. I let out a nervous laugh. "Or we can start with conjuring objects. You know, in case I don't have a weapon handy during an attack."

"Conjuring is a good idea," he says, once the shock has worn off. "It's next on the list anyway."

I give him what I hope looks like an innocent smile.

"Okay," he says. "What's been the most important principle you've learned so far about magic?"

"I didn't know there'd be a test," I say.

He grins. "Come on, you know this."

I sigh. "Um, something about energy? That it can't be created, just manipulated?"

"Exactly! So when moving objects you manipulate energy that already exists, and when flying you manipulate the air currents that already exist. When you conjure an object, you aren't creating energy, but borrowing existing energy and using it to take the shape of the item you want. It's pretty hard, but once you learn an object it's easier each time to make it appear again. I'm good at money." He winks at me. "So what do you want to try?"

I blow out a breath, thinking of what could best fend off another Bat Boy attack in Los Demonios. "I don't know. How about a gun?"

His nose scrunches up. "You don't want to do that."

"Why not? The purpose is to protect myself," I reason.

"Because using a gun against a sorcerer more skilled than you is the surest way to get yourself killed. They'd just reverse the bullet direction and you'd shoot yourself. And anyway, that's too complicated for your first attempt. A knife is smarter."

"Well, a knife isn't going to help me much. I'd have to get too close to use it. And plus, I feel kind of weird using a knife. After, you know . . ."

I don't say the words aloud—that Mom was killed with a knife. But I don't have to.

"Sorry, I didn't think of that," he says. "But we have lots of time to work up to something bigger. Let's start simple."

A memory flashes into my head. "I know! What about a shield? The day Frederick took my mom, he trapped me in some sort of invisible box so that I couldn't try to go after them. Isn't there something I can learn that works the same way, except keeps anything from coming in?"

"Easy, Tiger. You're talking about top-level skills here."

I sigh, my shoulders slumping.

"Relax," Bishop says, shaking me lightly. "You don't pick

up a guitar and right away play like Jimi Hendrix. You've got to start somewhere. Try a candle."

I roll my eyes. What the hell can I do with a candle in Los Demonios? Cast some unflattering light on my enemies? But Bishop won't take no for an answer, pulling my hands up in front of me. He turns me around so that his chest presses into my back, and speaks into my ear.

"Instead of pushing the energy down, away from you, like when you fly, feel around for it with your mind and bring it in front of you. The word for 'candle' is *candela*."

I clear my head and stare at the middle distance. Since I've gotten better at flying, I'm more aware of the earth's energy moving all around me. I can feel it in the warmth of the sun, hot and intense, and in the air, fast and thrumming. I can even feel it in inanimate objects—this dull, still presence. I focus on the energy in the room and try to pull it into me.

"Candela," I whisper.

But instead of a candle appearing, my bedroom attacks me. The clothes strewn across my floor, the papers and bottles of nail polish scattered all over my desk, the duvet on my bed, and even the curtains around my window fling themselves at me all at once. I have to cover my face as I'm pelted with my own stuff. I release the energy, and they fall to the carpet.

Bishop's laughing.

"It's not funny!" I cry, slapping his chest.

"And back to the violence," he says through his laughter.

I cross my arms.

"Oh, don't be so mad," he says, trying his best to sober up. "Try it again."

But my heart isn't in making a stupid candle. I want to learn something helpful. I tap my foot, thinking.

"I've got it," I say suddenly. "What about wind? Like I used that day on Jezebel. Say someone tries to attack me with an arrow or a bullet or anything that flies—I can knock it back with force."

"Deadly wind," he says. "Awesome, if we could figure out how you did it. Controlling the natural elements—the sun, the wind, et cetera—that's not something we're supposed to be able to do. I've researched this in everything I can get my hands on, but I can't find anything to explain what you did. Hey, are you sure you didn't do something else? Maybe Jezebel flew backward and you thought you pushed her with the wind?"

I glare at him.

"Okay, okay," he says, hands held up defensively. "I believe you. I just don't know how to help you with that. Maybe just try to simulate the situation. What were you feeling when it happened?"

"Anger," I say, remembering that night. "But fear mostly. That she was going to hurt me."

"Okay, so let's try that."

Except I've already tried. If I couldn't summon it when a

massive bat was attacking me, I'm not sure anything Bishop could try on me now would help.

I dig my fingers into my scalp and pace around the room. I'm fully aware of how impatient and unreasonable I must appear to him, but Paige doesn't have time for me to slowly improve. I need to get better, fast.

I can feel Bishop watching me. Finally, I turn to him again.

"Isn't there some other way?" Desperation clings to my voice.

"What do you mean?" he asks.

I throw my hands up. "I don't know. That I could learn faster?"

"You tried for like, two seconds," he says. "You need to relax—"

"Don't tell me to relax!" I yell. I feel guilty as soon as the words are out of my mouth, but seriously—who has ever actually relaxed when someone has said that?

"I'm sorry," I say. "It's just that since the moment I found out I was a witch I've been hunted. And my mom . . . I just want to get good at this fast. I don't want to practice for weeks or months or years."

I take a shaky breath. When I look at him, I know he sees the naked desperation in my eyes, and it makes me feel so exposed. I pace to the window and look out at Paige's room. The curtains are up, and I can see the yellow paint on her walls. I wonder how long her parents will keep her room this way. When they'll realize she's not coming back. Whether

her room is going to become some shrine to the daughter they once had.

"This is really important to you?" Bishop asks.

I don't answer. I can feel tears hot in my throat, and I don't want to cry right now.

"There is something we can try," Bishop finally says. His voice is dark, hinting at something dangerous.

I turn around.

He glances at the door as if to confirm Aunt Penny isn't listening in, and then crosses over to me. "There's this spell," he whispers. "I heard my uncle talking about it once."

I nod, urging him to continue.

"You know how scientists say that humans use only ten percent of their brain's capacity at any given moment? Well, it's the same thing for us. Even the most powerful witches and warlocks on the planet use only a small portion of the power that's available to them. The rest is there, but you can't access it all at the same time."

"And this spell gives you access?" I ask, hope blooming in my chest.

"For a short time, if you can do it."

"So why didn't you teach this to me ages ago?" I ask. "It's not like we've been short on occasions where it would have been helpful."

"Well, mostly because I like my girlfriends alive," he says. "I mean, I may not have been too discriminating in the past, but I do draw the line at necrophilia."

I shake my head. "What are you even talking about?"

"It's dangerous," he says. "Like, *very* dangerous. We're talking about black magic, Ind."

A shiver moves down my spine. "Dangerous? How so?"

"Because black magic comes with a price."

"Well, that's vague," I answer.

"All that power can be too"—he waves a hand absently, as if searching for a way to explain—"too overwhelming for your brain, I guess. It can put you out of your mind. It's just ugly, okay? Let's stop talking about it. It was a bad idea. Are you hungry? I could really go for—"

"Wait a minute," I interrupt. "How do you know about all this?"

"From the *So You're a Warlock* pamphlet the Family gave me on my sixteenth birthday." I kick him in the shin. "My uncle's friend tried it," he amends. "He was a warlock with twenty years of practice under his belt, and he ended up setting himself on fire. Don't ask me how. Another guy got himself admitted to a mental hospital."

"Really?" I ask, disbelieving.

"Opening those pathways in your brain is dangerous. But that's not the worst part. There's a price you pay when you do black magic. It could be big, it could be small, but the point is, you don't know what it will be, or how badly it will affect you. Most people just know better than to try. It's not worth the risk."

I chew the inside of my cheek as I consider. I'm willing

to try anything, but I have to admit that becoming a burn victim or mental patient does give me a bit of pause.

"But you said it's for only a short time, right?" I ask.

"A couple of hours," he says.

"And you'd be there helping me. I mean, you wouldn't let me do anything stupid. Your uncle's friend was probably alone when he tried the spell—you wouldn't let me burn. You'd help me."

"Listen, I shouldn't have mentioned it—" he starts.

"Don't be like that," I interrupt. "When I met you, you were fun and spontaneous. Aren't you even curious about it?"

It's a low blow, and I feel a pang of guilt.

He looks at me for a long time, fingering the chunky silver ring engraved with the Roman numeral one that's on his middle finger. I wish I could erase the look on his face—like he's considering doing something he really doesn't want to do just to make me happy. But I need this. I can feel how close he is to agreeing.

He keeps twisting the ring around. The ring that, given to Bishop by his mother on her deathbed, gave him extra lives and saved him from dying in the swamp after Leo stabbed him not long ago. Now it's just a chunk of useless metal. I wonder why he still wears it.

"Fine," he finally says. But when he smiles, it doesn't reach his eyes. "I'll ask my uncle about it tonight."

I smile back. "Or how about right now?"

11

Bishop drums his hands on the steering wheel to a punk-rock song blasting from the speakers. His leather jacket is pushed up to his elbows, revealing part of the sleeve of colorful tattoos on his right arm. The setting sun glints off his aviator sunglasses and makes the dark hair around his jaw shine copper.

I smile at my sexy boyfriend. In fact, if I weren't on my way to try out black magic that could set me on fire if it doesn't send me to a mental hospital first, I'd probably tell him to pull over right now so we could make out.

Cars whiz past on the freeway. Houses and shops slowly give way to desert the farther we get from L.A.

I had to lie to Aunt Penny and say I had cheerleading practice to score myself a few hours of free time after school. If she weren't so overwhelmed by the influx of Halloween shoppers down at the Black Cat, I'm sure she would have noticed that it was a Wednesday, and we only practice on Tuesdays and Thursdays. And, ya know, that I'm not a cheerleader anymore.

Double score that the shop has extended hours and doesn't close until ten tonight, giving me a bit of extra time before I have to be home.

"So where are we going anyway, Antarctica?" I ask.

Bishop grins. "We're almost there."

A noise from the backseat makes me jump. I swing around. An old army-green canvas backpack I didn't notice before lies across the faded red leather seat. I can distinctly make out the shape of a box inside the backpack.

"What's in there?" I ask.

"You'll see."

The backpack shakes, and I nearly leap out of my skin. "It moved!" I shriek.

Bishop glances at me, his eyebrows pinched together. "If you're that scared when it's inside the bag, I'm not sure how you're going to do this spell."

I want to demand that he tell me what the hell is in the bag already, but I'm determined to prove that I'm not a wuss, so I pointedly turn around and don't look back even when the bag rocks so violently I have to bite down on my lip to keep from yelping.

A half hour ticks by on the dashboard clock. Soon, we come to a massive mountain range topped with bright green trees that go on for as far as the eye can see. A big sign that reads ANGELES NATIONAL FOREST passes by on the left.

Bishop turns off onto a dirt road.

"Isn't this a popular area for hikers?" I ask. "I thought the point was privacy."

"Yeah, it's popular," he answers. "But haven't you heard of all the dead bodies they find dumped here?"

Um. What the hell do dead bodies have to do with our excursion?

Bishop catches the apprehension on my face and explains. "Some of the places in these mountains are so remote you're unlikely to ever pass another human, unless they wandered off the paths or got lost or something."

Joy. Glad we cleared that up.

Bishop pulls into a small lot in front of a little white information building. He reaches into the backseat and pulls out a pair of knee-high rubber boots. "Put these on," he says. "I'll just be a minute."

"Shouldn't I be wearing hiking boots?" I ask as he climbs out of the car.

"You need these," he says.

He closes the door before I can protest further, leaving me alone in the car with the mystery bag and a lot of questions. I can't get out of there fast enough.

Outside, a cool breeze makes goose bumps rise on my bare

arms. It's at least a few degrees cooler than when we left the house an hour ago. The scent of turned soil and pine trees fills the air, and insects chirp loudly within the thick tree cover. I kick off my wedge sandals and slip into the rain boots.

Bishop's back in a moment, carrying two hiking passes on lanyards. He reaches into the backseat and pulls out the backpack, then slips the straps over his shoulders. He links arms with me, and we set off into the forest.

We walk for a while on a wide path dotted with educational signs about the flora of the Angeles National Forest, but it's not long before Bishop pulls us off the path and the easy hike ends. Trees press in on either side of us, branches clawing at my bare skin as we climb over exposed tree roots and boulders. The boots are a half size too big, and they chafe against my heels as they slip up and down. It's slow and exhausting work.

"How far do we have to go?" I ask.

"Not much farther. We didn't see anyone on the trail, so I think we're pretty safe."

Finally, Bishop stops in a little clearing.

"Dear God, tell me we're here," I pant.

"This is good enough," he answers.

The sun is low enough now that what little light penetrates through the trees casts ominous shadows and makes the tree trunks look like skeletons in a graveyard.

Bishop shrugs out of his backpack, then starts walking around with his head down, kicking aside fallen leaves.

"What are you looking for?"

"A stick," he answers. He picks up a thick, ropy branch from the forest floor. Before I can ask what he needs it for, he starts carving a pattern into the dirt. The carving starts to take the shape of a large circle with seemingly random lines inside it—though I'm sure they're anything but random. I watch quietly as he works, my arms wrapped around myself to fend off the cold.

He stands up finally, a layer of sweat on his forehead. Satisfied, he tosses the branch aside, then crosses back to the bag. My heart is in my throat as he reaches around inside the backpack, but he only pulls out an intricately carved black candle.

"Here," he says, passing it to me. I take it, inspecting the swirling design in the cold wax.

"And this," he says.

I look down to see the hilt of an athame—a ceremonial dagger, like the ones sold at the Black Cat—held out to me. My stomach does a nervous flip, but I try not to let it show as I grab the handle. The dagger is much heavier than I expected, the ruby-encrusted gold hilt and five-inch blade glinting in the fading light.

Bishop reaches into the bag again and pulls out a small burlap satchel, tied at the top with twine. He returns to the circle drawn in the dirt.

"Salt," he explains as he opens the burlap bag. He does

a slow walk around the circle, the bag tipped over so that white crystals fall in a steady stream over the lines in the dirt.

When the bag is empty, Bishop crumples it up and stuffs it into his pocket. He kneels by the backpack, then pauses to look up at me. There are deep lines in his forehead, and his dark eyes are tense with worry.

"You sure you want to do this?" he asks. "Remember, black magic comes with a price."

I shiver at his words, but I'm willing to do anything to help Paige. "I have to try it," I say.

He sighs, like he was really hoping I would change my mind. "You can stop anytime," he says. I don't breathe as he pulls the canvas down around the base of a small glass tank. A flash of movement inside the tank makes me take an involuntary step back. Bishop pulls on a pair of gardening gloves, which does nothing to dispel the fear rippling through me, and then opens the lid of the tank. He plunges his hands inside, then pulls out a two-foot-long snake.

"Holy crap!" I scramble away from him. "What the hell is that for?"

He stands carefully, the snake wriggling in his grasp. Its scales are the deep blue color of the sky at midnight, so dark they almost look wet. Red eyes glow from the snake's triangular head; a forked tongue hisses from a jaw full of spiked teeth. I haven't had many run-ins with snakes in the past, but the ones I've seen didn't look like this. I doubt he picked it up at the local pet shop.

"Where'd you get that?" I ask, not taking my eyes from the snake's liquid scales.

"Irena hooked me up," he says.

Oh, just his insanely beautiful friend. Hooking him up.

"When you're ready, get inside the circle," he says.

Fear courses through me, but I hop into the circle. I expect to feel different being inside its lines, but I don't.

Bishop steps closer. His wary eyes never leave the snake as he holds it as far from his body as possible. The snake, for its part, looks like it doesn't want to be close to him either, recoiling like Bishop is the predator and not the other way around.

"The Bloodhound can smell the supernatural in our blood," Bishop explains, as if reading my mind. "They're more scared of us than we are of them."

Speak for yourself, buddy.

"But that doesn't mean they're not dangerous," he continues. "One bite from this sucker can knock you out for hours, if not days. But it won't try to attack you unless it feels threatened."

My heart races as Bishop approaches with the squirming blue-black mass. "So what do I do to make it feel unthreatened?" I ask.

He glances up at me, an eyebrow arched high.

"What?" The dagger feels heavy in my hand all of a sudden. "No, Bishop. . . ." I back up.

"I said you can stop anytime," he says.

"You want me to kill it?" I croak, like saying it out loud will make it untrue somehow.

"Blood sacrifice is the foundation of black magic," he explains.

"Kill an animal? That's so wrong." My voice sounds thick, my stomach abruptly uneasy.

"I never said it would be pleasant. Listen, Indie, I can put it away. Don't think just because we came out here that you have to go through with this. We can go home right now. I'll help you practice every day after school and all day on weekends. There isn't a rush."

The offer is tempting. I don't think I can kill a living creature, and I definitely don't want to. But as soon as that thought crosses my mind, I think of Paige. Of her unflinching loyalty and crazy-confident smile. She's in that place, facing down demons a million times worse than a snake. I need to do this for her.

"What do I do?" I ask, impressed that my voice comes out so sure, not at all the way I feel inside.

"You need to cut its head clean off."

I feel like I'm going to hurl, but I give a minute shake of my head before Bishop gets any more ideas that I want to stop. *I can do this,* I tell myself. I can kill this mother-effing snake.

"When I put it inside the circle, it'll be trapped by the salt," he explains. "The trick is to kill it before it gets a chance to bite you."

The circle, which had felt so large to me when Bishop was digging it, feels unbearably small now.

"You remember the words we practiced in the car?" he asks.

I nod.

"Okay," he says, bending down carefully. He looks at my left hand, which clutches the candle, and a flame bursts to life at the end of the wick. He leans into the circle, still firmly gripping the snake, then looks up at me for confirmation.

And then he lets go.

The snake slithers frantically over the leaves. I let out a yelp and jump back, my heels pressed up against the white lines behind me. The snake zips straight for the opposite side of the circle, but when it hits the salt, it lets out a hiss and its scales smoke as if burned. It's even more panicked now than before, darting around randomly desperate for a way out. I brace myself, trying to match its movements. I super wish I didn't have a massive bandage hindering my knife-wielding arm right now, making it hard to bend. Sweat slicks my palms, the knife cold in my grasp. My chest is so tight with terror I can't get a good breath.

"One firm hit," Bishop calls. "That's your best bet."

I leap out of the way as the snake darts past me.

Just do it, Indie. Do it for Paige.

I grip the knife tighter and focus on the snake flashing around the circle. I raise the knife over my head, then bring it down with all my might. It *thunks* into something solid, which sends a painful vibration through my injured arm. At first I think I've done it, but when I look down I see the knife is lodged in the earth. A hiss sounds behind me.

"Behind you!" Bishop yells.

I yank the knife out of the ground and spin around, holding the blade out in front of me. The snake has used the strength of its long tail to rise up. Its red eyes glow fiercely, its jaw opened wide to reveal sharp fangs and a flicking forked tongue.

It is pissed. Off.

It lunges at me. I duck just quick enough to avoid getting bit but not to avoid its scales from brushing against my arm. I let out a cry.

"You can do it, Indie!" Bishop cheers, but the nervous tremor in his voice is less than encouraging.

The snake lunges again. I panic and drop the candle, then slice the blade out in front of me with both hands. It makes contact with something solid, and wetness splatters my face. A heavy weight slumps onto my feet.

For a moment, I'm too stunned to move.

"Indie, the candle!"

Bishop's words sober me up enough to look down. The snake lies in two pieces at my feet, black sludge streaked across my boots. Flames from the dropped candle lick quickly along the dry leaves. I snatch up the candle and stomp on the fire until it's out. Smoke curls up from the blackened leaves. I look at the snake carcass again, and a violent gag rises through me.

Remorse and regret swim in my head, making me dizzy. I want to quit, stop this madness now, but then the snake's death would have been for nothing. I have to go through with this. I have to finish the spell.

I drag in a shaky breath and sweep my eyes over to Bishop. He stands with his hands clenched at his sides, like he's waiting to catch me if I collapse, but there's something besides apprehension in his eyes.

Respect. He didn't think I'd go through with it.

"Now chant the spell," he says.

I take a breath, calling the words to my head.

"Dame poderes, tres veces tres, dame poderes, tres veces tres, dame poderes, tres veces tres."

Nothing happens.

"Keep chanting," Bishop says.

"Dame poderes, tres veces tres, dame poderes, tres veces tres, dame poderes, tres veces tres."

"Are you sure we're doing it right?" I ask.

"Yes, I'm sure. I went over it three times with Irena."

Jealousy flashes hot in my stomach, but it's hardly the time, so I tamp it down and keep chanting over and over, until the words start slurring together and the sky grows darker by degrees.

"Do you feel any different?" Bishop asks after a while.

"I feel like an asshole, does that count? I murdered that snake for nothing." I blow out the candle.

"You don't know that," he says, but he doesn't sound very convinced.

Killing the snake seemed like a sacrifice I was willing to make if it gave me an edge to save Paige and those other kids, but to gain nothing at all from it? To have lied to Bishop for no reason? I squeeze my eyes shut against a rush of tears. I can feel him watching me and I wish I could disappear. I'm so disgusted with myself. I'm a terrible person.

"Indie . . ." He starts toward me when a boom of thunder sounds, so loud it makes us gasp. I look up just as a crack of lightning flashes across the sky. A fat raindrop falls on my forehead, quickly followed by more. Before long, my ears are filled with the sound of rain falling fast on the leaves.

"Awesome," I say, throwing my hands up at the sky. "It hardly ever rains in L.A. and it rains right now. The universe hates me."

"Come on, let's get out of here," Bishop says. He scoops the candle and athame out of the circle and dumps them into the backpack, then hikes the bag over his shoulder. He grabs my hand and pulls me through the forest. By the time we've made it back to the path, my hair is plastered to my head, my T-shirt wet and cold against my skin. I shiver so hard my teeth chatter.

"Sorry," Bishop calls over the rain. "I checked the weather, but I guess it's different up here in the mountains."

His words, meant as an apology, strike me like a punch to the gut. I'm being a brat. It's not his fault any of this is happening—he's done nothing but go out of his way to try to help. Sometimes I don't even recognize myself anymore.

I pull up short. He realizes I've stopped and spins around. His hair is wet against his cheeks, and he uselessly tries to shield his eyes from the rain. I wrap my arms around his neck and bury myself in his chest. He pulls me close.

"We'll practice every day," he says into my hair. "Every chance we get."

I squeeze him tighter.

We hold each other for a long time.

12

Aunt Penny knows something is up.

I stir my Cocoa Puffs with more interest than is strictly necessary as she eyes me over the top of the proof of the flyer for the Spooktacular Halloween Sale she's having at the Black Cat. She slowly bites into her toast, her eyes never leaving mine even though she's supposed to be checking the proof for typos.

"How was that math test?" she asks.

"Oh. Um. Good," I lie.

"Good? I haven't seen you crack a book in like . . . ever, actually."

"Well, okay," I admit. "It didn't go as well as I'd hoped.

But I'll make up for it, and my grades are so good it will hardly make a difference."

She's still staring at me.

"All right, what's up with you?" she asks.

I shake my hair around my face like a shield and take another big bite of cereal. "I don't know what you're talking about," I mumble.

Seriously, how could she possibly know about the spell? I had showered and was in bed, my wet clothes hidden beneath a pile of other laundry, *well* before Aunt Penny got home last night. But it's like the woman inherited some sort of parental bullshit radar the day she became my legal guardian.

"You seem unusually . . . distant today," she says.

I shrug. "Do I? Weird. I feel fine. So tell me about this sale. That's a good idea, by the way. I don't know why we haven't thought of it before. What kind of discount were you thinking of offering on the daggers? Thirty percent off, at least, right? I think way more people would buy them if they weren't so expensive." I force myself to quit talking. The kitchen is silent in the wake of my rambling.

Aunt Penny sets down her toast and straightens up. Dread pinches my stomach.

"Listen, Indie, I may be 'old,'" she says, making air quotes. "But I'm not stupid. You've changed."

I don't even know what to say. "Aunt Penny, I . . ."

"You had sex, didn't you?"

I stare at her, openmouthed.

"Knew it," she says.

Heat stains my cheeks. "No, Aunt Penny, that's not true."

"You don't have to be embarrassed, Indie. I mean, it's me. I know this happens when you have a boyfriend, okay? I just want to know you're being careful."

"Ugh!" I bury my burning face in my hands. "Aunt Penny, I'm eating, here."

"It's important I say this," she cries. When I peek through my fingers, she at least has the decency to look almost as embarrassed as I do.

"Trust me, this is as weird for me as it is for you," she says, "But I don't want you to get pregnant or catch some nasty disease because I was too embarrassed to bring it up. Just tell me you'll be careful."

"I'm not having sex!" Which was a feat after living with Bishop for sixteen days, I almost add.

"Just say it."

I huff. "Fine, I'll be careful. Happy now?"

She leans back in her chair. "Yes. Thank you."

I finally let my hands fall from my face.

"So," she says. "Do you love him?"

My cheeks flame a deeper red.

"You do!" she squeals, clapping her hands.

I can't help smiling. "I thought all the embarrassing questions were done."

"Aww, Indie's in *looove*," she coos. I swat at her

shoulder, but she just laughs. "Indie and Bishop, up in a tree, K-I-S-S-I-N-G!"

I stand up, taking my bowl to the sink. "That's really mature, Aunt Penny."

"First comes love, then comes marriage—"

"You're twenty-eight!" I call over her singing, though I'm laughing now too.

———•——•———

My plan seemed so sound last night. Even this morning, the idea of practicing every spare minute I get and then going back to Los Demonios on Saturday, when Aunt Penny has plans to go out for drinks with old friends after the shop closes, seemed logical. For once, I was thinking with my mind instead of just my heart.

But now that I've spent the past twenty-five minutes on a school bus full of gossipy girls and immature guys blowing spitballs at each other, it feels all wrong. It doesn't seem right to be at school while Paige is in that place, in danger.

Everything annoys me.

The bespectacled nerds loudly enjoying a game of mah-jongg on the floor. The football players play-tackling each other against the lockers. The Amy/Ashley twins gossiping about Bianca's Halloween party. The fact that they're wearing their cheerleading uniforms to school because it's a game day (even though just a few weeks ago I was doing the same thing). I want them all to shut up. To quit having so much fun and realize what an effed-up place this world is.

I'm probably jealous. None of them have a best friend who's missing, a dead mom, and a bandage that chafes as well as makes it hard to bend their arm.

Still. Annoying.

I slam my locker closed and turn to head for homeroom when someone knocks into my shoulder so hard I lose my balance.

I fall hard on my ass, my head banging against the locker. A gasp rises through the hallway. Every single person within a thirty-mile radius turns to stare at me.

I hear a snort and look up to see Bianca draped around Devon's shoulder, trying not to smile. With them dressed in matching blue, silver, and black cheerleader/football player uniforms, I can't help feeling even more like a loser splayed out awkwardly on the floor. Anger spikes inside me. I glare at Bianca, my breathing slowing. My stomach boils, and heat flares down to my fingertips.

But then Devon breaks away from Bianca, and I lose my focus. He's helping me up before I can even register what's happening.

"Devon!" Bianca hisses.

He ignores her, picking up my bag and slipping it over his own shoulder. I can feel the eyes of the school on us.

"Are you okay?" he asks. "That looked like it hurt."

"Yeah," I grumble. "It was more embarrassing than anything."

His eyes fall to my arm. "What happened?"

"Got mugged," I say.

His eyes go wide.

I hurry to change the topic before he asks for more details.

"Thanks for the help, but I should get to class."

"You should see the nurse," he says. "You could have a concussion."

"What?" I shake my head. "No, that's silly. It wasn't that bad."

"You're going to pass up a day in the nurse's office?"

I can't help giving a wan smile at the mischief in his blue eyes—dude is smarter than he looks. I look over at the spot where Bianca was, but she's gone. Probably to plot my destruction with the Pretty People Club.

Yay.

The crowd starts to disperse as Devon and I move down the hall. I stare straight ahead as we walk, my eyes focused on the neon-green flyer tacked to a bulletin board way at the end of the hall. It's still too weird to be this close to him. Cheating can have that effect.

"So," Devon says. "How are things? I mean, obviously not so good, with your mom and . . . everything."

"Good," I lie.

"Really?"

I glance over, hearing the genuine concern in his voice. His eyebrows pull together, and for a split second I can remember a time when I thought I loved that face, though I can't summon any of those feelings now. I look away.

"Not really. But, you know . . ."

The first bell rings, and noise picks up as students start filing through the hallway toward class.

I stop. "I can get to the nurse's office okay."

Devon pulls up short. "Oh. Are you sure? Because I don't mind helping. . . ."

"I'm all right. Thanks, though."

He gives me a sad smile, not moving from the middle of the hall as I turn my back on him. I feel sort of bad. I know I shouldn't, since I didn't do anything wrong, but still—he has to live with Bianca now, and that just sucks.

The good thing about the whole incident is that I get to spend all morning lying on a cot in the nurse's office. If I had known being knocked on my ass would get me out of Mrs. Davies's boring lectures and math tests, I would have gotten a head injury a long time ago.

I have a miraculous recovery at lunchtime. I'm in line for some oily cafeteria pizza when I hear someone yell, "Indie!" behind me.

Jessie. Again.

"Hey," she says. "I heard about your fall. Are you okay?"

I sigh. Who *hasn't* heard about my fall? "Yeah, I'm fine. Thanks for asking."

We inch forward. The hairnetted caf lady raises her eyebrows at me, which is her way of asking what I want.

"Pizza, please."

She tongs a slice onto a paper plate and slides it over the glass case.

"Same," Jessie says.

I leave her to pay at the cash register, all the while considering discreet places I can eat my pizza alone, with minimal embarrassment. Someone snags my arm. Lo and behold, it's Jessie again.

"Hey, you want to eat with me?"

I open my mouth to object, but the hope in her eyes—and okay, the fact that I don't have anywhere else to go—reminds me so much of Paige that I just nod and follow her.

Jessie sits at the front of the big hall, at what is politely termed the Loser Table. A few months ago, I would rather have eaten razor blades than sit there, but now, looking at all the faces that give me friendly smiles as I sit down, I couldn't think of anyplace I'd rather sit.

I take a big bite of my pizza, letting the conversation whirl around my head.

A burst of laughter comes from the caf entrance. I look up and see a blob of blue pleats and silver spankies in the form of Bianca, Julia, and half of the cheerleading squad walking in. They're all screeching with laughter at something Bianca's said—I can tell by the way she struts, a satisfied smile on her face.

My first instinct is to try to hide as she nears so that she won't notice me at the Loser table, but the second I have that thought, I feel a twinge of guilt and lift my chin up.

At first I think Bianca isn't going to notice me, but when her eyes sweep the caf, they land directly on me. She lets out a peal of maniacal laughter, her face radiating pure glee. The rest of the Bitch Brigade follows her line of sight. At least they have the decency to cover their mouths and try to stifle their laughter.

"Just ignore them," Jessie whispers.

But I can't. Anger burns up my chest.

"Something funny?" I call over.

The noise sucks out of the caf, and I can hear a person cough from across the room.

"How's your head?" Bianca asks, giving a small laugh. Chuckles come from the Pretty People table at the back of the room—the table I used to sit at—but otherwise the caf remains completely silent.

"It's fine," I say. "I didn't take you for a linebacker. You should try out for the team."

Light laughter erupts through the caf, and red blotches sprout up on Bianca's neck. She clenches her jaw and whips her head around, silencing everyone with a glare. Then she locks her eyes with mine again and levels me with a look of pure hatred.

"You know, people are only being nice to you because they feel bad for you."

Everyone oohs, and I can't help the heat that flashes to my cheeks. Of course by "everyone" she means Devon. For a moment I wonder if she's right, but then I remind myself that I don't care.

"Well, it's a good thing that worrying if everyone likes me is no longer my number one priority in life," I retort. "I don't care if I'm part of the Pretty People Club anymore."

"You're worse than not in the club," she answers, with enough venom that a chill reaches my bones. "You're a nobody."

I don't want to care, but I can't help feeling like the words are true. My eyes feel hot with the threat of tears. This can't be happening.

I don't consider myself religious, but I pray to God, to Allah, to the freaking Buddha to make Bianca walk away right now, but of course, she doesn't.

Bianca lights up like a Christmas tree when she notices I'm near tears.

"Aww!" She turns to the cheerleaders, who circle around her. "Look, she's going to cry."

A tear slips down my cheek. I wipe it away quickly.

Jessie squeezes my shoulder, but that only makes me angrier. Bianca gives me a little wave, a huge smile on her face, then turns on her heel. I glare at her retreating back as heat spreads through my body. The night in my bedroom when I lost my cool on Jezebel and regretted it the next morning comes flashing into my head, but I shove that thought aside.

I want Bianca to be as humiliated as I am, and right now, I don't care if that makes me a bad person. I want to hurt her.

The table begins to vibrate. At first I think I've imagined it, but then my cafeteria tray rocks so hard it clatters to the floor. The ground rumbles like it's being punched from beneath me, rattling my spine. Shrieks rise from all around me, just as a siren blares over the intercom.

Someone yells, "Earthquake!"

I panic. I've never experienced an earthquake this big before. I don't even remember what we're supposed to do.

"Indie, come on!"

Jessie stands next to the table. In the middle of the cafeteria, Bianca and Julia hold their arms out at their sides, trying to keep their balance as the ground rocks beneath them. Pieces of plaster rain down from the old roof.

A low-pitched groan sounds through the room. In a flash, a fissure forms at the center of the cafeteria floor. I can see what's going to happen.

"No!" I stand up, reaching a hand out. But it's too late.

The floor cracks open, and Bianca and Julia fall inside.

13

The windows shatter. I cover my head with my arms as glass rains down around me. And then: silence. Dust motes float in the sunlight blasting through the bare window frames. A few students stumble around, stunned.

My heart thrashes against my rib cage. What happened?

For a moment no one makes a sound, and then the wailing starts.

Bianca.

I dash to the wide, jagged crack that runs through the cafeteria and lean over the precipice. Bianca and Julia lie in a heap six feet below.

"Bianca!" I yell.

She moans. And then Julia whines, "Get off me, fatass."

"Fatass?" Bianca shrieks. "Have you looked in a mirror lately?"

I nearly collapse from relief.

"Are you guys okay?" I call down.

"We're buried in a hole in the freaking cafeteria, what do you think?" Bianca snaps.

And to think, for a second there, I had sympathy for her.

"Out of the way!"

I stumble up as Devon, Jarrod, and a few other football players rush past. Devon jumps into the hole, landing nimbly on his feet.

"Stabilize her neck!" someone yells.

"Devon Mills, get out of that hole this instant!" Mrs. Malone appears through the crowd, looking out of place in her red skirt suit and pumps amid all the destruction. I'm jostled to the back of the onlookers. Sirens wail in the distance, rising over the panicked cries around me.

The heat in my stomach simmers.

First, a rainstorm when I was frustrated. And now an earthquake after Bianca pushed me over the edge. Two freak weather phenomena in two days.

It can't be my fault. It has to be a coincidence.

But the wind that night in my bedroom—I know I didn't imagine that.

I slap my hand over my mouth, sick to my stomach at the possibility that I could have caused this. Someone could have died. And as much as I hate Bianca, have mentally wished she'd get hit by a bus or worse, I don't really want to be responsible for her death. The ground spins beneath me, but this time, it's not because of an earthquake.

An area of stillness among all the chaos catches my eye. I look across the cafeteria and spot Jessie staring at me. Not crying. Not panicked. Just suspicious.

She knows.

I turn and run.

———◆———

"You really think you caused it?" Bishop asks.

I scrub my forehead with the palm of my hand, pacing in the shadows outside the school. "I wanted her dead and the ground swallowed her up."

Bishop exhales through the phone. "Controlling the elements. It's not supposed to be possible."

"Well, it is."

Sirens wail and red lights flash as three ambulances and two fire trucks screech up to the school. It won't take long for the news crews to arrive. I sink down onto the grass as the chaos unfolds around me.

Bishop is quiet for a moment. "So the ceremony worked," he says.

"I thought so, but that was over twelve hours ago. The spell should have worn off by now."

"Well, the spell is obviously not what we thought it was."

I feel faint as the reality of it all sinks in; if this is true, I should be getting back to Los Demonios as quickly as possible. I'm suddenly desperate to end this call. The spell could be wearing off as we speak.

There's a beep from the phone. I hold it away from my face and see that I'm getting another call, from the Black Cat. The school didn't waste any time contacting parents.

"I have to go," I say. "Aunt Penny's calling me."

I switch over to the other line.

"Oh, thank God!" Aunt Penny says as soon as I say hello. "You heard?"

"Of course I heard. Are you okay?"

"Yeah, but Bianca and another girl were hurt."

She sucks in a breath. "*Bianca* Bianca? As in, your old best friend?"

"The same one."

"Oh, Indie," she says. In the background I hear someone ask how much for the bath salts. "Three fifty," she answers. And then, to me: "Indie, is she . . . ?"

"Alive?" I ask, realizing her question. "Oh God, yes. She's going to be fine."

At least, I hope she is. I didn't stick around long enough to find out. My stomach twists. How did I let myself lose control like that again? Do I even *know how* to control myself anymore?

"You sound shaken up," Aunt Penny says.

She has no idea. "I'm just weirded out. I mean, Bianca could have died. It's a miracle no one got hurt worse."

Someone calls for Aunt Penny's attention again. "One second." The mouthpiece of the phone is covered. "Can't you see I'm on the phone?" She huffs, speaking to me again. "Sorry about that. Where are you?"

"Outside the school."

"Okay, stay there. I'm going to close the shop and come get you."

"No!" I shout. "I mean, I'm okay. Don't close the shop. Halloween season is the busiest time of the year. And I'm fine. I think I'll just catch a ride home with someone and take a nap. I'm so tired I feel like I could sleep for ages."

There's a pause on the other end. "Are you sure?" she asks hesitantly. "I don't mind. I can be there in twenty minutes."

"I'm sure," I say. "But thanks for the offer."

"Well, okay. You do need to catch up on your sleep."

I breathe a sigh of relief and end the call.

It doesn't make sense for me to rush back to Los Demonios if I can't figure out how to produce similar results. I need to know that I can do this again. Or something like it, anyway.

I stare at the huge sycamore in the grassy quad, its trunk thick and twisted, its leaves unmoving in the still air. My breathing slows as the heat begins to simmer in my stomach. I stare at the tree and think about a gust of wind blowing through its branches. I think about it so hard that the rest of the world fades to gray.

A loud *crack* splits the air. I blink against the sound, my concentration shattered. When I open my eyes again, it's to see that the tree is split in half, its jagged edges pointing up at the sky.

Holy. Crap.

Cameramen just arriving on the scene swarm the devastated tree. I can already see the headlines: "Two Freak Events Occur Within Minutes at Local School."

My fingers shake as I text Bishop. I tell him the same story about going home for a nap, and then call a cab.

I've got powers that most witches can't even fathom, plus ten hours of free time before Aunt Penny is due home from the shop. The writing is on the wall for another trip to Los Demonios.

14

It's a miracle we don't get pulled over on the way to Venice Beach. The cab does twenty over the speed limit on the freeway, but I still feel like it's not fast enough. If traffic weren't miraculously sparse for midday, I wouldn't hesitate to climb out the window and fly the rest of the way. It's been so long since the spell—my powers could fade any minute.

When I finally reach the boardwalk, I practically sprint across the lot. The same freaks are out in force at the Black Market, but I don't even look twice at them now. To think, just last week I cowered from the cat-bone vendor and now I nod hello to her like we're best buds or something.

I slow to a jog in front of the old witch's booth, panting

for air. The black curtains are pulled back, but I don't see her inside the small shop. That's when I notice that the bottles and instruments on the worktable have been cleared away. Panic overwhelms me. Maybe the witch isn't here today. Or worse, maybe she's left the market for good.

I hang over the counter of the empty booth.

"Hello!" I call out. I want to yell her name but realize I don't know what it is. "Hello?" I repeat. "Anyone there?"

The back door swings open, and the witch is there. Her hands are white with a powder residue that is also dusted across the front of her tattered apron. I exhale a huge sigh of relief and slump onto the counter.

"Thank God," I say. "I need your help. Can I come in?" I don't bother to wait for an answer before letting myself in the side door. The witch's eyes flash with the first hint of life I've seen in them.

"Sorry," I say. "It's kind of an emergency."

She holds eye contact with me for a moment before wordlessly slipping back through the door at the rear of the shop. I follow her into the bowels of the market.

The scent of damp earth becomes stronger with each step I take down the rickety wooden steps, but instead of the darkness that met me last time, the cave is lit up with candles, the crags and cracks of the rock walls cast into deep shadow. The same worktable with bottles and jars strewn across its surface sits in the middle of the cave. The witch gets behind the table and resumes crushing what looks like amethysts into a crystalline gray dust with a mortar and pestle, like I'm not having a crisis.

"I want to go back," I announce loudly.

She lays the pestle down and uses a funnel to shake the dust into a round purple bottle with a small opening.

At first I think she must not have heard me, but then she wipes her wrinkled hands on her apron and looks up at me with eyes hazy with sadness.

"You have a death wish?"

"No." I shift my weight from foot to foot.

She shakes her head. "I trust you brought the payment, then?"

The money I stole from the lockbox feels heavy in my pocket. My whole life, I've never even considered taking money from my college fund. Mom worked so hard to save that money, put in every extra penny she could scrounge, and now here I am, just burning through it. Guilt hits me hard.

"Isn't there some way you could give me a deal? You know, since I'm a repeat customer."

"If you want a better deal you can find someone else to help you." She turns.

"Wait!"

I sigh, reaching into my back pocket for the wad of cash. I hold it out in front of me, and she snatches it, her mouth moving as she thumbs through the greenbacks.

"It's double the amount. I need my car back. I saw it in the parking lot, so I know you still have it."

Her sharp eyes consider me, then the bills, as if she's trying to figure out how I could be screwing her over, but then she puts the money inside her apron, grabs a lantern, and passes into a tunnel off the main room. I follow.

It doesn't seem to help that this is my second time going through with the spell. In fact, I'd argue that I'm more scared knowing what's coming as she leads me through the low-ceilinged tunnels into the back room with the old chair. She leaves me to gather the supplies. I remember the rusty knife, and the goblet to catch my blood, and feel suddenly sick to my stomach.

She's back too soon.

The items clank against the stone floor as she dumps them out of her apron. I catch the glint of the knife in the dim light of the lantern.

"What's your name, anyway?" I ask, my voice tremulous with anxiety or fear or both.

"Sit in the chair," she orders.

I swallow and do as she says, wiping my slick palms on my skirt. She grabs my wounded arm. I gasp.

"Wait, not that one," I say, pulling it out of her grasp.

She snatches it back. "Must be the right arm." She hastily pulls off the bandage, revealing a wound bright pink and puffy with scar tissue.

"But it's not even healed yet!" I complain.

Her wrinkled fingers hold my arm steady. I look away as the blade slices through my skin, sending waves of pain up my arm. I pass out before the cup's half full.

———◆———

It's the pain that wakes me. My arm throbs in time with my heartbeat, barbs of fire flashing up to my shoulder, stinging every nerve along the way. I look down at the wound and then wish I hadn't. A fresh gouge an inch deep and four wide stretches in a jagged line across the scar tissue in the crook of my elbow, like a toddler made it with a pair of rusty scissors. Which, actually, isn't that far off from what happened.

Blood oozes from the wound, saturating the golden sand beneath me. A wave of nausea comes over me and I have to look away before I hurl. I guess I can ixnay a career in medicine.

I listen for the sound of fireballs and lightning, but all I hear is water lapping against a shore and a lone seagull cawing as it circles in the clear blue sky overhead. The air is misty and scented with salt.

Did I travel to the wrong place? Is that even possible?

I rise to my feet on shaky legs, then reach into my pocket for the roll of gauze I brought along. I'd thought it was plenty at the time I found it in the back of the medicine cabinet at home, but the small roll looks painfully insufficient now. I wrap the gauze tight around my arm until I've used up the whole thing. A red stain quickly blooms through the fabric.

Super.

I reach back into my pocket and pull out the two painkillers I brought, which also seem insufficient now. I pop them into my mouth anyway and swallow without water. They sit awkwardly in the back of my throat until I can work up enough saliva to get them down.

And then I sit back down, fighting to catch my breath.

Dark golden sand stretches for a half mile behind me, until it reaches cement seawalls set into a grassy ledge. There's a lifeguard hut painted in a colorful seventies-flower pattern a few paces from me, and a small, red-roofed hut way off on the left. A modest mountain range speckled with houses rises up around the beach.

I've been here before, I realize. Torrance Beach. Bianca claimed it was *the* beach to visit and had forced me to come with her once. We'd quickly discovered it was filled with toddlers in soggy diapers instead of hot surfer dudes and never came back.

I panic as I realize I don't know if Torrance is in sorcerer territory. Cruz said rebel territory stretched all the way to Redondo Beach. My heart races. I can't believe I never thought of this possibility. If I run into Goth Woman or any of the other rebels again, my whole plan could be ruined.

I sit there for a few minutes, panicking and worrying and panicking, but no one comes for me. Of course, the one time it would be convenient to wake up near a battle zone, I get tossed onto an abandoned beach.

I stumble over to the lifeguard hut. The wood creaks as I climb the old steps. Once up top, I put my back to the ocean and shield my eyes from the glare of the sun, looking out over the horizon. But with all the mountains, I only get a better view of the parking lot.

I consider my options.

> Shitty Option A: I fly into sorcerer territory. But the closest would be East L.A., and that's still a major hike from here—I could easily get spotted by a rebel on my travels.
>
> Shitty Option B: I get to high ground in the mountains and try to see if there's activity anywhere around me. This seems like a solid plan until I consider that there could be rebels in the mountains.
>
> Shitty Option C: I use my magic to blow something up and watch from hiding to see who comes. This would work best if sorcerers wore identifying uniforms so I'd know if I should come out or not.

Ugh.

A thought strikes me: I don't even know if my magic still works. Who knows how long I was out for before I woke up? I'm hoping to get captured by sorcerers, but that wouldn't be such a good idea if I had only my basic magic skills.

I decide to try something small to test it.

I focus my stare at the glistening waves a mile out. The heat of my magic moves up quickly into my chest. I think of wind pushing through the calm water, and a ripple, large enough that I know it's unnatural, cuts through the blue. I have just enough time to smile at my success before the ripple grows so big it looks like a tsunami crashing toward the shore. Which is exactly what it is.

Awesome idea, Indie. A-plus decision.

I grip the beams of the lifeguard hut just as the massive wave arcs up over my head, casting me in its shadow.

I take a deep breath and hold on for dear life as the wave comes crashing down. It hurts worse than I expected, smashing into my body like a sledgehammer. In a moment, I'm completely submerged. The waves rip my body in every direction, pummeling me hard against the wood, churning me like I'm in a washing machine, but I cling to the beam with everything I have. The hut sways under the pressure, like it's going to uproot from the sand. I'm desperate for a breath, but the water is so vicious I'm afraid that if I let go, I'll be carried out to sea and pulled under with a current.

When my lungs feel like they're going to burst, the wave

finally recedes, and my head pops up above the water. I cough and sputter, black spots dancing in my eyes as oxygen slowly returns to my brain.

I don't know if it's my wet clothes, or fear, or both of those things, but my whole body is taken over by violent shivering that hurts the bruises quickly forming over every inch of my skin. My new bandage has been pulled loose and hangs in a sopping pile around my wrist, leaving my wound exposed and stinging from the salt water.

Awesome. I'll probably die from a bacterial infection before I save Paige.

I'm pulling off the useless gauze when I see movement flash through the sky. Three people land hard in the wet sand across from the hut.

One guy wears an oversized T-shirt, and a bandanna over his shaved head. A man with huge dreadlocks that reach halfway down his back and a jaw almost as hard as the body visible beneath his white tank top glares at me with contempt (or excitement—it's hard to tell). The lone woman wears a high ponytail, a sports bra, and a smirk I don't have to try hard to decipher.

"And what do we have here?" Sporty Spice says.

Please be a sorcerer, please be a sorcerer.

Magic bubbles hot in my stomach, the instinct to fight them almost too much to ignore. But if the plan is going to work, I need them to think I'm a human, and so I bite down on my lip until I draw blood. The heat doesn't go away.

"Wh-who are you?" I ask. The warble in my voice is a nice touch, though I didn't plan it. I scrabble back as they approach, but there isn't really anywhere I can go. They circle the hut like sharks scenting a bloody meal.

"Come on down, little girl," Eminem calls up. The rest of them cackle.

"We promise we won't hurt you!" Bob Marley says.

Yeah. Right.

I spin around, trying to follow their movements.

I don't notice that Eminem has vanished until he's right behind me, breathing down my neck. I shriek, which is apparently really funny. Sporty Spice rolls in the sand, kicking up her feet.

"How did you do that?" I ask. "Where am I?"

"Ah," Eminem says into my ear, making a shiver pass through me. "We got us another one. Lex?"

The girl rolls up into a tiger crouch.

"Let the fun begin," Bob Marley says. He rubs his hands together.

Fun? What the hell is that supposed to mean? The sorcerers seemed bent on kidnapping humans, and Goth Woman seemed to want answers. These three? They seem like they want blood.

"Don't be nervous," Eminem says. "Let's just go down for a little chat, shall we?"

He scoops me up so fast I gasp, then lobs me over the side. My scream lasts only a second before a pair of hard arms cushion my fall, then spring me out like we're practicing one of Bianca's basket tosses. I manage two disoriented steps in the doughy sand before someone grabs my arm and violently pulls me back. I stumble, just as a boot crashes into my ribs. I keel over, too stunned to feel pain. And then it hits me, white-hot pain bursting from my side, and my mouth opens in a soundless scream.

The guy behind me shakes with laughter. I force my body out of the fetal position and desperately try to pick myself up off the ground, but then a boot strikes the center of my back. I splatter face-first onto the beach, taking in a mouthful of sand. I cough and gag as pain splits my spine, my vision blurring at the edges. The last thing I see before darkness overtakes me is a boot coming for my temple.

15

I wake up to the face of God.

Actually, I think it's Jesus. His face is painted in an elaborate mural on the arched ceiling and surrounded by gilded halos and pink-cheeked cherubs. If my brain weren't banging against my skull so hard that my ears ring and if my ribs didn't feel like they were recently kicked in by a size 9 shoe—oh, and if not for the raised voices volleying swears back and forth at each other somewhere not far away—then I might think I'd died and gone to heaven.

I keep very still, trying to hear the conversation going on before anyone notices I'm conscious. I catch only bits and pieces.

"It's our standard agreement."

"That was before—"

"They're getting desperate. Haven't you seen—"

"She's worth more than that now."

"—probably can get them to toss in Santa Monica."

"After you three idiots roughed her up?"

A scuffle breaks out. I struggle up on my elbows, and a voice nearby cries, "She's awake!"

Before I can get all the way up, a dozen faces surround me, looking down from above. They exchange knowing looks with each other. I recognize the three from the beach among the group, but the rest are new faces. They range in age from early twenties, like Sporty Spice (I'm being generous here), to pushing sixty, like the guy wearing one of those really bad Hawaiian shirts that dads are famous for sporting on hot vacations, although he looks like he could probably bench-press me. I shrink under their assessment.

"Not so bad," Eminem says.

"Are you kidding?" someone pipes up. "Her damn face is purpler than a friggin' eggplant."

"They won't care about that," Sporty Spice says. "They just want a warm body."

"And how do you know that, huh?" The one who said that is a girl with a messy pixie cut wearing an oversized plaid shirt that comes down to her knees. "You have intimate knowledge of the sorcerer's plans?"

Her words are like a blow to my stomach: they're rebels.

What now?

I clear my throat, fighting to keep calm when they turn to face me. "You're Zeke's people?" I ask, remembering the name Cruz used for the leader of the rebels.

"How did you know that?" Sporty demands.

"How *do* you know about Zeke?" Bob Marley asks.

The rest of the rebels glare suspiciously at me.

Crap. How *do* I know that? Revealing my confrontation with Cruz doesn't seem like the best idea.

They wait for an answer I don't have. I think fast.

"I—I overheard it," I lie.

Pixie raises her eyebrows, so I continue.

"I was checking out that hut on the beach when I heard voices outside. I hid before I could see their faces, but I heard their conversation. They said something about this guy named the Chief and this other guy named Zeke."

A few people bark laughter. I don't know what's so funny.

"Zeke's a woman," Sporty explains. "And you're lucky she's not here or you'd be in for it."

"Oh." I remember Goth Woman from the night of the Bat Boy attack—maybe I came face to face with the leader of the rebels and didn't even know it.

"What happened to your arm?" Sporty asks.

"I got mugged yesterday," I answer easily. I've said it so many times it almost feels like it's true.

She assesses my wound for a long moment. "I think she's lying," she finally says.

"I'm not," I say.

"None of us were down at the beach earlier. We were all here for the meeting. How could you have heard anything?"

I swallow. "Well, maybe it wasn't one of you?"

"This is rebel territory," she says. "Who else would you have heard?"

"I don't know," I answer.

"Jason did see that guy nosing around the pier last week," a ginger guy says. "Maybe the Chief's sending spies."

The group breaks out into loud arguments. I don't know what's going on, but I feel really weird lying on the ground while the whole thing unfolds above me. I push myself up, and no one stops me.

I'm standing in front of an altar. Arched stained-glass windows refract colored beams onto the wooden pews stretched across the room, lighting up dust motes that float in the still air. If it weren't for the sleeping bags, pillows, and empty Coke cans littered around the church, it'd probably be beautiful.

I realize that the last time I was in a church was for Mom's funeral. The thought makes my chest constrict. The irony that I might be having my own funeral soon isn't lost on me. I miss Mom so bad it hurts in a place I didn't know existed before she died, but I want to live a long and—hopefully— happy life. I don't want it all to end in this place.

The arguing settles down, and it seems like they've come to some sort of decision. One that makes Sporty Spice very angry. She storms out of the church, the double doors smacking open, then closed in her wake. A few other people leave less dramatically, while still others separate into small groups, conversing in low tones and casting glances my way every now and then.

I wonder if I should make a break for it. I start moving slowly down the wide aisle between pews.

"Don't even think about it."

I gasp, turning to find Pixie staring at me with a very unimpressed look on her face.

"I wasn't—"

She raises her eyebrows, and I stop myself from saying anything else. It's very obvious that I *was*.

"Do you need food?" she asks.

Like I'd eat their food. "No thanks."

"It's safe," she says, guessing my train of thought. "We wouldn't, like, poison it or anything."

Right. Because the people who just beat me to a pulp are above that sort of thing. But anyway, I don't think I could eat even if I were sure the food wasn't laced. My stomach is a ball of nerves. I wonder idly if it's like this with criminals on death row, when they get to eat anything they want for their last meal.

"How about some ice for that head?" she asks.

On cue, my head gives a violent bang from the inside. I decide there's no possible way she could kill me with an ice pack, so I murmur an assent. I expect her to leave, but she just holds out her hand and an ice pack materializes. Of course. I hesitantly reach out and take it from her.

"Any chance you have some bandages where that came from?" I ask meekly.

She rolls her eyes, but complies. I try not to cry with relief when she hands me a huge roll of clean white bandages and a tube of antiseptic ointment.

"Thank you so much," I gush.

She doesn't answer, just turns around, her long flannel shirt flapping as she struts toward a door behind the altar. I sit in a pew and get to work cleaning up my arm. When I'm done, I press the ice pack against my temple and think.

I could use my magic right now, but there are so many people spread out through the church that I couldn't guarantee to get them all if I caused another earthquake or even the wind thing. It'd be as easy as one person noticing my attempt at escape for me to get killed. I need to wait until the room thins out, or they take me somewhere else. I just hope my magic still works then.

I watch the room, quietly assessing and hoping to come up with a better plan. The ice pack drips cold water down my arm. There isn't a clock in this place, but the light slanting through the stained-glass windows shifts, changing the shadows across the room. My stomach growls loudly.

Pixie returns and hurls a box of Ritz Crackers at me without pausing her steps. I'm not expecting it and bat the box away from me like it might be a grenade. She looks at me as if I'm challenged and then goes over to stand with a group of men.

When she's not watching, I crouch down and pick up the box. I'm biting into my third stale cracker when the back doors open, and all the noise sucks out of the room.

Two people stand in the doorway. One of them is a woman in her late forties. She's approximately the size of a tank and sports eighties-style peroxide-blond feathered bangs, too much makeup, and a leather vest (if she carried a purse, it'd be football hold, even if the purse had straps). The other person is the blond guy with the trucker hat who made the crude advance when Cruz had me in the back of the van.

Sorcerers.

I should be thrilled—this is exactly what I wanted—but as they stride down the aisle like they own the place, my stomach does a flip. I drop the box of crackers.

The rebels pull together at the altar as the sorcerers approach. Tension radiates through the air in palpable waves.

"You got us some humans?" Trucker Hat says.

"One human," Hawaiian Shirt answers.

"Just one?"

"Take it or leave it, Ace," Bob Marley answers.

Trucker/Ace/Whatever His Name Is locks eyes with Marley, who responds by sticking his rather large chin up at him. For a minute I'm sure they're going to come to some sort of testosterone-fueled blows, but then Ace glances at me. He pauses, and then his face lights up with a huge smile. Dread washes over me as he saunters toward me.

"Hey, I remember you," he drawls.

I shrink back into the pew, as far from him as possible.

"You're the girl went missing from Cruz last week, huh?"

His twangy voice sends shivers down my spine.

He takes another step closer, but Pixie appears out of nowhere and blocks his path.

"Not so fast," she says.

He looks her up and down and gives a dismissive shrug. Pig.

"Your part of the deal," Pixie says. She pokes him in the chest with her bony finger, even though she barely comes up to his shoulders. I decide I like her.

Ace eyes me over her shoulder, barely paying attention to her. My heart beats hard.

"Santa Monica or nothing," she says. "Safe passage for any rebel. We find a human, we'll turn 'em over, but no Chieftains on our land."

"Fine," Ace says quickly. Pixie is too shocked by his easy agreement to hurl an insult back at him before he passes around her. I scramble to my feet, stumbling backward, but he snatches me by the waist. The grin he gives me makes his green eyes sparkle and bile rise in my throat.

"You're coming with me, little lady. And this time, you *won't* get away."

16

He lifts me up and hefts me over his shoulder.

I scream.

I beat and pound on his back so hard that my already sore muscles flash with pain and my throbbing head feels like it's going to explode. But I don't stop.

"You're going to regret that," his accomplice says, striding behind us. I take a swipe at her, hoping to wipe the stupid grin off her face, but she recoils before I can make contact.

"Don't worry, Candy," Ace says. "I like a screamer."

Candy chuckles, her cheeks ruddy with pleasure. I glower at her, but I don't scream after that.

The church is too quiet. Around Candy's ample girth I

can see the rebels all standing at the altar. They watch my capture in silence, their expression a mixture of acceptance and happiness. Pixie has her back turned to me, pointedly looking away. I decide I don't like her after all.

We burst through the door into sunlight and birdsong. Ace carries me over a stretch of crunchy gravel before setting me down abruptly on my feet. I sway, trying to catch my balance as blood rushes from my head. All the while, Ace stands in front of me, close enough that I can feel his body heat radiating onto me and smell the cigarettes on his breath. I stagger backward, but I run into the warmed metal of a van.

He gives me a long up-and-down appraisal, then clucks his tongue. "Damn, girl. How Cruz let you get away is a mystery to me."

I wouldn't mind dropping this guy into a hole in the earth. I call my magic, and it answers instantly, bubbling hot as lava in my stomach.

"Save the Rico Suave stuff for later," Candy says. The van rocks as she hops into the passenger side. "We gotta be back, pronto."

Ace ignores his friend's comment and takes one of my blond curls in his fingers. He pulls it down, stretching it straight, then lets it go so that it springs back up. A chill seeps into my bones even as my magic pumps hot in my stomach. I will do it. I will kill him if he touches me.

A horn honks.

Ace gives me a long smile. "Later," he says. Like a promise *and* a threat.

He slides the back door open and spins me around. I gasp as he pulls my arms behind my back. Fabric binds so tightly around my wrists that my hands throb and I know that if I could see them they'd be a shade of purple. And then he shoves me into the van. The seats have been removed, and without my hands to brace my fall, my face slaps against gritty blue carpet. Pain bursts through my head. If I don't have a concussion by now, then I don't know what.

"Try anything stupid and I'll make you regret it." He slides the door closed. A moment later, the driver's-side door opens and he hops inside.

"Rock 'n' roll," he says, starting the engine. Country music blares through the speakers at a deafening volume. We jolt into drive.

From my slumped position in the back, I can only see the blue sky through the windshield as we fly across bumpy roads at breakneck speed. Ace taps the steering wheel and mumbles the occasional offbeat lyric. I can't believe the same thing is endearing when Bishop does it.

I remind myself that everything is going according to plan—that I shouldn't be trying to escape—but if this vehicle stops anywhere but sorcerer headquarters, if I even so much as suspect Trucker Hat's going to try something, it will take God himself to save him from the natural disaster I will strike on him.

The certainty is comforting.

After a while, I see flashes of tall buildings and burned billboards through the windshield. When I recognize the spherical shape of the Capitol Records building, hope flutters in my chest. We're in Hollywood.

Sorcerer turf.

I roll backward on the industrial carpet as the van moves up through the hills, the tops of trees cresting the windows. After a while, we stop.

Ace kills the engine, and a moment later, he slides the side door open. I'd expected to find we'd reached a busy headquarters, but all I see are trees.

And we're alone.

I try to scrabble away, but it's next to impossible while lying awkwardly on my side with my hands bound behind me. Ace grins as he pulls me out roughly by my ankles. I scream, my back stinging with rug burn as my shirt rumples up around my stomach.

"Let me go!" I yell as he pulls me up to my feet.

"Not on your life," he says.

I look around for Candy—she doesn't seem like the sympathetic type, but there must be a feminist bone in there somewhere—but she's disappeared. Panic swells inside me. But before Ace can hike me over his shoulder again, a door set into the side of a grassy outcrop swings open.

"Candy said you got another—"

The guy's words stop dead in his mouth.

For a split second I don't recognize him. His olive skin is scrubbed clean and closely shaved, and he's wearing a clean white fitted T-shirt instead of the grubby canvas jacket he wore on our first meeting. But I do recognize the bulky muscles under his shirt, the dark eyebrows drawn together in a brooding expression.

Cruz.

Relief floods through me. I don't for a second trust him, but I know that he has at least some feelings, based on the way he stiffened at my accusations of kidnapping. A person I can deal with. Ace, on the other hand, probably beheads bunnies for kicks.

"Help me!" I plead, before a hand slaps over my mouth.

"Shut up, or I'll make you shut up," Ace spits, pulling me against him. I bite his hand and he lets out a string of swears. His grip loosens momentarily, and I slide out from his grasp, stumbling back toward Cruz.

"What the hell is going on?" Cruz demands.

Ace cradles his wounded hand against his stomach. "Bitch!" he says through clenched teeth. He lunges at me, but Cruz steps between us.

"She's mine!" Ace yells.

I move out of his line of sight, trembling under his hate-filled glare.

Footsteps sound beyond the darkened doorway behind us, and then two more men emerge.

"Would someone tell me what's going on?" Cruz demands.

"I caught another human, that's what," Ace says.

"More like bought one," I say.

If it weren't for the witnesses, he'd kill me this instant. Of this I am sure.

"She's mine!" he repeats.

"Relax," Cruz says. "She's the Chief's." He nods at the two men who joined us. "Take her to the holding tank. And good job, Ace." He squeezes Ace's shoulder. The guards each grab one of my bound arms.

I can't breathe.

"Cruz!" I cry. But he doesn't so much as look at me as I'm ducked through the doorway. The small shred of hope I'd dared to have at the sight of him is snuffed out completely. The world sways under my feet.

The guards don't loosen their grip as they lead me through some sort of dank tunnel set inside the mountain, which is stupid since I can't exactly get far with my hands bound behind my back.

Low lights set at intervals into the curved walls paint strips of shadow onto the rock so that it looks like we're walking through the bowels of a petrified snake. Our footsteps echo against the stone ceiling. Otherwise, it's completely silent. The air is close and smells like dust.

The tunnel twists and turns through the mountain. I try to make a mental map of where they're taking me so that I can remember how to get out later, but after the first dozen turns, I give up.

The good news? We haven't passed another person the entire time we've been walking. If I don't find Paige in this place, it's nice to know I can search for an escape without worrying about getting past dozens of guards.

We stop suddenly in front of an unmarked metal door with thick metal straps bolted across it. One of the guards, a nondescript blond with a stony expression, lets go of my arm to press a fat key into the lock. The door creaks as he pulls it open.

It's dark inside the room, but a sconce in the hallway shines a pale beam of light inside. The walls, ceiling, and floor are made of dirt, with thick roots poking out at intervals.

"This is the holding tank?" I ask.

The guard doesn't answer, just grabs me by the wrist and tosses me inside. I stumble to my knees in the cold dirt. A beetle scuttles across the floor. I shriek, just as the door closes and I'm left in darkness. Boots clomp outside, and then the only sound is my heartbeat and my ragged breathing. I think of the beetle and struggle up. I know that I have much bigger things to worry about than bugs, but still—bugs.

I wonder how long they're going to leave me here. I tug at my wrists, trying to get free of the ropes, but they're bound so tight that all it does is make my hands go numb.

The walls of the minuscule room press in on me. It reminds me of the attic of the Black Cat, of the oppressive feeling of its close walls and secret places in the dark. I remember the last time I was up there, to look for *The Witch Hunter's Bible* for Mom while she remained downstairs with the nosy cop.

My heart gives a painful thump at the unexpected memory. I've been trying not to think of her, because every time I do, I end up a heap of tears and snot. It's normal for a grieving daughter to cry, but I haven't had the luxury of grieving properly. I've needed to search for Paige, and how was I going to do that if I was in bed crying?

But I think of her now.

I think of her radiant smile when I entered the Black Cat after school. Of her shining gray eyes and wild hair that matched my own. I think of the way she rocked into parent-teacher conferences wearing a half ton of silver jewelry and striped leggings, completely unashamed to be who she was even if it embarrassed the crap out of me. I think of her in the bleachers, cheering me on while I cheered on our football team. Of her ribbing me about my boyfriend choices, of her complaining about Aunt Penny's partying even while she made pancakes with ginger for her hungover sister. I wish I'd known how great I had it, that I'd told her I loved her every chance I got.

I'm so caught up in my memories that I don't hear the footsteps until they're outside my door.

The lock clanks, and then the door creaks open. The figure looking in at me is backlit by the pale light from the hallway, so I can't see his face, but I recognize the shape of his hat instantly.

Ace.

I open my mouth to scream, but with one movement of his hand, my voice dies in my throat. Terror rips through me. I try to run past him, out the door, but he gives me a hard shove in the center of my chest, knocking the wind out of me. He jumps into the room, swinging the door quickly closed behind him.

He's inside the room with me, in complete darkness. A bone-crushing fear that something Very Bad is about to happen overwhelms my senses.

I call my magic. I think of the earth swallowing Ace up. I think of a violent wind knocking him back. Desperately, I think of as many bad things happening to him as I can. But nothing happens. Not only is the spell over, but I can't even summon the usual heat of my magic.

The price, I realize with a start. Bishop said all black magic comes with a price, and you never know when you'll have to pay it.

I'm suddenly not so happy about the empty tunnels. I suddenly wish they were crawling with people. Anyone with the potential to stop Ace.

I can't see him, but I can feel his presence. I keep still, trying to hear better so I can anticipate his moves.

A hand brushes my shoulder blade. I spin around and kick

out, but my foot only sweeps through the air. In the moment it takes me to get stabilized on my feet again, he's behind me. His hands are low on my hips, his cigarette breath hot on my ear. I try to move, but he pulls my hips back hard, against him, then moves one arm around my shoulder to pin me to him.

He spins me quickly, and then his mouth is on mine. I bite down on his lip so hard my teeth smash together and I taste his blood. He roars as I spit his blood into his face, then tackles me against the wall. The air is punched out of me, but that doesn't stop me from delivering a swift knee to his groin.

The door swings open. Ace turns.

"What the—"

I have time only to register that the voice is Cruz's before he tackles Ace. Their bodies land with a *thump* that rattles the earth, and then the air is filled with the brutal sound of knuckles punching skin, vicious grunts, and ribs snapping. The space is so small I have to scuttle up against the wall, or get in the way of Cruz's flying fists. I watch in shock as he pummels Ace like he wants to kill him—which he's going to do if he doesn't stop. He just keeps hitting, even when Ace's body is covered in blood and immobile beneath him. I suspect he'd go on forever if he didn't run out of breath first. He stops, bent over Ace and heaving for air. Sweat glistens on his forehead and dampens the front of his shirt.

"You okay?" he asks.

Grateful tears spring to my eyes. I don't normally con-
done violence, but I can't imagine what might have happened to me if Cruz hadn't stepped in. (Well, I can. I just
don't want to.)

I open my mouth to speak, but no sound comes out.

"Of course," he mumbles angrily. He waves a hand,
and when I clear my throat, it makes a noise—my voice is
restored.

"Thanks," I say.

Cruz rises to his feet and uses his forearm to wipe the
blood oozing from his split lip, his chest still rising and falling fast. He looks me over.

"You hurt?"

I give a little shake of my head. The hurt I feel isn't what
he's asking about.

"Did he . . ."

The implication lingers heavy in the air.

"No. I mean, well, he did . . . but he didn't." I don't know
what to say about what Ace did.

He looks over at Ace like he wants to give him another
kick in the ribs.

"How did you know?" I ask.

"I didn't," he says. "I just came to check on you."

More footsteps sound from the hall, and then a voice:
"Hurry up, Cruz. The Chief's waiting."

Cruz reluctantly drags his eyes from Ace. When they meet
mine again, there's something pained there that I don't

understand. A switchblade materializes in his hand. I gasp as he takes a swift step closer to me. But then he reaches around me and cuts the fabric binding my hands in one quick movement. I shake my hands out, then rub my sore wrists.

He looks behind him at the door before continuing in a rush. "Look, if you want to leave, now's gonna be your only chance."

My heart races at his words. At the excitement flashing in his eyes.

"What do you mean?" I ask.

"Cruz!" someone yells down the hall.

His jaw clenches. "*Mierda*. We haven't got much time. It's now or never. You want to get out of this place or what?"

Footsteps sound nearby.

"Yes or no!" he hisses, waving a hand for me to hurry up and answer.

I freeze with indecision. Of course I want to leave—I want to get as far away from the guy on the ground as possible. But Paige might be in this place. I'm so close now.

A man pokes his head through the doorway. "The Chief's going to bust a nut if you don't . . ." His eyes fall to Ace. "What the hell happened to him?"

"We're coming," Cruz says.

The man stares mutely at Ace a moment longer before slowly backing out of the doorway.

"Let's go." Cruz motions for me to exit the holding tank. The excitement I'd seen in his eyes a moment before has been stamped out completely, and he looks at me like he's unbearably sad. I step around Ace's body. Cruz holds the door open for me, and I pause in front of him.

"Too late now," he whispers.

But that's not why I stopped.

I push my face into his chest, my damp cheek against his warm collarbone. He hesitates a moment before wrapping his arms around me.

"Thank you," I whisper, my voice hoarse. His heartbeat drums through his T-shirt.

"Cruz!"

Cruz pushes me off him. The girl standing outside the door looks at the small space between the two of us with an expression of utter disgust on her face. I want to explain so that he won't get in trouble, but I have a feeling it would be better to just shut up.

"Let's go," Cruz repeats, then takes off down the hall.

The girl grabs my wrist and gives me a shove in the opposite direction from Cruz. I walk dutifully, but I can't help turning to look back at him.

He's already gone.

17

Our footsteps echo through the tunnel. The girl's bright blond ponytail swings in front of me as she struts down the hall, not even bothering to turn to make sure I'm following. I could probably make a run for it right now. And I should probably try—it's what any human would do. But she's taking me to the Chief, the leader of the sorcerers. And if anyone knows where Paige is, it will be him.

My legs feel weak, and every time I think of Ace's mouth on mine I have to choke back vomit. I don't have to wonder if that moment will haunt me forever.

After a while, voices begin to echo from around a bend in the tunnel.

"Who's there?" a man's voice calls. We wheel around the corner and come to a stop in front of two beefy guards in tight shirts and skullcaps.

"New recruit," the girl says, like a soldier speaking to a drill sergeant.

The men eye me for what feels like a century before finally stepping aside. One of them pulls open a heavy metal door behind them.

"Sir, I have a new recruit for you," he says to whoever is inside. I never would have thought such a cloying tone possible from such a douche. The guy salutes, then turns to me, waving me forward impatiently. I swallow and take a hesitant step. The blond girl starts to come with me, but the other guard steps in front of her, blocking her path.

"Not you."

"But—"

"Recruits only," he says. The girl stomps off down the hall. I watch her swinging blond ponytail and suddenly feel very sad to see her go. I'm alone with these men.

I walk slowly up to the door. The guard huffs and yanks me over, shoving me inside and slamming the door with a clank so loud it makes me gasp.

The room I've entered is made of the same rock as the tunnel. There's a little round table set with fancy saucers for tea against one of the walls, and a red divan straight out of the 1800s against the other. A fancy lamp atop a heavy mahogany desk at the back of the room shines a circle of dim light on a braided rug.

And standing in front of the desk is the Chief.

He doesn't look anything like I'd expected him to. The name had inspired images of a long-haired, bare-chested Tarzan type, but the man standing before me wears a burgundy smoking jacket over a button-down shirt. His light blond hair is dusted with gray, and he wears it short, save for a cowlick that sweeps above his forehead. He watches me with interest, his eyes intelligent and calculating. When his mouth stretches into a wide smile, his teeth are so big they look like they belong in another man's face.

I shudder—I think I'd prefer the Tarzan type.

"Don't be scared," he says, still smiling that Cheshire cat smile. "I'm not going to hurt you."

I feel around inside for my magic. Nope, still not there.

"Would you like some tea?" he asks. "Coffee, perhaps?"

I give a tiny shake of my head, never breaking eye contact with him.

"Suit yourself. Why don't you have a seat?" He gestures to the divan. He watches me for so long and with such intensity that I move to the seat almost not of my own volition. I clasp my shaking hands in my lap as he walks over to the round table and pours himself a cup of tea.

I flash my eyes around the room.

"You can't escape," he says, without so much as a glance

my way. "The walls are solid rock for a half mile in any direction, and it's heavily guarded both inside and out." He sends me a sidelong smile meant to seem kind, but with his large teeth, it only seems demented. "You're probably very confused," he continues, stirring sugar into his cup. The spoon clanks against the china. "I bet you're wondering where you are. What's going on."

I manage to murmur "Yes."

"You needn't worry," he says. "You'll be at peace very soon."

I wonder if that's supposed to be comforting.

His eyebrows rise high as he slurps his drink. "Mmm, that is *fantastic*. Are you sure you don't want a cup?"

"Who are you?" I finally ask.

"Oh, how rude of me!" He sets his cup down and crosses over to me, stretching his hand out. "Everyone calls me the Chief." I reluctantly take his hand, trying to repress a shiver as he grips mine. "And your name?"

"Ind . . . dia. It's India."

I don't know why the fake name tumbles out of my mouth, just that it doesn't seem smart to tell him the truth if I don't have to.

He gives me a big-toothed smile. "India, what an unusual name—beautiful name. Welcome to my home."

He watches me for a long moment, and I have to scream at myself not to squirm under his stare. At first I think he's waiting for me to thank him for the compliment, but when he raises his hand up and points a long finger at my face, I realize it's something much worse.

I gasp, automatically covering my face with my hands.

But nothing happens.

I keep waiting, and after a while, I lower my hands. The Chief's grin slowly slides off his face.

"What did I just say to you?" he demands. I sink into myself at his angry tone.

"Um." I rack my brain for his last words, not at all sure what I did wrong or why he's suddenly so angry. "You said I had a beautiful name?"

"Impossible! Why didn't it work?" He kicks his leg out, and the tea cart goes crashing to the ground. The door opens.

"Everything okay, sir?" one of the guards asks.

"Did I tell you to enter?" he yells. "Did I tell you to open the goddamn door?"

The door is pulled closed. When the Chief faces me again, his eyes flash with a terrifying rage. He looks like he wants to rip off my face.

He points his finger at me again.

It comes to me in a flash—the sad look on Cruz's face, the Chief's words that I'd be at peace soon—he was trying to erase my memory. Only I'm a witch, so it didn't work. Holy crap. He's going to find out an enemy snuck into his camp. And then he's going to kill me.

His finger vibrates in the air. I realize with alarm that if I'm going to stay alive, I'll have to make him think his spell worked.

I fall back on the divan, pretending that I've passed out. And then I remember waking up seated in Mrs. Malone's office the day my memory really was wiped, which ixnays the possibility that passing out happens during the spell. I push myself up quickly, one hand pressed to my temple as I whip frantic looks around the room.

"Who are you?" I ask. "Where am I?"

The Chief's mouth twists into a smile.

"They call me the Chief." He reaches out his hand almost reverentially. I don't take it, but his smile never fades.

"Would you mind very much if I sat down?" he asks. "I'd like to tell you a story that might shed some light on where you are. Who you are. You're probably finding that you can't remember much right now."

He sits lightly on the end of the divan and smoothes his hands over his trousers.

"Once upon a time, there was a boy named"—he twirls a finger in the air—"Ivan. Ivan had a sister named Rowan. When he was just a very young boy, Ivan discovered that the world wasn't as he thought it was: it was filled with fantastical people—witches and warlocks and sorcerers. People who used magic. He learned that he had magical potential too, as did his sister. Their parents were both sorcerers. As you can imagine, young Ivan thought that life would always be grand with this power at his hands, but that wasn't so." The Chief's face grows serious.

"Ivan's parents were killed when he was just seventeen, his sister a mere nineteen. Brutally murdered at the hands of witches who feared his parents' power." He looks at me. I give a nod to show him I'm following.

"These witches," he continues, "were a part of a very corrupt organization called the Family. Their sole purpose in life was to rid the world of sorcerers so that they could be the only magical people on the planet. They were a very greedy and very evil bunch."

I want to interrupt and tell him that I know all about sorcerers, and that they're not so innocent themselves, but I'm smart enough to stay silent.

"Ivan and Rowan were justly angry at the loss of their parents, but they were only children, really, just two sorcerers against a massive, powerful organization. The people who were supposed to stand behind them—other sorcerers— agreed that the Family needed to be stopped. They told Ivan and Rowan not to try to exact revenge themselves. You see, due to a powerful spell, sorcerers could not kill a witch without being drained of their powers, thus leaving them defenseless. But these sorcerers—the Priory, they called themselves—they promised that they would do everything in their power to get the revenge that Ivan and Rowan so sorely desired. And so, trusting them, Ivan tried to live a normal life. He finished school. He met a girl. He even had a child. His sister, on the other hand—she never could forget. She got into quite a bit of trouble, and disappeared for a few years with some underground group of sorcerers. But Ivan was good. He listened to the rules the Priory had set out for him. He tried to be happy, but all the while he burned for the blood of his parents' killers to be on his hands. And then one day his sister returned: she'd heard of more murders. A group of a dozen sorcerers had been killed. No reason, just that the Family decided to do it. Can you imagine?"

The Chief dips his head toward his chest, pausing for effect. This guy deserves an Oscar.

"By this time, the Family had doubled in size and grown more powerful than ever. Ivan was angry—he'd trusted his people to protect them against further deaths, but they'd let him down. He decided in that moment to join his sister in her bid for revenge. But the Family were smart, constantly moving their headquarters, and Ivan and Rowan didn't know where to find the leaders. They decided that, instead of trying to scout them out, they would bring their enemies to them. Knowing that keeping the world of paranormals a secret was the most important value of the Family, Ivan killed a human. He cut off her head and raised it on a staff in the middle of a popular town monument."

He smiles as if the story were his own cherished memory, and a chill shudders through me. I suddenly realize how the Chief got his nickname—he is that murderous boy in the story. He is Ivan. I had an idea that he was sick and demented, but had no idea of the depths of it.

"But that didn't attract the Family," he continues. "Ivan and Rowan realized they'd have to match their brutality to the Family's to catch their attention. And so they killed dozens more this way. But as determined as the siblings were to best their enemies, the Family caught up to Ivan during an operation gone bad. He was captured. Thankfully, Rowan escaped."

His eyes turn dark at the memory, and he laughs without humor. "Oh, they pretended to give him a trial so that the other witches and warlocks would think they'd been fair, but it was no surprise to anyone when they found him guilty. The Family had access to a portal to another dimension, a dimension completely cut off from the rest of the world, filled with the dregs of the paranormal world. And this is where they sent him. His sister would be left to suffer alone with the debilitating grief of the loss of their parents. He would never see his wife again. Never see his baby grow. And the sorcerers who were supposed to be on his side, to protect him? They did nothing to stop it."

I can't keep quiet any longer. "If he cared so much about his wife and baby, then he should have thought about the consequences before murdering dozens of innocent people."

"Do *not* interrupt!" he yells.

I'm stunned into silence. The Chief closes his eyes for a

long moment, and when he opens them again, he's composed himself.

"This place, it looked like his home, but it wasn't. He tried everything to escape, but not even the wealth of magic available at his fingertips could take him home. Though time passed, his anger burned on inside him. He awoke every day with the singular goal of escape—of revenge against the Family. Over time his skills grew and he became a leader inside this horrid place. And then one day, many years after he'd been incarcerated, Ivan had a special visitor. His sister, Rowan, had bribed a witch for access to the Family's portal. Ivan thought his sister had forgotten him, but she assured him this wasn't so. She'd been planning a way to help him escape since the day he was sent away. Together they plotted. It was difficult for them to wait to enact their plans, but both of them knew everything had to be perfect this time, couldn't be rushed—they weren't going to risk getting caught trying to sneak out of the portal when Rowan left after one of her visits. And all of their patience was worth it. One day Rowan came to Ivan with great news: She'd found a way." The Chief's eyes get bright, the closest thing to a genuine smile possible on such an evil man lighting his face.

"The first part of the plan involved a Bible. You see, Rowan learned of a Bible that could be used to kill a witch without draining a sorcerer of his powers."

My stomach flips. *The Witch Hunter's Bible*. The thing

that got my mother killed. Got me into this whole, horrible mess.

"She would find the Bible, which they would then use when the second part of the plan went into effect."

A second part of the plan? Everything that had happened to me, every awful thing that I went through, it was all just part one of a larger plan? And if the Chief and his sister are really in charge of it all, then killing Frederick and Leo didn't stop the Priory after all, like we'd thought it had.

"Unfortunately, that part didn't go quite as planned," the Chief continues. "The Family struck again, killing three-quarters of the sorcerer population in our hometown. Fed them to crocodiles. Can you believe such evil people exist?"

I lower my eyes, the realization that he's talking about me and the swamp debacle the night after homecoming making heat blotch my cheeks. What would happen if he discovered I was the person who killed off the Priory?

"And worse," he continues, "they erased the memories of countless innocent young ones, such as yourself, for God knows what reason."

Liar. He just "erased" my memory five minutes ago. What other parts of the story are a lie?

"So why am I here?" I ask.

"I was getting to that." He smiles at me. "Because we saved you. The Family, they kidnapped you and erased your memory. You see, you'd been a witness to their crimes, and they didn't want you to spread the word. But we took you away in the cover of the night."

He stares at me so long that I feel like he's waiting for a response.

"Thank you," I mutter.

"We just couldn't *stand* that the Family was abusing innocent humans this way, and we couldn't be sure they wouldn't strike against you again. Fearing for your safety, we brought you here, to this place. To my home."

"When do I get to leave?" I ask.

His jaw tightens almost imperceptibly, but then he's back to smiling that menacing smile.

"Soon, dear. See, what we want to do for you—for others like you—is to offer you protection against these evil people. We want to make you one of us."

He wants to make me . . . a sorcerer? That's impossible. At least, I think it is.

"Hold out your hand," he says. I hesitate before I shakily offer it to him. He turns it so that my palm is facing up. A red spot appears in the center. I gasp as the spot blooms into a fresh red rose the size of an apple. Dewdrops cling to its velvety petals.

"Impressive, isn't it?" He takes the rose from me, inspecting it up close. "This, little lamb, is nothing compared with what you will be able to do with our powers. Fancy a new outfit? A sporty car? You can have them. Everything is in the palm of your hand. Wish to make a boy love you, to make yourself beautiful? Do you have an enemy?" His palm closes over the rose, the petals strangled by his grasp. "Crush him." He opens his palm and flourishes his hand— the petals turn to shimmering red dust that slowly sifts to the ground. His eyes glint as he smiles at me. "Would you like these powers?"

"What's the catch?" I ask.

He grins. "You're smart. See, there is a small catch. We will give you these wonderful, life-altering powers, send you back home to your friends and family with your memory restored. Life will be as it was, only better. And all we ask in return is that you show allegiance to us should a war erupt between factions. The chances of this are very slim—I can't emphasize that enough. With the numbers we'll have very soon, the Family won't want to go to war with us—they wouldn't take that risk. You likely wouldn't hear from us ever again, except of course to say hello from time to time."

"So what's the second part of the plan?"

"Pardon me?"

"You said the first part of the plan was to steal the Bible— what's the second part? Not to change me into a sorcerer just in case, right?"

"Well, unfortunately, that is highly sensitive, top-secret information. You'll just have to trust me."

I'll get right on it.

"And what if I don't agree?" I say. "Can I go home?"

His smile doesn't falter, but his hands clench his knees

like he might break them with his grip. "We've never had someone say no. But should you want to go home, to throw away all this potential, all this great power, then we certainly wouldn't stop you. Take a minute to think about it. *Really* think about it." He gets up and paces over to the desk, leaving me alone on the divan. He flips through papers with his back to me, though I can tell it's just an act to make it seem like he's not overly invested in my answer.

It's all a lie. He's using these humans for something else. Something much more sinister than what he's admitted to. All I know for sure is that he wants revenge on the Family. The fire in his eyes when he spoke of them—you can't fake that kind of hatred.

"I've made up my mind," I announce. He turns around slowly, his eyebrows raised so high that his forehead creases with wrinkles. "I want to become one of you."

His face breaks into a wide grin. "Excellent. I had a feeling you'd say that."

Just then, a knock sounds on the door.

"Enter," he calls cheerily. The door cracks open.

"Sorry to interrupt, sir," a female voice calls.

I recognize that voice.

"It's all right, dear, we're finished. What would you like?" He waves the female forward. The door groans open farther, and the girl comes into view.

Jezebel.

18

At first I think my eyes must be playing tricks on me—there's no way Jezebel could be in this place. And yet there she is, all five feet nine of her, gorgeous auburn waves trailing over the back of her moto jacket.

Has Jezebel been kidnapped too? If so, she's doing a good job of hiding her fear; she looks just as at ease in this place as the Chief himself.

"Rowan's sent through another three recruits," she says.

"This is good news," the Chief answers, smiling ear to ear as he steeples his fingers. "Delightful news."

Jezebel gives one of her trademark tight smiles. "The word is they landed in rebel territory, but we've got teams out there looking for them. They should be back before sundown."

"Excellent!"

"But there *is* a problem," she says. "Rowan says the media are starting to notice all the disappearances. It's made the national news, and she worries—"

"That's enough," he says, cutting her off. His smile vanishes. "Thank you for the information. I'll deal with it shortly."

Jezebel exhales sharply; it's obvious she's not used to being spoken to this way by him.

The full realization of what's happening sinks into me. Jezebel's betrayed us. She's working for the Chief.

I'm overcome with the desire to lunge at her. To tear out her gorgeous hair and smash her face into the ground. I dig my fingers into the velvet divan so hard I can't believe the fabric doesn't puncture.

Jezebel's eyes land on me, and she gasps. If it's true, and she's part of the Chief's plan, this could all end right now. All she has to do is out me as a witch and I'm a goner.

"You can leave now," the Chief says. "Thank you, Jezebel. Your hard work is appreciated."

Jezebel keeps staring. I beg with my eyes, *Please, Jezebel, don't say anything.*

But why should she do me any favors? Last time I checked, I did almost slam her into my bedroom wall.

Finally, she breaks eye contact with me. "Thank you, sir. I'll keep you updated." She retreats toward the door.

She didn't tell on me. It's shocking, but I don't for a second think it's because she's not up to something after all. This much is clear: Jezebel is a traitor. She's working for the same sorcerers who had my mother killed. Who kidnapped my best friend.

"Oh, and, Jezebel?" the Chief says. She stops in the doorway. "Please send in a guard on your way out."

She salutes, avoiding my eyes as she slips out.

I'm still reeling with anger when two beefy guards enter the room.

"Please escort Miss India to her living quarters. And remember to treat her nicely—she is our *special* guest."

It's impossible to suppress my shudder at his words.

I don't bother resisting as I'm escorted down more winding, nondescript rock hallways. Eventually, we come to a stop in front of heavy double doors. The muted chatter of voices filters into the hall.

The room is about as big as the cafeteria at school. Though its walls are the same dark rock as the rest of the place and there are no windows to the outside world, the track lighting overhead is so bright you almost don't notice. In addition to the puffy couches set up around big-screen TVs and card tables, there are braided rugs thrown down over the dark wood floors, modern art on the walls, and bright green planters springing up from every corner of the room. If it weren't for the glass cubicle hanging from the center of the ceiling that holds a guard who surveys everyone with his hands clasped behind his back, it might even be called cozy.

The room is filled to the brim with teens. They're wearing clean clothes and don't look like they've been tortured recently. More shocking: they look happy.

I take a tentative step inside, listening in on a conversation at a nearby table in hopes of overhearing something useful about this place, but they're just politely arguing the rules of rummy. People glance up as I pass and give me friendly smiles, which I find hard to return. I scan the group of teens around one TV, then another.

Finally I see her.

My heart lodges in my throat, the air punched out of my chest.

Paige looks exactly like she did the last time I saw her. Her shoulder-length brown hair is pulled back into a spiky ponytail, her bangs brush the rims of her leopard-print glasses. She's wearing a T-shirt with the name of some band I've never heard of and a pair of tweed trousers rolled up at the ankles to show off her Converse sneakers. She sits with her feet up on a coffee table, reading a large book spread open in her lap. Even the way she reads strikes a familiar chord in my heart.

I realize I'm smiling, and quickly wipe the grin off my face. I flick a glance up at the guard in the cubicle, but he's looking the other way.

All I want to do is run over and pull Paige into a hug, but I can't attract attention. I slowly cross the room, feeling the space between us shrink little by little. My chest is so tight I can't breathe properly. I scan Paige's arms as I approach, looking for signs she's been hurt in some way. . . . Nothing. Her face doesn't contain a pinch of worry.

She doesn't look up from her book until I'm standing over her and she's steeped in my shadow. I open my mouth, ready to blurt out that I'm here to save her, that she doesn't have to worry anymore, but the polite look she gives me stops me dead. She smiles and reaches out her hand. "You must be new. I'm Paige. Nice to meet you."

Pain bursts through my chest.

"Are you okay?" she asks, leaning forward. "I can call the guard."

"No," I answer too quickly. I wipe my slick hands on my pants and then reach out to shake her hand. "I'm fine. I'm . . ." I almost say India, but then I drop my voice an octave and say, "Indigo. Indigo Blackwood."

I watch her face closely for a flash of recognition, but she just smiles.

Oh, Paige. What have they done to you?

The discovery that she's happy here should be a comfort, but instead I feel more disturbed than if I'd found her bound and gagged. What they've done to her is almost worse than physical torture. They've taken away the part of her that is Paige and left a hollowed-out version of her in its place.

Our hands drop. The world sways at impossible angles beneath me. I fall into the nearest seat so I won't pass out.

She's eyeing me strangely now, so I grab the nearest book off an end table beside the couch and open it to the first page. The words blur together.

"It's strange the first day, but they're really nice here," Paige says.

I look up. Her face is so open—it's like she really believes what she's saying. My heart breaks.

I force a smile. "That's good."

She goes back to reading.

I don't know what to do. I've gotten this far, but none of it will matter if I can't get her to come with me.

She *has* to remember me. We have almost sixteen years of shared history—one spell can't possibly erase all that.

"Too bad they haven't got *Atlas Shrugged,*" I say, patting myself on the back for remembering the name of her favorite book.

"What's that one about?" she asks.

Strike one, Indie.

"Just some cool book," I mutter. God, how far back did they wipe?

She gives me a weak smile and returns to reading.

"Do they let us listen to music?" I ask.

She furrows her brow. "No, not really."

"Not even a radio? Why do you think that is?" I lean forward, but then I realize the guard is watching our interaction and force myself back against the couch. When I glance over at Paige again, she's still watching me.

"I don't know," she answers carefully.

I see it in her eyes—the spark of curiosity. The doubt.

"Do you think there's something they don't want us to hear?" I whisper.

She looks up at the guard's glass case.

I should shut up. I should stop talking to her when she's becoming anxious. But I'm so close now. I can feel it. She doesn't trust the guards or she wouldn't be nervous about them hearing our conversation. And Jezebel could tell on me any minute—this might be my only chance.

"They're not good people, are they?" I whisper.

She snaps her book closed.

"Paige, don't go." My words come out in a rush. "I have something important to tell you. I know you don't remember me, but that's because these people have erased your memories. We're best friends. These people killed my mom and they kidnapped you and took you here. They're not who they say they are. I can get us out of here."

She gets up.

"Paige!" I grab her wrist.

She glances down at my hand.

And then she screams.

19

I quickly release her wrist, but it's too late. An alarm sounds, and a red beam of light flashes across the hall. And over it all is Paige's screaming.

Four more guards appear in the glass cubicle. The first one points me out to the others.

No, no, no.

I get up and grip Paige by the forearms. She shrinks under my touch. The action burns like a slap to the face.

"Paige!" I cry. "Come with me. We have to get out of here. There's still time."

Tears well in her eyes. She glances around nervously, like

an animal backed into a corner. I hear heavy footsteps behind me.

"Paige, it's me! It's Indigo. You have to remember me."

I'm grabbed from behind. Her eyes are full of apology, but she gives a little shake of her head.

"I—I don't know who you are," she mutters.

I'm dragged away, but I don't fight back. The room has gone silent, the weight of dozens of eyes following me as I'm pulled away. I don't know if I could stand if it weren't for the people holding me up.

The next few hours pass by in a blur. I'm brought to some sort of examination room with only a steel table and a chair, and lit by a single bare bulb. One guard after another takes turns coming in to try to coax answers out of me ("What really happened in the mess hall? Why did Paige scream? Do you know that private conversations are strictly against the rules and can be viewed by the Chief as conspiracy to commit treason?"), but I don't talk to any of them. My tears have dried on my cheeks. I've finally stopped crying. I don't have the energy left.

It's impossible to tell time here, but it feels like I've been gone from Los Angeles for ages. I keep waiting for the head-splitting pain to signal that I'm getting shot back home, but it never comes.

Finally, a female guard lets me out of the examination room. I think she must be taking me to the Chief for some sort of punishment for insubordination, but I'm surprised when she opens a door to a dormitory full of military-style steel-frame bunk beds. The kids from the mess hall are inside. They stop chatting and watch as I'm led down the aisle between rows of beds.

My stomach is coiled into a knot at the thought of seeing Paige again, and I sweep my eyes over the room looking for her. The guard stops at an empty bunk at the back of the room.

"Change into the nightgown," she says dryly. "Bathroom is at the back." She turns to leave.

"Wait!" I say. "What happened to Paige?"

She looks back over her shoulder at me, one eyebrow quirked high. "The screamer? You're no longer allowed to associate with each other until one of you tells the truth." She gives me a pointed look before spinning on her heel.

I stare slack-jawed at her back as she retreats, her words spinning inside my head. Two male guards step aside from the double doors as she passes, then resume their post and watch over us.

I realize I'm smiling—Paige didn't tell them what I said. Strong, rebellious, independent Paige is in there somewhere.

I can feel everyone staring at me, so I wipe the goofy grin from my face and sit down on the hard bed. There's a thin green bedroll at the end; laid over it is a white nightgown and a ziplock bag containing a toothbrush, travel-sized toothpaste, and deodorant. I guess kidnapping is okay in their books, but not smelly victims.

Slowly, the silence gives way to chattering. The girls pass back and forth as they use the bathroom to get ready for bed and, I suspect, to get a better look at the crazy new girl. But I don't pay them any attention. I split my time between thinking about how I can find out where they've taken Paige, and how I can get her to come with me once I've found her.

A girl walks down the aisle toward the bathroom, and an idea strikes me. I grab the nightgown and bag-o'-supplies and follow her.

The bathroom has a dozen or so stalls opposite a wall of sinks, plus a row of open showers at the back. The girl I followed is standing at the sink, squeezing toothpaste onto her brush, when I enter. She freezes when she spots me.

"Hi," I say.

She must sense my intentions, because she runs, her bare feet slapping the gritty tile. I leap in front of her before she can pass me. She opens her mouth to scream but I clamp a hand over her mouth.

"Shhh, I won't hurt you," I whisper. "I just want to know where they're keeping Paige."

She whimpers, shaking her head.

"The girl from the mess hall—the one who screamed. Where would they be keeping her?"

The girl keeps shaking her head.

"Look," I hiss, my patience running out. "I said I wouldn't hurt you, but I will if you don't tell me the truth. Where is she? Speak. Now." I lower my hand to her chin.

"I—I really don't know," she stammers. Tears spill down her cheeks onto my hand. I drop my arm to my side.

"Say anything to the guards about this conversation and you'll regret it."

She stumbles out of the bathroom, whimpering quietly. I've hit a new low.

I go into a stall and change into the nightgown—the last thing I need is to arouse more suspicion. When I come out, I catch a glimpse of myself in the mirror. My bruises have faded to a pale purple, but dark rings lie under my eyes and my skin is the sallow kind of pale you see only on the sickly and those from Minnesota. I almost don't recognize myself.

When I walk back out to my bunk, I sweep my eyes over the room as inconspicuously as possible, looking for another exit besides the guarded double doors at the front. But there's nothing but rock, rock, and more rock. Obviously, these sorcerers don't care about fire code violations.

As soon as I crawl back into bed, the lights flick out. A few people have whispered conversations in the dark, but it's not long before the room goes silent, the only sound that of slow breathing.

I can't believe I'm spending the night in Los Demonios. The witch said the length of my visit would vary each time, but I must have been here for more than twelve hours already. Aunt Penny will have noticed my absence by now—and Bishop too. I cringe thinking about their reactions when they discover I've gone MIA again. Aunt Penny might try to send me away to that witch boarding school after all. I won't get another chance to come back here. I have to make this one worth it.

My eyes adjust to the dark, and the shapes in the room come into focus. The guards are silhouetted against the pale strips of light around the door. Surely they don't stand there all night. And when they leave, I'll make my escape. Finding Paige and getting out of a fortified mountain compound shouldn't be too difficult.

I groan inwardly. Sure, I passed long expanses of empty hallways when those guards dragged me in here earlier, but all it would take is coming across one sorcerer who sees us trying to escape and everything would be ruined. I need a weapon.

I rack my brain for something I can use against a guard, but the only thing remotely weapon-shaped I own is my sorcerer-issue Oral-B.

I get an idea.

I grip my toothbrush in one hand, then roll over in the bed and let my arm dangle over the side. Like I thought, the ground under my bed is made of rock. Huzzah. I press the handle end of my toothbrush firmly into the rock, then begin quietly grinding it back and forth. After a minute of this, I check my progress and am pleased to find that only a few more centuries of grinding should result in a fine shiv for combat. But I keep working at it anyway. It doesn't take long before my arms feel like they're made of gelatin and my eyelids are heavy with sleep.

I'm starting to doze off when the doors click quietly open. My breath hitches. A third guard enters, and the three of them talk in the doorway in low tones that I can't make out. I'm already planning my escape when the original two guards exit, leaving the new guard in their place. It must be change of shift.

I sag with disappointment, and I have to tell myself that this is still an improvement—one guard is better than two.

He starts padding down the center aisle, scanning the beds, for what I don't know. Ace pops into my head. What if he's returned to get another shot at me? I stiffen with fear, but I tell myself it can't be him. He was dead. Or very near it. This guy walks with a breezy swagger that would be near impossible after the beating Ace received.

Still. My heart races hard as footsteps approach. I'm not going to get a better chance than this—I need to get rid of this guy, whether it's Ace or not. If I can take him down, then maybe I can escape before anyone notices that something has gone wrong. And before anyone wakes up and screams loud enough to draw attention.

There are serious holes in the plan, but I don't see a better one emerging, so I choose to ignore them.

I grip my half-sharpened toothbrush and slowly slip out of the bedcovers, trying to make as little noise as possible.

The walkie-talkie clipped to the guard's pants hisses white noise as he nears. Each one of his footsteps sends a fresh bolt of fear through me, and when he's right next to my bed, my heart thumps so hard it's a miracle he doesn't turn and beam a flashlight in my eyes. But he doesn't stop. He passes right by me in the dark.

It's now or never. I leap out of bed and in one fluid motion land on his back as I jab the toothbrush into his neck. The guard grunts, but he doesn't go down like I expected him to. My arms cling to his neck, and I strain with all my muscle power to cut off circulation as I hit him hard and deep with the toothbrush. He stumbles left, then right. A few people shift in bed. Someone coughs.

"Stop, it's me," the man gasps.

I keep strangling. The singular goal in my mind is to get this guy down, one way or another.

"Stop. It's Cruz."

Finally, his words sink into my kill-happy mind. I let go of his neck and slide down to the floor, my bare feet landing on the cold tiles. My heart goes rapid fire in my chest as Cruz feels his neck for damage.

"Damn, girl," he whispers.

"I didn't know it was you," I hiss back.

He grabs my wrist and leads me quickly to the bathroom.

He lets go of my hand when we're inside and paces away from me. I shift from foot to foot.

"Sorry about the toothbrush," I say.

"Toothbrush—nice," he mutters. But he walks up to me. In the dim glow of a night-light set into a vanity, I can just make out the smooth contours of his face. In the short time since I last saw him, his black hair has started to grow out of the military style he wore it in, curling around the nape of his sun-bronzed neck. Which, I note, isn't even bleeding from where I jabbed him with the toothbrush.

"Some people saw us come in here," I say. "What if they tell?"

"They won't," he answers. "It's not the first time this sort of thing has happened."

My face flames in the dark, and I become hyperaware of the tiny white nightgown I'm wearing.

"I mean that a guard has snuck away with a girl," he explains. "Not me. I wouldn't do that. Not that it's any of your business."

"O-kay," I say cautiously.

He sighs. "What happened in the mess hall? Everyone's buzzing about it."

I cross my arms over my chest, reluctant to give away any information. "I don't know. You tell me."

"I'm trying to help you," he answers irritably.

"And how do I know I can trust you?"

He thinks about it for a minute. "You don't."

Awesome.

"Well, I'm not telling you anything," I say.

"Why didn't you leave when I gave you the chance? I gave you the perfect opportunity to escape and you blew me off. I don't get it."

"Not used to girls blowing you off?" I ask.

"You're avoiding my question."

I shrug. "I wasn't ready. *Not* that it's any of your business."

He eyes me a moment before taking a step closer and leaning to speak into my ear. "I know your secret."

His breath along my ear sends a shiver down my body. I tighten my arms over my chest, refusing to meet his eyes. "I don't know what you're talking about."

"Why do you remember blowing me off? You were taken to the Chief after I left you. Your memory should have been erased."

Crap.

I open my mouth, but no sound comes out.

"Don't," he whispers. "Don't lie."

I swallow, trying to hide my rising panic. "So what are you going to do, tell on me?" I ask.

"Yeah, that's why I changed shifts so I could be the one guarding you tonight. Just so I could tell on you. You caught me."

I don't get it. I shake my head. "So why are you here, then?"

"To help you," he says. Like it should be obvious.

I look into his eyes. Even though it's dark, I can still make out the intensity there. My heart does something I don't want to think about interpreting and my mouth feels like it's been filled with cotton. I don't know what to say.

"Why would you want to help me?" I finally manage.

He's quiet for so long I don't think he's going to answer. But he does. "I had brothers back home. If anything happened to them—" He shakes his head. "I admire what you're doing for your friend."

Tears prick my eyes unexpectedly, and I'm glad for the dark so he can't see.

"You have brothers?" I ask, just to get past the awkward moment.

"Two—they were five and eight when I was sent here. That was four years ago. Joel probably doesn't even remember me anymore."

I bite my lip, my chest squeezing up at the emotion in his voice. I'm not used to a guy wearing his heart on his sleeve. Bishop gets weird the minute girls get emotional. Forget about him crying himself.

"Four years," I say. "That's a long time."

He shakes his head as if coming back from a memory. Then he clears his throat, and when he speaks again, his voice is low and gruff. "Tell me about it."

"So how did you get sent here, anyway?" As soon as I ask, I'm not sure I want to know the answer.

"I did some stupid stuff when I was younger."

I raise my eyebrows, which makes him give a low chuckle.

"Don't worry. I didn't kill anyone."

"How reassuring."

"Do you trust me?" he asks.

I think about it. I don't know him, but for some reason, I do trust him. "Yes," I answer.

"Then that's all that matters."

His eyes are so intense as he looks at me. He has a way of stripping my guard with just one look, like he's seeing right through the tough-girl exterior to the fragile girl inside. It makes me feel utterly exposed, like I'm standing naked in front of Mrs. Davies's homeroom class, and yet I'm not uncomfortable.

Suddenly, the space between us feels small. "Um, sorry again. About the toothbrush and the strangling. I feel bad."

He smiles without breaking eye contact. "And I'm sorry about kidnapping you."

I can't help grinning now. "And about that time I left you with the bat thing. That was really rude of me."

He chuckles quietly. "Forgiven. . . . Friends?" He looks at me earnestly, his teeth biting into his bottom lip. My stomach does a massive flip.

"I thought you said there were no friends in Los Demonios," I say. Is it just me, or has my voice gone hoarse?

"Well, maybe I'm reconsidering that," he answers.

He takes a step closer, narrowing the already small space between us. Body heat radiates off him in waves, the scent of soap and sweat and *man* filling the air. I make the mistake of looking at his lips.

"I need to find Paige," I mutter.

He reaches up and brushes my hair behind my ear, tingles trailing where his fingers touch my skin. He cups my face with his hand, his thumb moving to graze my bottom lip. I can't seem to catch my breath. He tips his face to mine. I should leave. I need to leave. This is wrong, wrong, *wrong*. But I don't move. Anticipation builds up inside me until I feel like I might explode.

A firework of pain explodes in my temples. I gasp, my hands coming up around my ears.

"What's wrong?" Cruz asks.

Black spots flash in front of my eyes. I try to fight it, to stamp down the awful pain radiating inside my skull. I fall to my knees. Cruz's words float around my head.

One minute, I'm in Los Demonios. And the next minute, I'm gone.

20

If it weren't for the damp earth smell, I wouldn't know where I am. I'm lying in complete and utter darkness, the stone floor ice-cold through my thin nightgown. I keep waiting for my eyes to adjust so that I can see something—anything—but they don't. I can't even see my hand when I hold it up in front of my face; light doesn't penetrate the room.

Something drips from deep within the cave, but otherwise it's completely silent. The witch is gone, and more important, so are her painkillers. My head throbs like it has its own heartbeat.

A realization strikes: the witch didn't expect me to make it back.

Thanks a lot, lady.

Anger fires up inside me at her complete lack of confidence in me, but then I realize I'm being unfair. Even I didn't think I'd make it.

Cruz flashes into my head. His sexy smile. His fingers through my hair. And in the same flash, I think of Bishop. My gut throbs with guilt.

Nothing happened, I remind myself. *You haven't done anything wrong.* But I know it's not the truth. One more minute in that place and we would have kissed. I can't lie to myself that I wanted it then. That I want it even now.

I'm suddenly desperate to see Bishop again.

I try to get up, but my limbs feel like they've been strapped with weights and my head pounds in such intense waves that I think I'm going to puke. I sink back to the ground, gasping for air.

Do it, Blackwood. Get up.

Biting down hard on my lip, I push past the unbearable pain and force myself to my feet. I have to fight the urge to let myself fall back to the ground as I put one foot in front of the other, my hands reaching out in front of me. It feels like I've walked forever when my fingers finally bump into the cool, pebbly surface of a wall, and I almost cry with relief.

Keeping one hand against the wall, I move forward on shaky feet, following invisible twists and turns in the cave. My head brushes against the low ceiling at times when the path narrows. I'm thinking I can't keep myself upright any longer when finally, mercifully, a faint outline of light appears above my head, so pale that at first I think I've imagined it. But when I get closer, my feet run into something I realize are stairs: I'm back at the entrance to the witch's shop.

I fall onto the stairs, the last of my strength finally draining out of me.

"Help!" I call feebly.

There's no way I'm going to make it up these stairs. I won't make it a few more minutes unless I can get the witch to hear me. I swallow, then take a big breath.

"Help!"

A long moment passes. And then the door at the top of the stairs opens. The witch looks down at me like I might be a specter come to haunt her.

"Surprise," I say flatly. "I'm not dead."

———◆———

I know I should go straight home, but I need to see Bishop right now.

My head still thumps with the ghost of a headache as I drive. All the lights are off inside his house, but as soon as I pull into the driveway, he appears on the doorstep. I can't see his face, but I don't have to see it to know that he's angry. His arms are crossed over his chest, and he leans against the doorframe, waiting for me to come to him instead of meeting me halfway. My stomach clenches. He knows—somehow he knows about Cruz.

But that's impossible, I remind myself. There's no way.

I slip my keys into my purse and get out of the car, approaching Bishop slowly, like he's a wild animal instead of my boyfriend. He watches me almost clinically, and he doesn't look shocked that I've shown up to his house in the night, pale and bruised and wearing a strange nightgown. It makes me unbearably sad.

"Where were you?" he asks.

His lifeless tone hits me hard. I stop in front of him, but I can't look at his eyes.

"And don't say you were at work," he adds. "I talked to your aunt."

"Look, it's complicated—" I start.

"It's not complicated," he interrupts. "It's simple. You lied to me again. Why?"

I look up. His forehead is creased with wrinkles, and his mouth is set in a hard line. It's not the Bishop I know—the smiling, carefree, joking boyfriend I fell for. The worst part is it's my fault.

Desperation overwhelms me, and I grab hold of his wrists, tugging his hands away from his chest. He resists, but I pull his head down and kiss him hard. At first his mouth is rigid against mine, but before I can get too embarrassed, his lips soften and match mine, moving urgently until we're both short of breath and clutching at each other. I press myself against him, relishing his warmth, the feel of his body against mine, his apple-and-clean-laundry scent. Being with him feels so right it's overwhelming, and I fight the urge to let out a maniacal laugh. To push him to the ground and climb on top of him.

Cruz flashes into my head then, and the guilt of it is like a knife to my gut. I push him back out and kiss Bishop like it can erase the bad thoughts from my mind. The thoughts that I've turned into a terrible person. That I always was and am only just now realizing it.

Bishop stops suddenly and grabs me roughly by my wrists. I heave for breath.

"What's wrong?" I try to pull him closer but he's resistant.

"You have to tell me what's going on with you. You have to stop lying." His voice wavers, and I can't be sure in the dark, but I think his eyes might be brighter than usual.

I drop my gaze, studying the lettering on his Sex Pistols T-shirt. The water fountain in the driveway splashes quietly, and crickets chirp in the grassy hills around his home.

I know I can't lie anymore. And I don't want to.

"I've been going to Los Demonios," I say quietly.

He doesn't respond, and for a moment I worry he hasn't heard me. But when I look up, his face is hard and impassive.

"I'm sorry," I add. It sounds so insignificant.

His throat moves up and down as he swallows, his nostrils flaring. "More than once?" he asks. His voice cuts like glass.

"Twice," I admit. Tears prick my eyes. God, how did things get so out of control?

He exhales and rakes a hand through his hair. I've never seen him look so mad. I know instantly that I can't tell him about Cruz—not right now. Not yet.

"I was going to tell you," I start lamely.

He laces his hands behind his head, his elbows folded over his face as he paces the doorstep. My heart pulses with a profound ache.

"Bishop—"

"When?" he interrupts, spinning on me.

"The day we fought," I say, surprised at how hoarse my voice sounds.

"And tonight?"

I nod.

"How . . ." He stops, seeming to reconsider his line of questioning. He wipes a hand down his face. "Do you know how much danger you put yourself in? Do you have any idea?"

I look up at the softening of his voice. He quickly pulls me into a hug that I don't deserve. All the stress of the last few weeks releases in one big wave, and I let out a sob.

"You could have gotten yourself killed," he says into my hair, running his fingers down my back so that warm tingles spread through me. "You're crazy, Indie."

I don't deserve his kindness. I cry into his chest until his T-shirt is wet under my cheek and I don't have any tears left. And then he pulls me over to the stairs, and we sit down, leaning against each other in the dark. I trace the colorful tattoos snaking up his arm, while he absently plays with the ends of my hair. After so long the silence seems impossible to breech.

"Well, did you at least find her?" he finally asks.

I take a shuddery breath and nod. "They wiped her memory. She doesn't even recognize me."

He kisses my shoulder, saying so much without any words.

"How did you do it?" he asks. "Get there, I mean."

I wipe my cheeks, sniffling. "A witch at the black market has been helping me."

He looks at me, as if trying to decide if I'm telling the truth.

"What?" I say.

"You're amazing."

I am the opposite of amazing.

"I met someone inside who's been helping me," I spit out.

"Who?"

I hesitate.

"Come on, no more secrets," he says. "I want to hear all the details."

"His name is Cruz." My cheeks flood at the mention of his name in front of my boyfriend.

Bishop's eyebrows raise just the tiniest bit, like he can see right through me. I look into my lap and hope he hasn't noticed the guilt on my face.

"He kidnapped me the first time I went there. He was going to let me go before I got attacked by this gargoyle thing. And the second time he saved me from this guy who was attacking me, and he was going to break me out of the dorms where they keep the teens except I got shot back here before that could happen."

I realize I'm babbling and stop myself.

Bishop's quiet for a moment, and my chest tightens in anticipation of what he might say.

"That's great," he finally says. "I'm glad you've had help in there."

I'd thought I wanted him not to be mad at me, but hearing him be so charitable just makes me feel even worse. I'm a bad person.

We're quiet for too long.

"Come on," he says, giving me a gentle nudge with his shoulder. "Tell me what's going on. And start at the beginning. You weren't making a lot of sense back there."

I force a smile.

I tell him all about the teens who have mysteriously gone missing in L.A. and shown up in Los Demonios. I tell him about Jezebel and the Chief's speech, about the Chief's sister, Rowan, and everything in between. I talk for so long that my throat is sore when I'm done.

"That doesn't sound good," he says when I finally finish.

"Understatement of the century," I mutter. I pick up a pebble and toss it across the driveway. It plinks against the pavement.

"Don't get mad at me," Bishop says. "But . . . I think we should tell your aunt."

My instinct is to tell him he's crazy to even suggest doing that, but deep down, I know he's right. Something big is going on. Too big for us to handle alone.

------◆------

If my life were a book, it would need a whole chapter dedicated to Impromptu Meetings in Kitchens.

Aunt Penny sits across the table from me, Bishop at my side. They're both waiting for me to explain why we're gathered here.

"So listen," I start. "I'm going to be completely honest with you and tell you everything that's been going on, and in exchange I ask that you please, *please* consider cutting me some slack. I could keep this from you and you might never know about it."

For a second it looks like my aunt wants to give me a good old-fashioned spanking, but finally she nods. I take a deep breath.

"I've been going to Los Demonios."

"What?" She launches to her feet.

I sit there quietly while she loses her shit.

"How could you be so stupid?" she yells. "I can't believe it. Right under my nose!"

"Are you finished?" I ask. "Because there's more."

She slumps back into her chair, then waves a hand impatiently for me to continue.

"Remember on TV the other morning—there was a teen who was missing and you asked if I knew him?"

Angry blotches have sprouted up on her neck.

"Well, there have been more teens missing."

"So?" she says, shifting in her chair.

"So they're inside Los Demonios. Dozens of them. The Chief is collecting them for something—he says to save them from—"

"Wait a minute," she interrupts. "Did you just say the Chief?"

"Yeah, why?"

"And you talked to him?" she asks, staring at me with a scary intensity.

"Yes . . . ," I answer cautiously.

She slaps a hand over her mouth. Her eyes triple in size as the reality of what I'm saying sinks in. "Never again," she says. "That man is dangerous. Stay far, far away from him, okay? Promise me."

I exchange a glance with Bishop.

"Why?" I ask.

"Because he's a disgusting man," she spits, shaking her head. "Worse than the Family. Worse than anyone. Why do you think he's in that place?"

The hate coming from her is so uncharacteristic I don't know how to react.

"Is there something you're not telling me?" I ask.

She pauses a beat too long, and I know that I've hit on the truth.

"Aunt Penny, you have to tell me what you know."

"I don't have to tell you anything," she retorts. "I'm the adult here. I'm your guardian, not the other way around. It's time you started acting like the kid in this relationship."

"How can I trust you when I know you're keeping things from me?"

The hypocrisy of my words hits me. But if Aunt Penny recognizes it too, she doesn't show it. She puts her head in her hands, and I can't be sure that she's not crying. I wait for her to look up.

I wait a long time.

When she does, her eyes are filled with remorse. Suddenly, I'm not so sure I want to know what she has to say.

"Gwen and I," she starts. "We were so different in so many ways, but one thing we had in common was bad taste in men."

I sit up straighter, my throat going dry at the mention of Mom. "What does my mom have to do with this?"

"No . . . ," Bishop says. I look across at him, then back at Aunt Penny, my chest constricting with panic.

"What?" I ask, feeling like I'm missing something important.

And then it hits me.

I shake my head.

Aunt Penny's face is full of apology. "Indie, the Chief is your dad."

21

The ground sways violently under my feet.

She's lying. She has to be lying. The Chief is a sorcerer; there's no way he could be my dad.

But even in my haze, the devil on my shoulder asks, "Why not?" My dad's been gone since I was three, and Mom never kept any pictures of him. I don't have a single memory of the man, and I never really cared until now—I had Mom, and she was all I needed. I could never understand why some people would go to such lengths to find a person who'd dumped them like week-old trash.

I think back to the day I met the Chief in Los Demonios. To his calculating eyes and too-large teeth. Besides the blond hair—his straight, mine fiercely curly—we look nothing alike.

"You're wrong." I send Aunt Penny a challenging glare. Bishop rubs my back, but I shrug off his touch. "She's wrong! You're wrong!"

But Aunt Penny just gives me this infuriating apologetic smile. All of the fears I've had about myself in the past few months, that I'm a bad person, ugly in some deep, fundamental way, come crashing back into my mind. Could it be that I've been fighting against my true nature all along, that the black parts of myself are just the real me pushing through?

I get up and walk away from the table, my fingers trembling at my temples. "I would know my dad if I saw him. And that monster is not my dad." Of course my argument is ridiculous. I don't give her a chance to say so. "How can you be so sure? You've always said you never met my dad."

Aunt Penny drops her gaze into her lap.

I give a snort of derision. "Oh, so you were lying about that too?"

"It was just easier than answering questions about him," she says. "Your grandma thought it was better if you didn't know about him."

I swallow the panic rising in my throat, hot tears blurring my vision.

"Nothing you've said proves he's my dad."

Aunt Penny gives a resigned sigh. "Your dad is a sorcerer.

He's cruel and has no regard for anyone besides himself, and his nickname is the Chief because he killed dozens of humans and carried their heads around on staffs, which got him tossed into Los Demonios. What are the chances there are two people who meet all those descriptions in the world? What more proof do you need?"

I can't pull in enough oxygen.

"We look nothing alike," I whisper. But even now, I have to admit there are similarities. The light eyes. The fine bone structure and full lips.

"And what about Rowan?" I ask, remembering the Chief's speech about his sister.

"Rowan's there too?" Aunt Penny gasps.

"She's been to visit him."

"God," she says. "That woman is vile—nothing but a troublemaker. Constantly stirring up problems for the Family. It doesn't surprise me that she's part of this. You need to stay away from her."

Acid burns my throat. This can't be happening to me. This can't be true. Yet more and more, it seems impossible to deny.

I'm part sorcerer.

A moan escapes me. Bishop pulls me back into my chair, and I bury my face in my hands. I can feel the weight of their stares on me as I cry.

I'm made of evil.

"Indie," Bishop pleads.

I wish he would just leave. Doesn't he get it? What it all means?

He pulls my hands from my face. "Indie. It doesn't matter if he's your dad. All of that—it's just biology."

I take a shuddery breath, but I won't look at him. I'm so ashamed.

"Who you are isn't about your DNA," he continues. "I mean, it is, but it's not what makes you *you*. You're nothing like him—you're *good*."

I look at him then. I don't know what I expected to see in his face, but it wasn't this deep understanding, like he gets just what's going through my mind, like he can see every dark part of me and he doesn't think less of me for them.

Like he loves me.

Instantly, I remember crashing upstairs after Aunt Penny told me about her love affair with a sorcerer. I hadn't said so, but I'd thought it was vile that she'd considered one of them worthy of her. And now here was Bishop, accepting me without batting an eye. I could probably announce I was also one-quarter alien and he'd be cool with it.

Bishop brushes his fingers over mine. I'm so sorry about Cruz in this moment that I almost break down and tell him everything. I don't deserve him.

"Bishop is right," Aunt Penny says, interrupting my train of thought. "Me and your mom, we're your family. Not him."

My throat constricts at the mention of Mom. I want so

badly for her to be here right now. I need answers. I need to know why she kept all this from me.

"How?" I start. "How could she?" Bishop rubs my back in small circles. This time, I don't shrug him off.

"Haven't you always wondered how Gwen could possibly know nothing about witches?" Aunt Penny asks.

"She was a human," I answer defensively. "She wasn't supposed to know."

"But her own mother was a witch. Her sister too. Don't you think she'd have caught on that something was up?"

"She *did* own an occult shop," I spit. "She practiced Wicca."

"She had her memory erased," my aunt says.

"Wh-what do you mean?"

Aunt Penny takes a big breath, as if about to tell a long story. "Your mom, she was always so trusting. So openhearted. Ivan would do the meanest things to her and she'd always take him back. When our mother found out Gwen was pregnant with Ivan's child, she was so worried he'd harm her that she moved us across the country, here. But he found us, and Gwen took him back again, just like she always did." Aunt Penny shakes her head. "She thought she could change him, that you guys would be this nice, happy family. She couldn't believe it when the Family found him guilty of murder and threw him in Los Demonios. She cried for *months* after he was gone. We all thought she'd get over it eventually, but she just didn't get better.

Our mother had to do something. Gwen had you to look after. . . ." She trails off, leaving the implication hanging in the air.

"So she erased her own daughter's memory?" I ask, incredulous.

"It was the only option," Aunt Penny answers quickly. "If there had been any other way, she wouldn't have done it."

My heart aches suddenly for my mother, for her violation. I can't believe they did this to her. I press the backs of my hands into my eyes, the promise of another headache throbbing against my skull.

"You make it seem so bad," Aunt Penny says.

"It *is* bad."

"She didn't know the difference. She was cured!"

I feel sick. Overwhelmed. Exhausted.

I put up my hands. "Can I just—can I just have a minute to digest this?"

The room falls quiet, and there's just the sound of the grandfather clock ticking away.

My thoughts speed in so many different directions I don't know how to start processing them.

Mom's memory was erased. I hate that so much that it hurts in a physical way, but there's nothing I can do about it now.

The Chief is probably my dad. Bishop says it doesn't matter, and I desperately want that to be true. Maybe I could shrug it off if I'd discovered my dad was some deadbeat living off welfare in Illinois, but my dad is an evil sorcerer bent on killing people. A murderer. And I can't help asking myself, can evil be inherited?

Finally, I allow myself to think of the scariest part, the part that sends a cold shiver straight down into my bones: if I'm going to save Paige and the rest of the teens, I'm going to have to go up against my dad. The only parent I have left. Could I kill him if it came to that? The thought makes me sick, but I know one thing for certain.

"I have to go back," I say.

Bishop speaks first.

"Indie, I know this is shocking, but you can't seriously be talking about going to Los Demonios again. We can work out a plan that doesn't put you in mortal danger."

"Listen," I start. "I know you guys think I'm just saying all this because I have some vendetta against the Chief—I don't. I don't care if he's my dad. I mean, yes, it's shocking, but who he is isn't what's important right now. It's what he's doing. Something is going on in Los Demonios. Something big. And it's not just Paige who is in trouble. There are dozens of kids in there, and something really bad is going to happen to them if we don't stop him." I take a measured breath. "I know it would be easier and safer if I just forgot about what I saw in there and let someone else worry about it, but I can't do that, okay?"

I look from Bishop to Aunt Penny, waiting for the on-slaught of arguments to fly at me from both sides.

"You're right," Aunt Penny whispers.

I lean forward, sure that I misheard her.

Aunt Penny covers her face with her hands. "I can't be-lieve I'm saying this." She sighs, then drops her hands back into her lap. "Look. I don't want you to go, but I don't want you to live the rest of your life full of regrets because I stopped you from doing this. If you listen to everything I have to say and still feel like you need to go back there"—she shrugs—"then I'm not going to stop you."

"You're joking, right?" Bishop says.

"No."

"Hello? Human heads on staffs? Didn't we just talk about how sick the Chief is? And you want to let her go straight to him?"

"I can't control her for the rest of her life, Bishop. I think the two times she managed to go to Los Demonios behind my back—behind both of our backs—are evidence of that."

"And if she kept sneaking away to shoot up heroin you'd say the same thing? Oh well, can't stop her! That's some twisted logic you have there."

"The last time I checked, you weren't her guardian," Aunt Penny retorts.

Bishop gets up so fast his chair crashes to the ground. A moment later, the front door bangs shut.

I desperately want to go after him and tell him that

everything is going to be okay, but I can't make that promise, and I can't let an opportunity like this one slip away. Aunt Penny could change her mind any minute.

We're quiet a moment, the weight of our situation sinking in.

"We better get some sleep," Aunt Penny says. "We've got a long day ahead of us."

"We?" I ask, surprise written all over my face.

"Well, you're not going alone. I'll have to cancel drinks and apps with Chels, but I do what I gotta do."

"You can't come to Los Demonios," I say. "You've got that AMO tracker thing."

She shrugs nonchalantly, but she can't hide the fear in her eyes. I won't let her come—I won't let another person I love get killed because of me—but the idea that she would bring on the wrath of the Family to help me makes me smile. In this moment, I feel the invisible wall that's been between us since Mom died break down, and I'm suddenly looking at the old Aunt Penny again.

"I'm coming."

Bishop's voice shatters the intense quiet. I didn't even hear him come back in. He's leaning against the doorframe with his arms crossed over his chest and his lips pulled into a thin line. "I'll go with Indie."

"That's a great idea," Aunt Penny says. "Indie?"

Yes. It's a great idea. So why am I not as happy as my aunt?

Bishop raises an eyebrow. "What's wrong, Indie? Is there a reason you don't want me to come?"

My cheeks flame at his accusatory tone, at the hint of a challenge in his eyes. I think of Cruz. Maybe Bishop suspects more than he's let on.

I make myself meet his stare. "No. Of course not."

"Good," he says. "Then it's settled. I'm coming with you to Los Demonios. So what's our plan?"

"Plan?" I sputter.

"Well, we're not going to just go in guns blazing, are we? We don't even know what the Chief is up to. Have you talked to the families of the kidnapping victims?"

"Um, no," I admit.

"That's our first goal, then. See if they saw or heard anything that will give us a hint what the Chief wanted those kids for. If we're going into that place, we need to be smart about it."

I can't help smiling. A genuine smile. Because for the first time since I learned that Paige was in that awful place, I feel like there's a chance we might actually get her out.

22

Bishop leans across the dashboard, squinting up at the mansion on the hill.

"Man, Bianca has a lot of time on her hands, doesn't she?"

Bianca's place has been completely transformed for her Halloween party. Caution tape borders the property, and dozens of headstones and zombies stick out from mounds of dirt on the lawn. Flickering jack-o'-lanterns lead up to the front door, which is covered in cobwebs and creepily lit by a spotlight; orange pumpkin lights (which I know from experience that Bianca got some minions from the cheerleading squad to put up for her) are strung around all the windows and in the big poplar out front.

"You are cordially invited to Bianca's *HallowSCREAM!* party," Bishop says, mocking Bianca's girlie, high-pitched voice. "The When: Saturday, October thirtieth. The Who: anyone who's anyone." He gives a hearty chuckle, crumpling up the party invitation I got from the trash at school. "Is she for real?"

"Unfortunately," I mutter.

But actually, I used to love Bianca's annual Halloween rager. I mean, who doesn't like getting dressed up in a crazy costume and dancing till you can hardly breathe? But the last place I thought I'd be while my best friend was missing is at a party, let alone one at my sworn enemy's house. But Bishop and I didn't have any luck speaking to Samantha's parents (and trust me, we tried—over and over and over. Mrs. Hornby wouldn't even come to the door when I said I just needed to talk to her about getting back on the cheerleading squad). We *did,* however, find out that the friend who'd gone to school with Samantha the day she went missing was Brooke McDonald.

Here's what I know about Brooke:

1) She's the forward on the girls' soccer team and has the calf muscles to prove it.
2) She could drink any member of the football team under the table.

3) She gave Misty Carey a black eye freshman year after she found out that Misty had made out with her boyfriend.

4) She scares the crap out of me.

Suffice it to say, I've kept my distance from the girl. But the last person to see Samantha Hornby before she was kidnapped *must* know something. And according to the infallible Internet, this is where Brooke is going to be tonight.

"Are we going to do this or what?" Bishop asks.

I'd rather jump into the path of an oncoming train, but I sigh, "All right. Let's go."

Music spills out of the mansion's open windows and rattles the pavement so hard that it feels like a minor earthquake under my feet. Chants of "Fight, fight, fight" emanate from the backyard, and I can spot the shadow of a person bent over puking in Bianca's rosebushes.

It's only ten o'clock.

"Don't forget this." Bishop tosses something over the roof of the car. I catch it and groan.

"Don't be such a poor sport," he says.

I put on the fluffy bunny ears as Bishop pulls a hockey jersey over his head. He grins at me.

"I don't see why we have to wear costumes," I mutter.

"Because it makes us stand out less," he says, rounding the car. "And because you look cute." He gives me a peck on the cheek and pulls me across the front lawn.

My stomach roils with nerves. Going into Bianca's house could end badly. Scratch that—*will* end badly. I wouldn't dream of setting foot in her place if I wasn't seriously desperate and seriously short on time.

"Myra Mains. Ima Goner," Bishop says, checking out the names on the headstones as we pass. "Nice."

"Trust me. You haven't seen anything yet."

I lead him through the front door.

Even jam-packed with sloppy-drunk teens and covered in plastic cups and beer bottles, the inside of Bianca's house doesn't disappoint.

All the furniture has been draped with tattered white sheets, as if the house has been abandoned for ages. The ceiling drips cobwebs and spiders and bats, and Gothic candelabra cover nearly every surface. There's a bar in one corner called "Boos and Spirits," which serves Bianca's signature bright green punch with floating ice "fingers," and the dining room table has been set for an elaborate dinner for five skeletons, with fake maggots crawling out of the turkey-dinner feast. A football player dances suggestively with a female skeleton while a crowd cackling with laughter gathers around him.

"Whoa," Bishop says.

It's pretty impressive when you can shock a warlock.

I thread my fingers through his and pull him farther into the house.

The party might as well be the set of a porno. In three seconds flat, I spot a sexy cat, a sexy nurse, a sexy cop, and a couple making out so vigorously that they bump a framed family photo off the wall. Three girls run giggling down the stairs in nothing but their underwear while boys hoot their approval.

Bishop's smiling a little too brightly. I roll my eyes.

"Okay. She's got short black hair and she usually wears a headband," I say.

"Got it."

We push through the crowded living room, scanning the faces for a sign of Brooke.

Someone jumps out in front of me and yells, "Boo!"

I gasp, more so because of the screaming-in-my-face part than the demented clown mask with leering smile and rotten teeth.

"Did I scare you?" Jarrod pushes the mask up onto his head and gives me a big, goofy grin that makes his glassy eyes sparkle.

"Yeah, I almost peed my pants," I say flatly.

He doesn't seem to notice my lack of enthusiasm. "Where the hell you been? We missed you."

I wince as his toxic booze breath wafts over me.

"Around," I choke out. "Hey, have you seen Brooke McDonald?"

His eyes move over to Bishop, then down over our outfits. "What are you guys supposed to be?"

"Hockey player and puck bunny," Bishop chimes in proudly.

Jarrod keels over laughing, slapping his knee. "That's

good, man." He straightens up and does a little unbalanced flourish with his arms. "Can you guess what I am?"

I take in the rest of his outfit, which consists of a pair of jean overalls over a bare chest. "Uh, a dead clown farmer?" I guess, indulging him.

He reels with shock. "Man, you're good!"

I sigh. "So, Brooke McDonald? From the soccer team?"

"Does Bianca know you're here?" he asks, ignoring my question. "'Cause she's gonna, like, bust a nut if she catches you." He laughs so hard at his own joke that his face turns red.

"'K, nice seeing you." I start to pass around him.

"Hey, wait." He get so close that I have to remind myself it's rude to wave someone's bad breath away. "Have you . . . talked to Paige lately?" he asks.

I'm too stunned to answer.

"Because I kind of miss her, you know?" he adds. "She just left so suddenly." His cheeks flush.

Paige? And . . . Jarrod? I don't think I'd be more shocked if he'd announced his bid to run for the presidency, with Devon acting as vice.

"Um, yeah," I say, once I've recovered. "She's good."

He smiles, swaying on the spot. "Well, tell her I said . . . just tell her I said hi."

I think I'd keep staring at him all night if it weren't for Bishop pulling me away. We work our way down the hall, flattening ourselves against the walls as two guys dressed as conjoined twins pass by (sharing a pair of massive boobs, obviously).

Bishop gives a low whistle, and I elbow him in the gut.

In the kitchen, there's a rowdy game of flip cup happening across the island, and two guys from the football team are hoisting a guy dressed as a Grim Reaper up to do a keg stand. The girls who ran through the living room have joined up with a group of equally pantless guys, and they all squeeze out through the patio doors toward the pool. I guess they "forgot" their suits and were "forced" to strip down to their underwear.

The patio doors slide open again, and a group fresh from the pool loudly enters the kitchen. Right away I spot Devon's floppy blond waves. He's calling to a friend to get him a beer from the cooler while he towels off his wet hair, his washboard abs on full display. It's not hard to guess from his tight red board shorts and yellow towel that he's dressed up as a Ken doll. Mostly because he wears the same costume every year.

Where Devon goes, Bianca is not far behind. And if she catches me, she might kick me out before I get a chance to talk to Brooke.

I start to shrink behind Bishop, but Devon looks up just in time to spot me. His face cracks into a huge smile. He drapes his towel around his neck and crosses over to me.

"Ind! I never thought I'd see you here." He smiles down at me, his wet curls plastered against his forehead.

I suddenly feel Bishop's eyes on me.

"Last place I thought I'd be," I answer.

Devon just keeps smiling that huge, brilliant smile of his.

"Where's Bianca?" I can't help blurting out.

He shrugs. "I don't know, probably sucking face with that college dude or something."

So all's not well in paradise, then. It shouldn't make me this happy.

His friend shoves a beer into his chest, which he absently accepts. Devon can't take his eyes off me.

"So what have you been up to?" he asks, with more interest than is strictly necessary.

I shrug. "Oh, you know—"

"Just slaying the same old dragons," Bishop interrupts.

I cut him a look that could kill—I was under the strict impression we weren't going to mention the dragon—but he just winks at me.

When I look back at Devon, he's got his eyes narrowed on Bishop, his gaze moving from Bishop's tattooed neck to his long hair to his leather jacket. Devon pushes his shoulders back and puffs up his chest in that characteristic way that announces a challenge. I sigh.

"Devon, meet my boyfriend, Bishop," I say.

"Boyfriend?" Devon says.

Bishop gives him a cocky smile and waggles his eyebrows. Oh man.

"Sorry, Devon, but we're actually looking for someone: Brooke McDonald. Have you seen her?"

Devon continues to eye Bishop, but then he finally sweeps his gaze over to me. "Yeah, she's outside. Why're you looking for Brooke?"

I wave off his question. "Oh, just, you know, just some homework I missed." I give a stiff laugh.

Devon's brow creases, and he gives a little shake of his head. "She's out back, by the pool. Hey, are you coming to the game next weekend? We're playing L.A. High."

"Oh, um, maybe." I grab Bishop's hand. "Nice chatting. Talk to you later!"

Bishop gives Devon a little salute as I pull him toward the patio door.

I spot Brooke right away. I mean, it's kind of hard not to spot Brooke. She's double-fisting drinks as she dances sloppily to an electronica song, sloshing beer everywhere so no one stands near her. She's stripped down to boy shorts and a lacy bra, and someone's drawn crude images across her stomach and arms with a Sharpie. I don't know what she's supposed to be dressed up as, except maybe the token drunk girl. A group of boys laugh at her, but she's completely oblivious.

Huffing, I slide the door open. It's hard to decide what I want to do first: get Brooke out of here to salvage some of her dignity, or sock every single one of the assholes laughing in the face.

I reach out and touch her shoulder. She startles, swinging around to see who's touched her. Her glassy eyes finally focus on me, standing right in front of her.

"Look, isss Indigo," she slurs to no one in particular. She tries to stand still, but her body sways like she just hit land after a long boat ride.

"Can we go somewhere to talk?" I ask.

"'Bout what? I'm having fffun." She lists sideways and beer sloshes out of her bottles, down the front of my shirt.

Ugh.

I look at Bishop.

"About Samantha," he says. "Your friend who went missing."

Brooke's face darkens, her lip jutting out in a pout. "I don't wanna talk about her. It makes me sssad." She takes a swig of her beer, then coughs uncontrollably.

I snag the bottles out of her hands and slam them down on the patio table.

"Hey!" she protests. "Give that back."

She tries to lunge for the bottles, but loses her footing and stumbles to the ground. Bishop catches her before her head smacks the pavement. I crouch down on my knees to get to eye level.

"Brooke, this is important. We need to know what happened when Samantha was kidnapped."

"I don't know anything," she says. Her head bobs, like she's struggling to stay conscious. I bite my lip in frustration.

"You must—you were there. Come on, any details. Anything at all could help. Just think."

"Who the hell said you could come in?"

I stiffen at the sound of Bianca's voice. I look over my shoulder and find her framed in the patio doorway, hands on hips, but it's hard to take her seriously when she's dressed in only a white corset that leaves little to the imagination. Judging by the elbow-length gloves, half ton of jewelry, and hair teased into a big eighties pouf, she's going for "Like a Virgin"–era Madonna. Ironic.

"I distinctly remember not sending you an invitation," she adds. Julia comes up to her side. She's wearing the usual Fairfax High cheerleader's uniform of blue pleated skirt, silver spankies, and a fitted silver shell, but she's got fake rot on her cheeks and blood dripping from her mouth. She eyes my jeans, tank top, and bunny ears and gives a condescending little snort.

"Nice costume."

"Thanks," I say, feigning nonchalance. "You should have dressed up too. I mean, you do the whole brain-dead-cheerleader thing every day. Where's the fun in that?"

Snickers burst out around me. Julia's cheeks flame, and she flares her nostrils like she's a bull considering charging.

"Come on, let's get out of here," I say to Bishop. "Pick Brooke up."

"We're taking her with us?"

"Well, we're not leaving her like this!"

He shrugs, then hefts a now-unconscious Brooke over his shoulder. Together, we push past Bianca.

"I wasn't done talking to you!" Bianca shrieks, grabbing my arm. "This is private property and you're trespassing. I should call the cops!"

Someone starts up another chant of "Fight, fight, fight!" All of a sudden, everyone from inside the house is spilling outside to see what's going on.

I look down at Bianca's hand, then up at her face. "Then call the cops," I say, barely restraining myself from pulling her hair out. "I bet they'd *love* all the underage drinking going on here."

"So you'd narc on us? You're even more of a loser than I thought."

"What?" I shake my head at her moronic words.

I could just leave—actually, I really should just leave. But as much as I've tried to tell myself otherwise, the way Bianca has been treating me ever since I caught her with Devon has upset me. We'd been friends since the first grade, and sure, her personality took a nosedive in recent years, but did all that history mean nothing to her? How could she treat me so badly? Where is the friend I once knew?

Strictly speaking, a party with hundreds of my peers isn't the best place to have this conversation, but I can't help myself.

"What happened to you?" I blurt out.

She crosses her arms. "Oh please. Don't be so dramatic. Nothing happened to me."

"No, it did," I insist. "You changed. Don't you remember . . ." I stop myself from listing some of the great times we had together—dressing up in furry hats and trying to convince people we were Russian sisters, singing and dancing in the car at stoplights to embarrass her mom, staying up until four a.m. watching marathons of our favorite reality TV shows—there's no point. Nothing I can say is going to make her suddenly realize she's become a horrible person. I have to let go. But I have one more question before I do.

"Listen, Bianca. Things might not have been good with me and Devon, but I trusted you. The least you could have done was be sorry about it after I caught you. Instead, you've treated me like scum. And I just want to know . . . why?"

She bites her lip, and I feel a tiny flicker of hope come to life inside me. Bishop adjusts the weight of Brooke in his arms. I wait. And wait. But Bianca doesn't speak. Finally, I shake my head and turn my back.

"Stop."

She says it so quietly I might not have heard her if a deafening silence hadn't descended over the party. I glance at Bianca.

She hesitates, and in that moment, Julia drapes her arms around Bianca's shoulder.

"This is a no-losers party," she says. "So why don't you scram."

I wait for Bianca to come to my defense or at least say whatever she wanted to say, but she just gives a brittle laugh.

I give them my back again. I don't need Bianca to apologize—just saying what's been on my mind lifts a weight I didn't know I was carrying from my shoulders.

We push through the crowds until we make it out the front door. I keep waiting for someone to complain about this strange guy carrying Brooke out of the house in her underwear, but no one does, which makes me even happier we aren't leaving her here.

"I think that went well," I say.

Bishop gives me a sweet smile as he lugs Brooke. "You did good. I'm proud of you."

"I'm proud of me, too," I say. "I really wanted to punch her in the face for a minute there."

He laughs. "I would have liked to see that."

I open the car door, and Bishop carefully lays Brooke across the backseat. Then the two of us look at her with our hands on our hips, as if we're two maintenance workers assessing a job.

"So what are we going to do with her?" Bishop asks.

I lean into the car and give Brooke a little slap on the cheek. Her eyes flutter open.

"Wake up," I say.

She groans.

"We need to know where you live."

She goes back to sleep.

"Brooke!" I shout.

Nothing.

Great.

I notice a bulge inside her bra. Well, it's not the strangest thing to happen tonight. I reach inside and am pleased my guess was right when I pull out a cell phone.

I feel like a jerk going through her personal stuff, but how else am I supposed to find out where she lives? I see an entry called Mom in her contacts. My finger hesitates over the Call button. Contacting her mom will get Brooke into some *serious* trouble.

Finally, I hit the button.

It rings three times before a tired-sounding lady picks up. When I tell her why I'm calling, she doesn't sound the least bit surprised that her daughter is drunk. It occurs to me that Brooke's lost her best friend too. That maybe this is how she's been coping. If there's one thing this strange night has taught me, it's that I didn't know Brooke like I thought I did. I'm not scared of her anymore—I don't think I'll ever be able to look at her again and feel anything but sadness.

Her mom rattles off her address, and Bishop and I get into the car.

Despite telling Bianca how I feel, the night feels like one gigantic failure. We came here looking for answers, wasted all this time, and we're still no closer to finding Paige than we were hours ago.

Hopelessness descends over me, the landscape outside the window blurring behind my tears. Bishop grabs my hand and gives a little squeeze.

We get to Brooke's house twenty minutes later. She groans when Bishop hauls her out of the backseat.

"Where am I?" she asks, looking around confused.

"Home," I answer.

"Oh no," she says. "My mom's gonna be pissssed."

Bishop hoists her into his arms, and I lead the way up the path toward her house.

"I miss her," Brooke blurts out. "I've known her since I was three. Did you know that?" Her head is lolled back on Bishop's arm, but she lifts it to look at me with glassy eyes.

"I didn't," I say. "I'm sorry."

"You know who I *really* hate?" she asks.

"Who?" I say, humoring her.

The porch lights flick on, and Brooke's mom appears in the doorway, pulling a bathrobe around her chest.

"The cops," Brooke slurs. "I hate 'em. All of 'em."

"Oh yeah, why is that?" Bishop says.

"They wouldn't listen to me. I told them the woman was talking about sacrifice, but they said I must have misheard. I didn't mishear." She belches loudly, then laughs.

Bishop stops dead. I whirl on her, my heart thumping wildly.

"What did you just say?"

"I said Bianca's a bitch. That was mean of her to talk to you that way."

"No, about the woman and the sacrifice," I say.

She swallows, wetting her lips. "They made me sign papers. They threatened my family if I told anyone."

"Who?" I demand. "The cops? Who is this woman?"

She starts gagging.

"Not on the leather!" Bishop shouts. He practically drops her onto the grass. Brooke's mom runs down the porch steps and falls to her daughter's side, holding back her hair.

"Thank you," she says to me, with a strained smile. "I've got it from here."

23

I used to hate the attic of the Black Cat. It's a tiny, un-finished space with exposed insulation for walls and a low ceiling with a single, flickering overhead bulb. Cobwebs are strung between the boxes that fill up the space, and it smells like moldy cardboard and cigarettes.

When Mom was alive, I did everything possible to avoid coming up here. But after what I've had to go through, a creepy attic is the least of my concerns.

Bishop is stretched out in front of a stack of boxes across from me, while I sit cross-legged with a giant tome open in my lap.

After Brooke's little barf-fest in the front yard last night, her mom ushered her inside and practically slammed the door in our faces. And despite my calling Brooke so many times this morning it nearly bordered on harassment, I couldn't convince her to tell me anything else. She even denied the whole thing about the cops threatening her, saying it must have been drunk talk.

Aunt Penny hasn't been much help either. She said that child sacrifice was a cornerstone of black magic at one time, but it had been outlawed for so long she didn't know much about it. But if killing one snake meant powers that could cause an earthquake, I don't even want to know what sacrificing a bunch of teenagers could do for the Chief. Whatever it is, I doubt it's going to mean great things for the general population.

And so, since before the Black Cat opened this morning, Bishop and I have been poring through every book that has even the remotest possibility of containing information on human sacrifice. So far the most useful thing we've found is a spell to combat body odor. I've been reading for so long that the text is starting to bleed together and my eyes are crossing.

Our determination from this morning has taken a nosedive. I don't think either one of us wants to admit it, but chances are good we aren't going to find anything in these pages. We don't even know what we're looking for, and besides, it's unlikely we're going to come across a chapter titled "Creepy Ceremonies Requiring Much Human Sacrifice."

I finally break the silence.

"Find anything yet?"

Bishop sighs. "Nothing. You?"

"Nada."

I return his sigh and go back to skimming my finger across the ancient paper. Through the thin floorboards, I can faintly make out the chatter of customers and hear Aunt Penny's greeting as the bell jangles and someone new enters the store. My mind drifts back to this morning.

We started out reading downstairs, until the influx of shoppers for the big Spooktacular Halloween Sale forced us to move somewhere with more space and privacy. But in the short time that I saw Aunt Penny in the role of shopkeeper, I was shocked to discover she's become as possessive of the place as Mom once was. When a snarky customer demanded to know why the athames were priced so high, she delved into an in-depth explanation involving the price of gold and manufacturers in Scotland that left me gaping at her. I always thought she was just doing this job because she had to in order to keep a roof over my head and her ass in designer jeans, but in that moment it seemed like maybe she was doing it to honor Mom, who loved this place like a second home.

A rattling jars me from my memory. I look over at the trapdoor, expecting to see Aunt Penny emerging, but instead Jessie Colburn is poking her head into the attic.

"Jessie, what are you doing here?" I slam the book closed,

my heart racing hard. How did Aunt Penny not notice her come up? She was supposed to be watching.

"I was looking for you," Jessie answers. Her eyes zero in on my face. "What *happened* to you?"

My cheeks blaze with heat, every single fading purple bruise beating in time with my heart. I shouldn't have skipped the makeup this morning. I scour my brain for an excuse that sounds legit, but all I come up with is a mugging gone bad, and I've already used that one.

"This area isn't open to customers," I say.

"Good thing I'm not buying," she replies. "And you didn't answer my question. What happened to you?"

"It was my fault," Bishop cuts in. "Her aunt called me looking for her. I threw my cell to her, but she didn't react in time and it smacked her in the face."

It sounds totally made up, but I giggle and give a self-deprecating roll of the eyes anyway, playing along.

Jessie's eyebrows pull together. She doesn't believe us, but she isn't going to argue. Good enough.

"So did you need something?" I ask, which might as well have been "Go away." But instead of leaving, she climbs up the rest of the steps. I send a panicked look to Bishop, but he just shrugs.

Jessie sits down heavily across from me.

"Listen," she starts. "I know something is up."

I try to find words—any words—but she holds a hand up. "No, let me finish. I called every single music school in North America and not a single one has any record of a student named Paige Abernathy."

My heart thumps so hard I'm sure she can hear it.

"You'd think her parents would have looked into that, right?" she continues. "Would have noticed by now that something was wrong? And yet every time I go over there, it's like nothing happened."

She's gone over there?

"It's weird," she says. "It's like her mom has been brainwashed or something. And then there's you." She tilts her head to the side, assessing me. I feel like the words LYING WITCH are stamped across my forehead. I should have been more careful when I noticed Jessie was on to me. I shouldn't have underestimated her.

"You go missing from school for weeks at a time," she says, "and when you come back you're different."

"My mom just died!" I cut in.

"I know," she answers, totally unruffled by my outburst. "This is different. You're different. And that's saying nothing of your injuries. Have you looked in the mirror lately? You look like you got in a fight with a meat tenderizer. And lost."

I shrink under her penetrating gaze.

"Look," she says. "I know you're probably going to say that I'm crazy, but I'm not going to leave and I'm not going to stop bothering you until you give me something, okay? I want Paige back just as much as you do."

Until her last comment, I would have told her she could eff off with her stupid suspicions, but at the mention of Paige's name, I come undone. I know that I don't really know Jessie—I know I shouldn't trust her and I should keep her out of it, even if for her own safety—but I also know that Paige trusted her.

"She's not at music school, is she?" Jessie asks quietly.

I give an infinitesimal shake of my head.

"Is she in danger?"

I look into my lap, at my callused fingers and unpainted nails. My silence is an answer.

She lets out a pressurized breath. "Okay. What can I do to help?"

I'm so relieved she's not pressing me for more information that I grab the first book off the stack that I haven't gone through already and toss it to her. She catches it like a football against her chest, then turns it over to read the title on the faded red leather cover.

"Practical Magic for the Modern Witch," she mumbles.

Her eyes go wide, but to her credit, she doesn't run away screaming. She cracks the spine to the first page. "So what are we looking for?"

I exchange a glance with Bishop.

"Anything about a mass spell or ceremony," he says.

"Especially if it involves human sacrifice," I add.

"And anything about alternate dimensions or prisons," Bishop chimes in.

Jessie blows out another breath, her face suddenly so pale that, for a minute, I wonder if she's going to go down. But then she leans over the book and starts reading.

I can't help smiling at her then. Paige was right about Jessie.

For the next few hours, the only sound is the shuffling of pages and the occasional battle cry as I release my frustration. I'm ready to suggest taking a quick break for food when Jessie sucks in a breath. She leans in close to a passage.

"What?" I ask.

"I think I found something."

Bishop and I scramble up to lean over her shoulder.

"Right here," she says, pointing to a paragraph in the middle of the page.

"'All magic works on the basis of manipulating energy already in existence,'" I read. "'Energy cannot be created or destroyed, only transferred into other forms. These are the foundations of our science, the only Truth not to be questioned. Only one magician of the dark arts has ever speculated that this was incorrect.'"

My mouth runs dry. I wet my lips and keep reading. "'He claimed that, under a full moon on All Hallows' Eve, he'd sacrificed his child as part of a spell that he hoped would create a well to combat the twelve-year drought. He claimed that instead of a well, he'd accidentally ripped a hole in the fabric between dimensions. However, all efforts to re-create this spell failed, and he was tried for murder. The man argued that his child had given his life willingly, but he was found guilty by a jury of his peers, and was hanged, drawn, and quartered in the town square.'"

I skim the rest of the page, but it says nothing more about the spell or the dark magician.

"What could this mean?" I ask.

"I don't know," Jessie says, her tone a bit deflated. "It mentioned sacrifice, so I thought it was important."

"'A hole in the fabric between dimensions,'" Bishop mumbles. "What if this hole was a door between dimensions?"

"You mean a portal?" I ask.

He shrugs as he chews the corner of a blunt nail, but his eyes tell me he thinks we're on to something.

"A portal," I repeat. "Maybe the Chief is trying to re-create the spell."

"Who's the Chief?" Jessie asks.

"But why?" I say, ignoring her question.

"To escape Los Demonios," Bishop says.

I realize it's true the moment he says the words. "Oh my God. That's it. That's what he wants—the second part of the plan. Sacrifice teens to try to make a portal out."

"Could be, anyway," Bishop says.

"It is. What else could this mean? We know he wants out. We know he's kidnapped kids."

"Who kidnapped who?" Jessie asks. "Are we talking about Paige? What's this about a portal? You guys are really freaking me out here."

"What would happen if it worked?" I ask Bishop.

"It wouldn't be pretty." Bishop paces the attic, raking his hands through his hair. "No one could stop them. Not even the Family." He lets out a humorless laugh. "Actually, if Jezebel's involved there a one hundred percent chance the Family would be their first targets—it's got to be why she's helping them. They have a shared enemy. She must have turned to them after we refused to help her."

My stomach hollows out. "Well, what are we going to do?" I ask.

The attic descends back into silence, the muted chatter of customers filtering up the stairs. We turn back to the book passage, looking for more answers.

"All Hallows' Eve," Jessie says. "That means Halloween, right?"

"Yeah," I say absently, skimming the words.

"Indie." Bishop's eyes flash.

And then it hits me what Jessie's suggesting.

The blood rushes from my head.

"This is it," Bishop mumbles.

"What? What does it mean?" Jessie asks.

I look at Bishop, then back to the page again, realization slamming into me like a Mack truck.

"The spell is happening tonight."

24

Aunt Penny takes one look at my face and the book clutched in my hands before she goes into evacuation mode.

"Store's closed, everybody out!" she yells. The Halloween shoppers packed into the Black Cat gape at her like she's crazy. She whirls around the counter, snatches a package of bath salts from the customer considering it, and dumps it back on the shelf.

"Come on, get moving!" She gives a teen a shove toward the door. He hurls an insult at her as he stumbles out. The rest of the customers start to follow suit, grumbling and sending annoyed looks at my aunt.

"You too," she says to Jessie.

Two big red circles bloom on her cheeks. She's already started for the door when I grab her wrist. "She can stay."

Aunt Penny starts to argue, but I level her with a glare. She huffs and turns her energy back to kicking out the stragglers who haven't gotten the hint yet.

Jessie gives me a small smile of gratitude—I just hope I made the right decision.

When the last customer is out the door, Aunt Penny flips the dead bolt and turns off the neon Open sign. And then she turns to me.

"Tell me."

I look over at Bishop. He's casually leaning against the big front window, but I can tell by the way he's flicking his jacket zipper that he's as anxious about our discovery as I am.

"Jessie found something." I hand Aunt Penny the book. "The third paragraph."

She brings the red leather book close to her face, her lips moving as her eyes dart over the words. I pace the store while she reads, wiping my damp palms on my pants.

"I don't get it," she says, looking up.

"Child sacrifice," I say. "A hole—a portal—between dimensions. All Hallows' Eve."

Her face pales. She reads the passage again. I want to tell her not to bother—the words aren't going to change the more times she reads them. I've already tried.

The setting sun spills orange-pink light through the window. Why didn't we find that passage six hours ago? There's not enough time. It's all happening too fast.

"This could explain everything," Aunt Penny says. "They could have just kidnapped the teens, but they went to all the effort of mind-wiping them too. Maybe it's because they're trying to replicate this spell as closely as possible. Maybe they want *willing* sacrifices, like this kid in the story."

I press a hand to my temple. "Sure, there are witches and warlocks in Los Demonios, but the Family's been dumping the Priory's best sorcerers in there for decades. The place is jam-packed with them. If they get out, they'll be more powerful than the Family—than anyone on the planet. Nothing will stop them from killing anyone they want."

Every time I think things couldn't possibly get worse, they do.

"What do we do?"

All three of us spin around at the sound of Jessie's voice. She's been so quiet that I'd almost forgotten she was here. She has her hands balled at her sides and her jaw thrust up as if ready to challenge Aunt Penny should she try to kick her out again.

"I'm sorry to interrupt," she says. "I don't know what's going on, but if this is happening tonight, we don't have time to waste. Yes, it's horrible, but what are we going to do about it?"

"She's right," Bishop says. "We've got to get there right away. We don't know how long we'll be out before we wake up, and if it's longer than a few hours . . ." He shrugs. He doesn't have to say "It could be too late."

"We need to do the spell again," I announce. "The amplification spell." Though my magic finally returned after its disappearance following the spell, I would still be nothing against the sorcerers in Los Demonios at its regular strength.

"We don't have time," Bishop says.

"But I can't go back there like this! I'll be useless."

"I'll go alone then," Bishop says.

"You don't know the place. You need me."

"Then we go together."

Aunt Penny closes her eyes. It's quiet for a long moment, and I know what we're all thinking. That we're in way over our heads. That it's a stupid, reckless plan that will probably end badly. But also that we'll do it anyway for a chance to save those kids. And then Bishop claps his hands and breaks the spell.

"All right. So when do we leave?"

Jessie's the one who came up with the backpack idea. I don't know why I didn't think of it before. My clothes and everything in my pockets got to come with me into Los Demonios, and my big, fancy plan to get Paige back involved clinging to her when the horrible headache came on—so why not take a backpack and cram it full of goodies?

We've filled it with rolls of gauze and medical tape for wounds—which God, I don't even want to think about—plus pain pills and weapons for me, since I still haven't mastered conjuring objects yet. I want to protest out of pride, but the truth is, I really could use something to defend myself with in that place.

I pull the backpack over my shoulders and look at myself in the mirror hanging on the back of my closet door. The backpack combined with my black tank, short shorts optimal for running, and combat boots makes me look like Lara Croft in *Tomb Raider*.

"How do you feel?" Jessie asks.

Nervous. Scared shitless. Like I'm about to go to battle with hundreds of powerful sorcerers, including my dad. "Good," I say. "I feel ready."

"That's great," she says.

Someone clears their throat. I spin around and find Bishop standing in the doorway. He's got his hair pulled into a messy bun at the top of his head, with a few pieces hanging loose in the back and around the Betty Boop tattoo peeking out from his collar. He's wearing a black T-shirt and black cargo pants tucked into lace-up combat boots.

"We're wearing matching outfits," I say. "This is sad."

"I kind of like it." He gives me a wolfish grin as he crosses over to me.

He tugs me against him. His dark eyes burn into mine, and I can tell before his lips touch mine that it's not going to be some sweet, romantic kiss. His lips crush against mine. I moan into his mouth, a thrill passing into my stomach.

"Hello, I'm still here."

Jessie's voice snaps me back to reality. I start to pull away, but Bishop takes my head in his hands and keeps kissing me, softer this time, his fingers brushing through my hair and trailing along the back of my neck, cupping my cheek and smoothing over my jaw, as if he's memorizing my face, as if he might never kiss me again and wants to remember everything about the way this feels. And then he presses his forehead against mine. The ghost of his wood-and-mint taste fills my mouth as his dark eyes penetrate mine, his chest rising and falling quickly as he takes me in. I wish I could stay like this forever.

And then he lets go.

Aunt Penny is waiting for us downstairs.

"We're ready," I announce.

"Almost." She holds out her hand. Two necklaces made of braided leather dangle from her fingers. I grab them and hand one to Bishop. A little wooden box splashed with red paint and inscribed on all sides with symbols I don't understand hangs from the leather.

"It's a protection amulet," Aunt Penny explains. "It's mostly folklore, and any sorcerer with a lick of talent can overpower it, but I thought you should wear it anyway."

"Thank you," I gush. I pull the necklace around my neck, turning so that Aunt Penny can do up the clasp. The box feels heavy on my collarbone, already making me feel safer just by its presence.

When I turn back around, there are tears in Aunt Penny's eyes. She gives me a melancholy smile. I pull her into a hug, and she breaks down, sobbing against my neck.

"Oh, Aunt Penny," I say, pressing down her hair. "This isn't goodbye. I'm going to come back."

We both know it may be a lie, that there's no way I can be sure of that. She sucks in a shuddery breath.

"I know. I know that. It's just—" She pulls back, wiping her cheeks with the backs of her hands. She gives a self-conscious laugh. "I worry about you, you know? I know it's been only a little while since I've become your legal guardian, but I just feel like in that time I've become sort of, you know . . ."

"Like a second mom," I finish. She gives me a weak smile. I pull her into a hug again. "I love you, Aunt Penny."

"And I love you," she whispers. "Your mom would have been so proud of you."

I feel my breath hitch in my chest. We hold each other for so long that Bishop clears his throat. We break the hug.

"We better get going," I say. "It's getting late."

"Just one last thing." She disappears into the kitchen and comes back a moment later. She shoves a handful of bills into my hands.

"What's this?"

"I want to pay for it. No more taking money out of your college savings for these trips."

"You knew?" I ask, heat staining my cheeks.

"I knew that you were using it for something," she says. "I kind of hoped it was for booze and drugs."

I laugh, shaking my head. "Why didn't you say something? I can't take this. It's too much." I push the money back toward her, but she shoves it at me again.

"Just take it. You're going to need your college fund for when you actually *go* to college. And besides, we do know a warlock who can conjure more for you."

Tears sting my eyes. I can tell how much this means to her—the physical symbol that I'm coming back—so I pull off my backpack and stuff the money inside. I stand, hiking the bag back over my shoulder.

She hesitates, and I know exactly what's going through her mind before she can get a word out.

"There's nothing more you can do," I say. "There's nothing to feel guilty about."

She gives me a wan smile. "Just . . . come back safe, okay? And bring Paige with you."

I smile at her. "I will."

I turn to Jessie, who has been watching the whole thing from the stairs with her sleeves pulled down over her hands. Looking at this girl, who has done so much to help and on so little information, who has put herself out there even though I've done nothing but push her away, I can't help but be reminded of Paige.

Chasing me around my house when we were kids, trying to get me to play dress-up with her. Jogging across the street at whatever ungodly hour it was that I interrupted her pajama party with Jessie, ready to help at the drop of a dime even though I'd been nothing but shitty to her for years. Looking up at me as Bishop flew with me in his arms, concern and fear stamped across her brow.

"Thank you," I say now to Jessie.

And then I take one last look around my Mexican knickknack-littered house and engrave it in my memory. As much as Aunt Penny wants to believe I'm coming back, the reality is that this might be the last time I see this house again. I wish I had more time.

I give them one last wave before I go outside.

The sun has dipped behind the houses of Fuller Avenue, painting the sky with thick brushstrokes of orange and pink. A few trick-or-treaters already skip down the street with bags full of candy. It's just another Halloween for them.

Bishop takes my hand and leads me toward his Mustang, the shiny red paint glinting in the fading sun.

We don't have more time. All we have is now.

25

"Indie. Indie, wake up."

A warm hand brushes my cheek. When I open my eyes, Bishop is standing over me, backlit by a blue-black sky studded with stars. His brow is creased with concern.

I gasp, a vague recollection of the spell at the boardwalk flashing into my mind. We did it. We got back to Los Demonios.

All of sudden, I realize that my arm isn't screeching with pain, like the last two times I woke up in this place. The wound has already been wrapped in clean white gauze. It throbs dully under the bandage, but nothing like the pain before. Bishop kneels beside me, the backpack I wore into

Los Demonios open at my feet. His arm is also bandaged, albeit more messily than mine. He's been up for a while. A flash of jealousy spikes through me. He's handling this like a pro, like coming here was no more challenging than a harrowing trip to the grocery store.

"Here, take this." He passes me two pain pills and holds a bottle of water up to my lips. I gulp greedily, then wipe my chin as I heave for air. He watches me carefully.

"What?" I ask.

"You're amazing. I can't believe you did this twice on your own. I could barely look at my arm and this is your third time."

It's like the guy could read my mind. I'm not sure if he's just being kind, or if he really is impressed with me, but I probably should take the compliment.

"I'm glad you're here," I say. And I mean it.

We're on the flat roof of a tall building. Storefronts in various states of disrepair spread out below us like rotten teeth. I spin around and scan the horizon for a hint of where we've landed. We need to get to the Chief's headquarters ASAP. It could be too late already.

I hear something in the distance. Far away, across the storefronts, I can just make out the glisten of moonlight on water. Something big and round sticks up against the dark sky like the spokes of a giant bike wheel.

A Ferris wheel, I realize with a start.

"We're in Santa Monica," I say.

"How do you know?"

Bishop follows my finger as I point. "That's the pier. Or what's left of it. We're in rebel territory. They got it in a deal a few weeks ago."

Bishop blows out a breath. I can't help the feeling of pride that swells inside me at knowing something helpful.

"We should fly low to the ground until we get out of their territory," I say. "Once we get far enough we should try to steal a car so we can save some of our energy for later. Hopefully, with the spell going on tonight, the Chief won't have as many guards out this way."

"All right, let's do it," Bishop says.

I reach into the backpack and pull out the dagger we packed, slipping it into the sheath on my belt. And then I pull out a knife and slip it into my boot. I feel better already.

When I'm done arming myself, I kick the bag aside. I won't be needing it anymore.

"Ready?" he says.

"As I'll ever be."

Bishop gives me a quick last-minute kiss on the lips. And then we jump off the edge of the roof.

My stomach does a somersault as the cracked pavement nears, faster by the second. But I call the heat of my magic and push it down hard, until I'm floating on the wind.

We fly fast and low to the ground, slipping between buildings like ghosts in the night. We make a turn between two buildings, and the sounds of laughter and club music get so loud it's like we're right in the middle of a party. A man stumbles through the street, singing an off-key tune. Panic seizes my chest, but Bishop tows me quickly through a narrow alley before the man can spot us.

The cool wind dries the sweat on my temple, my pulse pounding in time with the music that follows us through the dark streets.

We keep flying long after the noises fade away, the bitter wind nipping at our skin. After a while the landscape beneath us begins to change from city to residential. If we're going to steal a car, we need to do it now, before it's nothing but barren highway.

I tug Bishop's T-shirt, and we touch down in front of a small neighborhood strip mall, strangely intact despite it being in Los Demonios. It should be reassuring, but instead it makes a cold shiver creep down my spine.

One of the shops is called Nails! Nails! Nails!, and a sign plastered across the big front window claims they do the best acrylics in Los Angeles County. Next to it is a restaurant that announces they serve the cheapest Thai food in the area, which I'm not sure is such a great thing, and next to that is a Buck-O-Rama. A half-dozen cars are parked in the small lot out front.

Bishop strides up to a Toyota hatchback—sadly, the most reliable-looking vehicle in the lot. He waves his hand at the lock. It pops open with a click, and he lets himself inside, falling into the driver's seat. "No keys," he mutters. "Not a problem." He climbs back out and pops the hood, his head disappearing into the engine block.

I hug myself against the biting-cold wind, casting nervous glances over my shoulder. "Can't you just use magic on it?" I whisper.

"Relax," he answers. "This isn't my first rodeo."

A second later, the engine rumbles to life. Relief floods through me. Bishop lowers the hood, a triumphant smile on his lips.

"Hate to say I told you so," he says.

I gasp.

Goth Woman—Zeke—stands behind Bishop, her Mohawk sticking straight into the air in messy spikes.

"Nice work," she says.

"Couldn't have done better myself."

I whirl around at the man's voice. Eminem grins at me from the parking lot, a dozen other rebels scattered behind him.

Bishop leaps over to stand in front of me. He holds his hands out in a defensive pose as I reach into my belt and unsheathe the dagger. Its heavy metal shakes in my hand as Bishop and I spin back to back, trying to keep our eyes on our enemies. But if they're scared of us, they don't show it. I spot Sporty Spice at the back, rubbing her palms together like she's been waiting for this moment for ages. Bob Marley puffs his chest out, while Hawaiian Shirt picks his teeth with a toothpick, a scary gleam in his eye.

"Care to explain what you're doing in our territory?" Zeke asks. She takes a casual step closer, her boot heels clacking against the pavement. Up close, her dark eye makeup looks like it was smeared on with a spatula. I'd love to take a baby wipe to her face, but it's probably not the best time.

"You don't want to get any closer," Bishop says in a cool, confident tone.

"Is that right?" she asks, smirking. "Says who?"

"Bishop. Nice to meet you," he answers breezily. Zeke's people instinctively move in around us at his cocky tone.

I grip the knife tighter, sweat slicking my palms, but Zeke holds up a hand, and the rebels stop their advance. My pulse races as her eyes narrow on my face.

"You're the human we sold to the Chief a few weeks ago," she says.

"Except I'm not a human," I spit. "I'm a witch."

Surprise flashes across her face, a low buzz of whispers rising up from the crowd around us. She looks at Bishop.

"Warlock," he says. He gives her a little wave, a smug smile on his face.

"Might want to check your facts next time," I add.

"She's a spy!" someone yells. The rebels charge forward, but with another raise of her hand, Zeke stops them.

The moon sits fat and heavy in the sky. The spell could be happening this minute. I fight a wave of panic. Every wasted second means Paige could be dead.

"I'm going to ask you this again," Zeke says. "I want an honest answer. If you lie to me you'll get no mercy from my people. *What* are you doing in my territory?"

Bishop looks back at me, a question in his eyes: *What do we do?*

"Be very careful," Zeke warns.

I close my eyes. We've come this far to save Paige, gone through so much, and it could all end now. I press my lips together so I don't cry out in frustration.

Unless . . .

An idea rapidly forms in my mind. From what I've learned from my forays into Los Demonios, the rebels hate the Chief almost as much I do. If I can somehow convince them to ally with us, we'd massively increase our chances of stopping the ceremony. Plus they wouldn't kill us—I hope. (Note to self: don't let it slip that the Chief's my dad.)

The more I think about it, the more it makes sense.

"Time's running out," Zeke singsongs.

I take a measured breath and lock eyes with her. "We came from Los Angeles to stop the Chief from killing my best friend."

I don't know what I expected—that she'd be surprised the Chief entertained ideas of murder? But she doesn't even blink.

I swallow. "Except now we know it's not just my friend in danger. The Chief's sister, Rowan, has been kidnapping teens to use as sacrifices in a spell he's doing tonight. He's going to try to open up a portal so he can escape this place and overthrow the Family."

The rebels break into chatter. Bishop tugs hard on my arm, but I won't look at him.

"Hmm," Zeke says, as if I were reporting the weather.

"You have to help us," I plead.

She chuckles darkly. "Really. And why do I *have* to do that?"

Somehow I don't think "Because it's wrong to sacrifice teenagers" is going to be a convincing argument.

"Because we'll help you get out of here," Bishop says.

I spin to face him.

"Help us and I'll talk to the Family about getting you out of here," he continues.

Zeke barks a laugh. "And why would the Family care what some teenager has to say about me? I've murdered humans. You're going to say something to change their mind about me?"

I pale at her words, but Bishop doesn't falter.

"My uncle is in the Family—high up too. If I tell him you helped us stop the Chief from escaping and overthrowing them, he'd have to recognize that. He'd convince the rest of the council to let you out, or at the very least, to cut your sentences down to nothing."

She doesn't look convinced. She's quiet for so long I expect her to launch her goons at us with every passing second, but she surprises me by nodding.

"Fine. We'll help you stop the Chief, but the deal is you get us out of here—every single one of us—and if you don't? We won't stop hunting you down until you and every single one of your family members dies in the most brutal way we can think up. Have I made myself clear?"

An involuntary shudder passes through me. I want to ask how she's going to do that from in here, but I get the feeling she'd find a way. It's a risk, but it's not like I have a choice.

I reach my hand out. She clasps it.

"Deal," I say in a voice more confident than I feel. "And my name is Indigo."

26

We drive in a caravan toward the Hollywood Hills. The rebels yip and holler over their music, a scary excitement radiating through the air. Zeke drives the car at reckless speeds, taking turns so hard it's like she's *trying* to get us into an accident. But no one else seems to care. I can't believe we've put our trust in these people—the same people who recently beat the crap out of me and sold me to the highest bidder. Not for the first time, I wonder just what we've gotten ourselves into.

Bishop and I huddle in the backseat as the car bumps along. I lean my head against his chest, and he wraps his arms around me, resting his chin on my head. Strangely, it's the most romantic moment we've shared in too long.

"Remember the time you attacked me in the sand dunes?" he asks.

Heat flashes across my cheeks.

Bishop chuckles softly, rubbing small circles into my arm. "Don't be embarrassed. It was cute."

If someone had told me a few weeks ago that I'd one day look back on the memory of Bishop rejecting me and laugh, I would have smacked them. And yet here I am, chuckling along with him as he holds me close. I wish we had more time—we don't have enough good memories together.

All at once, in this singular moment in the back of a car full of sweaty rebels, I know: I want Bishop. I don't know what happened with Cruz, why I let him get so close to kissing me, or why I would have risked everything in one stupid moment. All I know is that I want a future with Bishop, and only Bishop.

We peer out the dirty windows, on the lookout for an attack that could take place at any moment. But nothing happens except the sky grows darker by degrees. It should make me happy. Like Mom used to say, I shouldn't look a gift horse in the mouth, whatever that's supposed to mean. But something about the lack of action feels off, and my nerves are on edge more than if we'd had to pick off thousands of armed sorcerers on the way to the Chief's headquarters.

After too much driving, the landscape finally morphs into the Hollywood Hills. I sit up straighter.

"All right, where is this place?" Zeke calls back. "All I see is forest."

"It's inside the mountains," I answer. "The door is set into the trees."

Zeke shakes her head. "No wonder we couldn't find it."

I scan the woods in the light of the full moon, looking for a sign of the headquarters, but everything looks the same. Trees, trees, and more trees. I worry we won't be able to find the door in time, and panic tightens my chest.

"So am I just going to drive around forever, or are you going to tell me where to go?" Zeke asks.

"I'm looking," I snap. "Just give me a minute." I bite my lip and stare out the window as if looking intently enough will make the secret door pop up out of nowhere. If I just had a bit more light. A bit more time.

Finally, I see it.

"Stop!"

Zeke slams on the brakes so hard I crash into the back of her seat. Grumbling, I open the door and jump out. I expected the door to the compound to be invisible in the grassy hillside but instead it hangs wide open.

Two more cars screech to a halt behind us, and the rest of the rebels pile out, the crisscrossing headlights of our vehicles beaming across the mountain.

"They're gone," I announce, staring at the open door.

"How do you know?" Zeke asks.

"The Chief wouldn't leave the door to his stronghold wide

open and unguarded. The fact that he has means he doesn't care who finds it or gets inside. Wherever they are, they expect the ritual to succeed and they don't plan on coming back."

"Great, so what now?" Bob Marley asks.

"Yeah, what now?" another echoes. A stir goes through their ranks. I need to take control before they start getting angry and taking it out on me for leading them here.

"We search the place," I say. "Try to find clues about where they went. Anything could help, so keep your eyes peeled. We'll meet back here in ten minutes. Make that five."

"Who put you in charge?" Sporty asks.

I so don't have time for this crap.

"Listen," I say. "You don't have to like me, but I'm the only one here with a *clue* what the Chief is up to. So if you have a problem taking orders from me, then I suggest sitting this one out. No one is going to mind."

Her mouth falls open.

"She's right."

The two of us look over at Zeke.

"You're going to let her talk to us this way?" Sporty sputters.

Zeke raises a pointed eyebrow at her before crossing to the door. She disappears inside, and the rest of the rebels soon follow suit. Sporty looks after them, paused by indecision, before sending me a nasty glare and trotting off after the others.

"Good job," Bishop says, grinning at me. "I didn't know you'd become such a badass."

He takes my hand, and together we enter the Chief's headquarters.

The rebels have split up, taking off in all different directions through the snaking tunnels. I'd hoped to have some bearings in the place since I'd been here before, but it all looks the same. I pick a direction at random and set off at a jog, Bishop at my side.

The place feels different. It's not just that all of the heavy metal doors set into the rock walls are open—the air itself seems zapped of the charge that it used to hold.

Up ahead, a group of rebels file through a set of double doors. I slow behind them. It's the dormitory. The sheets are rumpled at the ends of the military beds as if everyone got up and left in the middle of the night. Where are the teens? What's happened to Paige?

"Clear!" someone yells.

Bishop tugs my arm, and I follow him out of the room.

Shouts ring out from deep inside the tunnels. We break into a sprint toward the noise. After a few twists and turns, we find the source.

The rebels have found the Chief's office. A half dozen of them pore through the files and maps spilled out across his desk, cackling with glee at each new discovery.

"He's got maps of our locations," one says. "He knew about our Redondo camp."

"No wonder those jack-offs knew about the March raid."

"How do I look?" Eminem says. He's got one of the

Chief's velvet jackets on and is modeling it like a lady. I dig my fingers into my scalp.

"Hello!" I yell. "You're supposed to be looking for clues!"

One of them pitches over the tea cart, and china goes crashing to the ground. They holler like a bunch of wild dogs.

I don't have time to babysit these idiots.

I dash over to the desk and start frantically going through the papers. Bishop takes the hint and joins me.

A rebel smashes the red velvet divan against a wall. A resounding *crack* splits the air, and splintered wood flies everywhere as a chorus of maniacal laughter rises up around me. My heart races as I riffle through the papers.

"What's this?" Bishop stamps his finger down on a page. In the center of a large piece of graph paper is a drawing of a circle with horizontal lines stretching around half of it.

"I don't know—do you think it could be important?"

He pulls the paper close to his face, quickly scanning it. "I don't know." He hands it to me.

Footsteps and shouts ring out through the hallway. Sporty stops in the doorway, huffing for air.

"Found anything?" I ask hopefully.

She shakes her head. "Nothing. Just some sorcerer tied up in the basement. Practically dead by the looks of it."

I drop the paper. "Where is he?"

She scrunches her nose at me. "What's it to you?"

Idiot. She. Is. An idiot.

"Did you try to revive him?" I ask.

"And why the hell would I do that?" she retorts.

Isn't it obvious? "Because we could make him tell us where they're doing the spell!"

She opens her mouth to retort, but Zeke steps inside the room.

"It's a good idea. You should have thought of it yourself."

Sporty's jaw tenses as rebels come running in, bent over and heaving for breath.

"Well, are you going to take us to him, or pout all night?" Zeke asks.

I have to restrain myself from smiling triumphantly at Sporty—I'm afraid she'll try to kill me if I do. She turns on her heel. Zeke jogs off behind her, and Bishop and I hurry to follow.

We're led through a series of tunnels twisting down into the bowels of the building. The farther we get, the narrower the paths become; jagged rock presses into us from all sides. It smells like damp and mildew and there's the sound of steady dripping coming from somewhere deep in the shadows. The only light comes from a lantern swinging from Sporty's arm that I'm guessing she magicked into existence.

Finally, the rebels stop in a small alcove that definitely doesn't qualify as a basement. It looks more like a place used to torture prisoners in medieval times. Which, from the looks of it, isn't too far off the mark.

The space is so small that with the rebels crowded around, I can see only the sorcerer's hands chained over his head and the splatters of blood on the stone wall behind him. I start to move closer to try to get a better look, but Bishop pulls me back.

"It could be dangerous," he whispers. "We don't know what this guy is capable of. Let them take the risks."

I want to argue that tied up and unconscious, surrounded by a dozen angry rebels, he doesn't look capable of much, but what Bishop is saying makes sense, so I press myself back into the shadows with him.

Zeke pushes through the crowd and stops in front of the man.

"Wake up," she demands.

Silence.

There's the sound of an impact, then a quiet grunt from the prisoner.

"Wake up," Zeke repeats. "You don't want me to have to ask you again."

More silence, broken only by that same dripping sounding from the dark.

Coming down here seemed like such a good idea only minutes ago, but it's beginning to feel like a waste of time. And we didn't have a lot of time to begin with.

"Ah, there he is," Zeke says.

Thank God. I rise up on my toes, trying to get a better look.

"Who are you?" Zeke asks. "And why are you down here?"

The guy lets out a painful groan. It's quiet for a moment. And then:

"Cruz. My name is Cruz."

I gasp, all the blood draining out of my head.

Bishop tries to grab my arm as I launch forward, but I slip free of his grip and push through the rebels.

Cruz's head is slumped against his chest, whatever energy he summoned to speak zapped out of him. There's a dark circle in the center of his T-shirt, and I don't need more light to guess that it's blood. I fall to my knees in front of him and grab his face in my hands, lifting his head up. His skin is too cold, his head dead weight in my hands. His eyes are circled with two violent black bruises, and there's dried blood in the cuts on his swollen, cracked lips.

"Cruz, wake up," I say, my voice faltering. "It's me, Indie."

A long moment passes before his eyes flutter open.

"Indie," he whispers, his voice hoarse. A sad smile quirks his lips. "Hey, *chica*."

"You know this guy?" Zeke asks.

"What happened to you?" I say, ignoring her.

Cruz lets out a soft chuckle, then wets his lips. "Turns out the Chief doesn't like humans disappearing on my watch."

His words slam the air out of my lungs. He was punished because I disappeared on his watch. It's my fault that this has happened to him. That he's been tortured, beaten.

"I'm so sorry," I breathe. The words sound so inadequate to my ears. Tears spill down my cheeks faster than I can check them. "I never would have—"

"Don't," he interrupts. "It's not your fault."

There's something behind his eyes I haven't seen before—resignation. It makes a fresh wave of fear take hold of me. He can't die down here. Not because of me.

"We don't have time for this," Zeke says. "Where is the Chief? Where is the ceremony being held?"

I turn to face the rebels. "Get him out of these chains," I demand. I don't wait for them to answer before I start frantically pulling at Cruz's chains, as if I have enough strength to break two inches of solid metal. I wheel around, searching for support, but no one's looking at me.

"Hello? Why are you all just standing there. Help me get him out!"

"Stop," Cruz whispers.

"What do you mean?" I say, giving a bitter laugh. "Don't be stupid. You're not thinking straight. You're sick."

"They're not regular cuffs."

I stiffen at the sound of Pixie's voice. The rebels part to reveal the small girl standing in the entryway to the alcove.

"The only person who can remove them is the person who put them on," she says.

The ground sways underneath me. It can't be true. I look at the faces around me—everyone except Bishop, who pointedly looks away. And then I look at Cruz. His head is slumped against his chest again.

"Then blast the wall! If you can't break the chains, just dig them out of the wall. We can't just leave him here—he'll die."

"Of course he's going to die," Sporty says. "Look at him."

I flash my eyes to her. She grins, and it makes such intense anger rise up in me that I could probably kill her with my bare hands.

Cruz mumbles something.

I reluctantly break my stare from Sporty's. "What did you say?"

He licks his lips slowly, then takes a big breath, as if what he's about to say requires all of his energy. "Go," he mutters. "Save Paige."

I shake my head. "No. We won't leave you here. We'll get something for your wounds. We'll stop the bleeding and get you out. It'll be okay. You just have to hold on."

He coughs then, and blood spurts out of his mouth. Hot tears spill down my cheeks. I squeeze his cold hand.

"The Hollywood B-B-," he whispers.

I lean in closer. "What did you say? Cruz, stay with me."

He doesn't answer.

"The Hollywood Bowl," Bishop says. "That's got to be what that drawing in the Chief's office was of."

Murmurs rise up through the alcove.

"Cruz." I shake his shoulder. "Cruz, wake up!"

He doesn't answer.

I press a panicked finger to his neck, feeling for a pulse the way they do in the movies.

Nothing.

He's dead.

27

The world goes out of focus. The ragged hole in my chest rips open and a choked cry pushes out of my mouth.

Arms wrap around me.

"Come on. We have to get out of here."

Bishop's voice brings me back to reality long enough that I realize he's pulling me out of the room.

"No," I say. I become dimly aware that the rebels have left, and we're alone.

"Time is running out," he says.

"You don't understand," I say, shaking my head.

"I think I do." Though his voice isn't entirely unkind, I

can't help but notice that it's cut through with pain. "We *need* to go. There's nothing we can do for him."

I want to fight him, tell him that he's wrong, but I know what he's saying is true. That doesn't make it hurt less.

I gulp for air as Bishop leads me back through the tunnels, supporting the weight of my body. Cruz tried to help me, and because of that, he's dead. Everyone who cares about me ends up paying a price.

Bishop stops short and holds me by the forearms.

"Enough," he says. His fingers dig into my arms more roughly than I'm used to. "Listen to me," he continues, shaking me until I look up at him. "What the Chief did to him? That or worse could be happening to Paige and those other teens right now. Okay? So get it together."

My mouth falls open at his harsh words, but he doesn't soften his grip.

He's right. Of course he's right. Still, a part of me can't help but wonder what he's really mad at.

I take a shuddery breath and push all the pain and hurt back to that place in my chest where I keep memories of Mom. It will haunt me in my dreams, but right now, I can't think about it. Paige needs me.

I give a terse nod, and Bishop lets me go.

We hear them first.

We're barely to the parking lot of the Hollywood Bowl before the sound of hundreds of people chanting in time with a drumbeat spills through the open windows of the rebels' car.

My first thought: Cruz was right.

My second thought: I wish he wasn't.

In Los Angeles, the Hollywood Bowl is a popular venue for outdoor concerts. I can already picture the white domed amphitheater that sits in a giant crater dug out from the scrubby mountaintop, wooden benches rising up all around the hillside. It seems crazy that the last time I was here I was watching Lady Gaga strut around in a bedazzled leather bikini, and now I'm back to stop evil sorcerers from sacrificing my best friend.

Zeke slams on the brakes just outside the lot—any closer and our headlights might be spotted shining over the top of the sunken amphitheater.

Bishop and I hop out of the backseat as the rest of the caravan screeches up behind us.

The acrid smell of smoke fills the air, black clouds of it rising up toward the fat moon. Anxiety grips my chest. The rebels start running toward the wide stone steps that lead down to the theater.

"Stop!" Zeke hisses. "We go through the trees. It's sparse cover, but it's our best chance to get close before they see us. This is the closest we've ever come to crushing these

guys—let's not ruin it because we didn't think it through."
She raises her eyebrows at her people. They nod. Sporty
huffs, but thankfully she doesn't spend twenty minutes arguing and just follows orders.

We move through the cover of the ash trees on the hillside. Some areas are thickly wooded, some are so barren we
have to dash ten feet across open land before we're covered
by another patch of trees. Adrenaline courses through me
as we crest the top of the hill. The Hollywood Bowl finally
comes into view through the trees.

Wooden benches wrap around the mountainside like in
Los Angeles, but here, where the amphitheater is supposed
to be, are a dozen or so massive rectangular stones in a large
circle like some sort of Stonehenge. Hundreds of sorcerers
holding torches that send huge orange flames into the sky
form a second circle around the stone formation.

I don't see Paige, or any of the other humans.

"We need to get closer," I whisper.

Silently, we move across the hill. It's pretty amazing how
well we work together when everyone shares the same goal:
stop the Chief.

The closer we get, the louder the chanting becomes. I
don't recognize the strange language they're speaking, but
I know it's the same one the Priory used in the swamp ceremony after homecoming. I shudder.

We need a plan. Though we have the rebels on our side
now, we're only just over a dozen people against hundreds

of sorcerers. Like Bishop said, we can't go in guns blazing and hope for the best.

We reach a point in the hillside where the tree cover ends abruptly. There are a few single ash trees sticking up here and there, but nothing that could hide a baker's dozen of rebels. We hunker down and look out over the hill.

What I see sends a chill into my bones.

The sorcerers sport the same dark brown robes that the Priory wore during the ceremony in the swamp, except over their heads are the skins of dead animals. I spot a wolf, a bull, a bear. Something about the sheen of the pelts, the dead, glassy eyes, and the mouths opened in perpetual roar tells me they didn't pick these up at a costume supply store.

Their bodies jerk and sway in a strange, primal dance that makes my stomach clench.

I still don't see the humans. And then one of the sorcerers moves just enough that I catch a glimpse into the inner circle.

And there they are.

My heart sinks. Now that I know what to look for, I can make out the distinct shape of dozens of people crowded around what looks like some sort of altar.

But they're not dead. We're not too late.

The sorcerers sway in time with their chanting, the slow drumbeat pounding hard as their voices rise to a crescendo.

Bishop and I huddle with the rebels, watching the sorcerers through a break in the trees. This would all be so much easier if the sorcerers weren't crowded around the humans, making so many options—namely, bombs and guns—too dangerous to try.

"What are they doing?" Eminem asks. "That looks like some weird shit."

"They're trying to open a portal to another dimension," I answer. "And they're going to sacrifice all those kids to do it."

"That's bullcrap," he says. "No way can they do that. That's creating energy."

"Well, something tells me they're going to try it anyway," Pixie says.

They bicker back and forth, and I can feel my blood pressure mounting by the second.

But before I can suggest they sort this out later in couples therapy, a blast of heat and light flashes up into the trees. I cover my eyes from the searing white, as screams from below pierce the air. The sorcerers' chanting sputters to a halt. Through my spotty vision I can make out the robed men and women shielding their eyes. The light winks out, the air still pulsing where it had been.

All of us gape down at the scene.

Holy. Crap.

The sorcerers resume their chanting.

"We need to do something," I hiss.

"All right," Bishop says. "We split into two groups. One goes around the side of the hill and creates a distraction. The Chief will send sorcerers to investigate, and while their numbers are down, the second group will attack."

"That's a good idea," I say. "Zeke?" I look over my shoulder at her. She's watching the sorcerers thoughtfully, almost as if she hasn't heard us.

"Zeke!"

She looks up suddenly.

"What do you think of the idea?" I say.

"It's good."

"All right, let's do it," I say.

Bishop reaches up to brush a big branch out of our way, but his hand pauses in the air.

"Move it." I give him a little shove. "There's no time to waste!"

He doesn't respond. Doesn't move an inch.

"Bishop!" I hiss. It's too dark to tell for sure, but it looks as if his face has taken on a bluish-white sheen. A quiet *crack* and *pop* comes off his skin.

I have just enough time to register that something Very Bad has happened before a chill races through me, as if my veins were made of ice. I can feel my blood suck into my core as icicles spread over my skin and frost mists off my body. My teeth chatter involuntarily before my jaw locks and even chattering becomes impossible.

We're frozen. Someone has frozen us.

I try to scream, but with my jaw locked, all that comes out is a zombielike moan.

Zeke passes in front of me.

"We hate the Chief, but we *really* hate Los Demonios," she says. "Sorry to go back on our word, but we can't let you ruin our only chance of getting out of this place."

The truth hits me.

"You traitor!" I growl, but it's hardly effective when it comes out just a mumble of gibberish.

I want to lunge at her and rip that stupid eighties Mohawk right off her head, but I can't move. Despite my frustration, my heartbeat slows and my breath turns shallow. It's like my body is shutting down.

The rebels chortle quietly as they move around in front of us. I spot Sporty. She gives me a pouty face as she passes.

"Don't worry," she says, walking backward. "You'll thaw in a couple of hours. Hopefully, you're still alive by then." She winks at me, then turns on her heel to watch the ceremony with the rest of the rebels.

Pixie passes me. I try to catch her eye, but she refuses to look at me. Eminem pulls my knife and dagger out of their sheaths. He grins at me. "Thanks. These might come in handy."

The rest don't give us even a second glance. They hunker down just yards away, watching the ceremony with scary intensity.

Why did we for a second think we could trust prison inmates to be good on their word?

The chanting resumes. My heart beats weakly in rhythm with the slow drumbeat.

Oh God. We're going to be forced to watch the ceremony—forced to watch Paige and the other teens die—and there won't be a single thing we can do about it. I let out a frustrated groan. I try to look at Bishop, but the muscles behind my eyes are too sluggish to respond to my mental command and eventually I give up. I summon my magic with every ounce of concentration in me, but there isn't a stitch of warmth in my body.

This must be what it feels like when you're awake during surgery, I think. Completely alert and aware, yet unable to move a muscle.

The bright light flares again. I try to close my eyes, but my lids are frozen open. White light sears my retinas, which causes tears to slip down my frozen cheeks. For a minute I can't see anything but spots of black and I think I've gone blind, but then the world comes into focus again. A ball of purplish-white light the size of a grapefruit swirls over the top of the stone formation, emitting a misty gas.

And then I see him.

A sorcerer wearing the head of a huge white ox with curling horns steps atop the altar in the middle of the stone circle. The Chief. He holds up a limp body in offering to the light. It blazes a bit brighter.

"It's working," one of the rebels says. He starts to move forward, but Zeke grabs his shirt and yanks him back.

"Not until the last minute," she says. "The portal isn't fully formed yet."

The rebels lean forward on the balls of their feet, ready to pounce at any moment. They practically vibrate with anticipation.

The Chief tosses the body to the side. Another teen climbs shakily up to the altar. My mind screams out a plea for him to stop, but the rest of my body behaves like I'm going to sleep. The Chief lifts the boy up to the light.

A stir goes through the ranks of sorcerers. That's when I notice a robed body slumped on the ground near the back of the huge group, his torch spilled in front of him and an arrow sticking out of his back. Another sorcerer quickly picks up the torch and stomps on its flame, but an arrow pierces his side too, and a second later, he's fallen on top of the first downed man. Two more sorcerers go down within seconds. A dark shape whizzes across the sky.

"What the . . . ," Eminem mutters.

Someone's picking off the sorcerers. Hope flashes hot inside my ice-cold body.

"Stop him!" the Chief yells.

Three sorcerers leap up from the ground and set off

toward the mysterious archer. One holds out his hand, and a fireball blasts from his palm. It misses by a wide margin and strikes the mountainside so hard that the ground rumbles under my feet. Huge flames soar into the sky.

The figure moves fast, dodging his pursuers as he circles around the mountain so quickly I can hardly follow his movements. He swoops in close to the stone formation and picks off one, two, three more sorcerers in the span of a second. But in that short amount of time, the sorcerers in pursuit close the gap between them.

They launch another fireball—this time directed right at him. My heart moves to my throat, but the man zips out of the way just in time, and the fireball blasts into the mountainside.

"Who the hell is that?" Zeke asks.

Three more sorcerers fly up from the ceremony to help. They close in on the man from different directions. He's completely surrounded—there's no way he could dodge an attack now. I had dared to hope, but how could one person stop this many sorcerers, no matter how incredible his magic?

A half-dozen fireballs flash across the sky, all trained on the man. But an instant before the flames make contact, he disappears into thin air. The mountainside rocks from the blow of the fireballs, pebbles tumbling into the amphitheater. The sorcerers let out angry roars over the chanting still going on below. Flames lick fast along the dry scrub—pretty soon the whole place is going to be up in flames.

"There!" One of the rebels points at a spot on the hillside right behind the stone formation.

"We have to stop him before he ruins the spell," another says.

Zeke leaps up from her hiding spot and soars into the sky after the man. The rest of the rebels take flight behind her.

I watch as the dauntless archer pulls arrows from a quiver on his back, picking off two more sorcerers before any of them have even noticed his new location. He's too far away for me to see his face, but I notice a shock of blond hair that seems vaguely familiar.

Rebels and sorcerers alike descend on the man. He disappears again, bullets and arrows and fireballs landing on the spot where he had just been standing.

He appears again, only ten feet in front of me, crouched outside the line of trees Bishop and I are hidden behind.

Only it's not a he.

It's Aunt Penny.

28

She's got a quiver of arrows strapped across her back, and she heaves for breath, sweat slicking the tendrils of hair that have escaped her ponytail against her face.

Who replaced my bar-star aunt with a freaking superhero? And more important, what is she doing here?

I moan as loudly as I can to get her attention. She glances behind her, and her eyes go as wide as saucers when she sees Bishop and me.

"Indie!" she gasps. She turns to face me. That's when I notice the fireball hurtling toward her.

I moan frantically, trying to get her to move. Aunt Penny flicks her eyes over her shoulder just in time to put her hands up in front of her face. She's blasted off her feet, the flames engulfing her. She disappears before her body hits the ground.

I let out a gut-wrenching groan.

No. No, this can't be happening.

A robed sorcerer lands in front of the flames.

I shrink into myself, praying he doesn't spot us. He howls with rage and kicks a tree so hard that leaves break free and flutter to the fiery ground. He takes off again. If Aunt Penny isn't already dead, he's on his way right now to finish her off.

The flames spread quickly into the trees around us. The heat sears my face, and pinpricks of pain flash all over my skin. For a second I think we're going to burn and there won't be a thing we can do about it, but then I realize that this fire is what will free us.

The pinpricks spread along my body as my blood flow is restored. My skin drips water as the icicles melt, and color slowly returns to my blue skin. Bishop curls his outstretched hand into a fist. I try to do the same. My fingers move in slow motion, icicles popping as my joints flex, but they move. My heart rate speeds up. In a few more minutes, I'll be able to move normally.

The Chief stands atop the stone altar as another teen is pushed toward him. I recognize her instantly. She's the girl I saw my first day in Los Demonios—Mrs. Hornby's daughter, Samantha. She shakes so hard I can see it from a half mile away. The Chief hoists her up over his head in offering. I desperately want to do something—anything—but my core is still too cold to summon my magic, my body too sluggish to respond to my commands.

The chanting builds to a wail. Slowly, Samantha's body goes slack, wilts as if drained of its life force, and as it does, the ball of light glows bigger and brighter. It swirls and pulses like a living thing, giving the air a charge.

Samantha's dead.

Something flips inside of me. Anger flashes hot in my stomach, my blood turning molten.

These people have taken so much from me. My mom, Cruz, maybe Aunt Penny—the only family I have left. They took Samantha, and they'll take Paige too, and the rest of these teens who just happened to be in the wrong place at the wrong time.

I stare at the stone formation, at the sorcerers circled around, swaying and chanting in time to the drumbeat. I know in this instant that I could kill them. I could kill every single one of them and not feel a bit of regret for doing it.

The single thought in my mind is death. I can feel the dark part of myself like it's a separate thing, but instead of feeling shame and embarrassment about it, I give in to it, letting the rage and anger consume me until I'm sure that if I could see myself, I'd look demented. Magic courses hot through my veins.

"Indie," Bishop says, through his still-tense jaw, "are you okay?"

I clench and curl my hands at my sides, ignoring Bishop as I stare at the Chief. At my dad.

"I will kill him," I say.

I take a step forward. My joints crack like I'm a hundred years old. But I take another step, and then another, and the more I move, the looser my limbs become. I can feel myself thawing out by the second.

Explosions sound all around me, the chanting and drumbeat rising up in a din of bone-shaking noise. Sorcerers and rebels zigzag through the air, too intent on killing the archer—and now each other—to notice our approach down below.

I give into the black part of myself, letting the darkness unfurl around me like a cloak. My heart pumps with black blood, my breath coming hard and fast as magic pulses scorching hot through my veins. The ground rumbles under my feet. I walk faster and faster.

And then I run.

I'm just twenty feet from the stone formation when the first attack comes.

Two sorcerers leap forward. I hold out my hand, and a violent blast of wind slams them back so hard they land on their backs with a resounding *crack*. They don't get up. They don't move.

Good.

"Holy shit," Bishop mutters behind me. He's finally thawed and caught up with me. "Indie, how did you—"

His words are cut short as two more sorcerers challenge me. Scratch that—rebels. Sporty and Zeke land in front of me. I knock them away, barely raising my hand. The power surges through me in palpable waves.

Another sorcerer leaps into my path, bent low and ready for a fight.

"Come on, little girl," he says. "I look forward to making you scream."

Terror rips into me at the sound of Ace's twangy voice. For a split second my concentration is thrown and I'm no longer this powerful force, but a scared girl cornered in the dark. Ace raises his hands, those hands that touched me against my will.

I can't move.

I don't see Bishop until he's already tackled Ace to the ground. They twist left and right, a tangle of grappling bodies and grunts. Bishop delivers a punch to Ace's cheek that knocks his mask clean off his head and throws him three feet. His body skids along the ground, sending up sprays of dirt in its wake. Bishop doesn't let him recover before he yanks him up by the front of his robe and hurls him at a nearby tree. There's a loud *crack* as he smacks into the trunk, but he stumbles up again and levels a glare at Bishop.

There's a whistling noise behind me. I spin around to find four more sorcerers advancing in the air.

A blast of fire shoots toward me. I leap to the left just in time—the fireball whizzes past me, so close it singes the hair on my arms and I taste smoke at the back of my throat. I've barely registered that I'm not dead before the sorcerers launch another. I duck this time and it whistles over my head, striking the earth just behind me. The ground rumbles so hard I'm knocked off-balance. I stumble backward, thudding onto my ass. The sorcerers close in above me, the vacant, dead eyes of their animal masks staring me down. Sense comes flooding back and I throw my hands up, but before I can unleash my magic, the sorcerers drop from the sky. One lands right on top of me, knocking the wind out of me. I see a dagger lodged in his back.

I shove the dead weight off me and scuttle backward. Bishop reaches down a bloody hand to help me up. Sweat glistens on his forehead, but his face is the picture of calm.

"Sorry I took so long. Dude just wouldn't die."

I grasp his hand and pull to my feet.

"Thanks," I say. "I—I don't know what happened. I just choked."

"Don't worry about it," he answers. "Heads up!"

I turn just as more sorcerers flash through the sky toward me. I throw my hands up, flinging people away without discretion. But they come at us relentlessly. A long sword appears in Bishop's hand. The blade arcs over his head, then brutally slashes at the people in front of him. Someone slams into me from the side. I'm blasted off my feet, my head smacking into the dirt so hard my ears ring. A sorcerer stands over me, grinning, but Bishop lands the sword in his gut. The color drains from the sorcerer's face and he spits blood. Gritting my teeth, I roll out of the way before another dead body can fall on me. I detect movement from the stone formation and snap my head up.

The Chief holds up another teenager, who kicks and screams against his grip. The other teens howl and scream uncontrollably—I guess they've figured out from the pile of bodies on the ground that they're not going to become sorcerers and go home.

A torrent of anger courses through me, and the ground rocks so violently under my magic that one of the massive stone pillars rattles backward with a boom. Some of the teenagers try to run out of the circle, but they're snagged back by their shirts and easily overpowered by the sorcerers without even using their magic. The Chief's ox mask flashes toward me.

"Stop her!" he bellows. Dozens of masked sorcerers turn to face me.

Six of them leap from the ceremony, the rest continuing the chanting.

They circle around Bishop and me, caging us in.

"Bishop, behind you!" I scream.

Bishop spins around just in time to dodge a dagger hurtling toward his head. While he ducks, I send a blast of wind over his crouched body. The sorcerer skids backward, his body digging a trench in the dirt. Bishop pops up and delivers a roundhouse kick to another sorcerer's face while simultaneously slashing out with his sword. I blast two more sorcerers back, then another two. A sorcerer noticeably larger than the rest approaches us, shuffling side to side like a boxer getting ready to strike an opponent. Candy—Ace's accomplice from the rebel camp. She launches a dagger at me, but Bishop reverses its direction so that it lands in her own gut.

We fight back to back, killing sorcerers in tandem as if we'd trained all our whole lives to do it. Teens break away from the stone formation and run in all different directions across the blazing mountaintop like headless chickens. But the sorcerers keep chanting, the sphere of light above them glowing brighter and brighter. I head straight for the Chief.

Sorcerer after sorcerer intercepts me, but I blow them off easily. Someone steps out from the crowd. She pulls off her wolf mask, revealing a shock of too-white hair and skin so pale she looks albino. I can tell from the confident way she carries herself that she's the Chief's sister, Rowan.

My aunt. The person responsible for kidnapping all these teens, for kidnapping Paige. It isn't lost on me how ironic it is that I've got one aunt trying to kill off a bunch of innocent kids while another is selflessly trying to save them. To save me.

Rowan sneers at me, like the prospect of killing me is fun. Rage sinks its ugly teeth into me. I look just left of her face, at the giant stone pillar behind her. It lifts from the ground, casting a shadow over her. She glances over her shoulder just as the stone tips forward. It happens too fast for her to move. The stone smashes her into the ground, a boom echoing through the theater.

"Indie," Bishop breathes. And I can't tell whether it's respect or fear I catch in his voice.

I step around the pillar.

That's when I see her. Paige has been herded into the middle of a panicked group of humans. Tears flood down her cheeks, her bangs are plastered against her damp forehead, and her glasses are askew on her nose. She looks at me.

My heart squeezes hard.

I'll save you, Paige.

I turn my attention back to the Chief, but he's already watching me intently. He unceremoniously drops the teen he was holding. I can see what he's going to do before he does it, but it happens too quickly for me to stop him. He's behind Paige in a flash, an elbow hooked around her neck and one hand fisted in her hair. The rest of the humans shriek and run around the circle, looking for an escape. The sorcerers push and shove them brutally back inside. I hear a *crack* as fist meets bone.

"Any closer and I'll snap her neck," the Chief says. The calmness in his voice raises the hair on the back of my neck.

The chanting sputters to a halt, and the light above him shrinks.

"Keep going, you fools!" the Chief orders.

"Let her go!" I demand, with more confidence than I feel.

He tosses his head back and laughs. "And why would I do that?"

It comes out before I can think it through. "Because you broke my mom's heart and you haven't done a single thing for me since I was three and it's all I'm asking of you."

His laughter dies, and he pushes his mask up onto his head, narrowing his eyes on my face.

"I-Indigo?" he asks.

I fight the impulse to cross my arms, to make myself smaller. I ball my hands into fists at my sides.

He exhales, his face twisted in confusion. I can see him thinking it over, trying to decide whether or not it's possible. I feel like I'm on an episode of a trashy daytime talk show that specializes in paternity reveals.

His grip around Paige's neck relaxes, and she takes huge, gulping breaths. For a split second I think he'll do it—he'll let her go—but then something in him snaps and he snags her neck, his arm taut again.

Of course. Why would he care about me now? All that talk about family back in his office—it was just part of the ruse, to make the teenagers feel bad for him. He has no heart.

I feel a twinge inside my chest, but I refuse to believe it's because I'm hurt. I don't care about him. He isn't family.

"Take me instead," I say, changing tack. "Look." I point

to the dimming light of the portal overhead. "They're not willing sacrifices anymore. They can see what you're doing. My energy is worth more than a human's. My blood is both sorcerer and witch." I have no idea if any of what I'm saying is true, but I'm desperate.

"Indie, no," Bishop says, grabbing my arm. I shake him off and lift my chin.

The Chief's eyebrows raise, his jaw moving as he thinks. "Now, that is an offer I'm willing to consider."

He shoves Paige back into the herd of teens.

"Come," he says, beckoning me forward with his hand. His eyes are filled with a disgusting longing at the prospect of murdering his own daughter, using my blood for his dark magic.

"Indie, don't do this," Bishop pleads.

I take a step forward. The rest of the battle falls away as I lock eyes with my dad. Magic pours through me like lava, getting hotter and hotter until it's unbearable to hold it in any longer. Still, I wait. My whole body feels like a flame, and I'm sure I've caught fire. Black clouds scud across the moon too fast to be natural; the air crackles with electricity. The heat flows down to my fingertips in a painful swell of magic dying to be released. I wait a moment longer.

And then I let it go.

The clouds break apart, and a bolt of lightning strikes the Chief. He's lifted a foot off the ground, captured in a flash of white light, his back bent unnaturally, his eyes wide, and his mouth open in an O. And then he slumps to the ground. His ox mask is singed black and wisps of smoke curl into the air. He doesn't move.

I did it. I killed my dad.

"Whoa," Bishop breathes.

A violent gag chokes me, and I fall to my knees.

The place becomes absolute bedlam. A ragged crew of sorcerers keeps up with their chanting, while the rest come at me from all sides. Shouts and cries ring out through the night, fire and arrows flashing past too quickly to follow. I would be dead if it weren't for Bishop, defending me as I heave vomit into the dirt.

I killed my dad.

But then the lights in the sky dim, then flicker, and the place goes silent. I haul myself up and look out over the hillside.

A hundred people stand along the brim of the Hollywood Bowl, looking down into the amphitheater with an eerie calm. It takes me a moment to figure out who they are. Not sorcerers—they're all here for the ceremony. Not rebels—there are just too many of them. But who else would be in Los Demonios?

And then I put it together. The flickering light. The people with a secret entrance into this place—a portal used to shove inmates inside.

It's the Family.

29

Everyone flees. Sorcerers and rebels alike fly in every direction, like they can't get away from the Family fast enough. What's left of the pitiful portal of light above the stone formation winks out completely. The humans huddle together in the circle as fires blaze all around. Two girls whimper loudly. Paige looks around dazedly.

All the while, the Family floats calmly down the mountainside toward us. I leap in front of Paige, shielding her body with my own. Bishop follows, his arms out at his sides to cover the humans. I don't know what they want, how they found us here—all I know is that I'll do anything to keep the teens safe.

The Family members range from fresh-faced teenagers to adults in their fifties, but they all share one thing in common: eyes so hard they lack even a glimmer of empathy.

"So you're in charge, then?"

A man glides forward, landing lightly in the charred earth across from me and Bishop. He's wearing one of those pinstriped suits that have a long, forked tail at the back. His sideburns are just a bit too long and pointed, and he wears his hair parted down the middle and slicked flat against his head. Despite the fact that he's dressed like a circus trainer from the 1930s, he's handsome. He clasps his hands behind his back, assessing me.

"Where is she?" he asks.

And all of a sudden I realize how they knew: they followed Aunt Penny's tracker.

"I—I don't know what you're talking about," I stammer.

"Here!" someone shouts. A man steps over the crest of the hillside to our left, carrying Aunt Penny's body in his arms.

"Aunt Penny!"

I stagger forward. Two warlocks move to block me, but I blast past them until I'm right in front of Penny. I desperately want to pull her into my arms, but I stop short at the sight of her. Her arms are ravaged with angry-looking pink burns, which slowly seep blood. Her face is pale, with a sheen of sweat, and a frightening amount of blood is streaked through her blond hair.

No, no, no.

"Aunt Penny!" I cry, my chin wavering uncontrollably. Her eyes flutter open at the sound of my voice.

"Not looking so good, Penny Blackwood."

Aunt Penny shrinks into herself at the sound of the voice.

"Damien," she croaks.

I recognize the name. Damien—the leader of the Family who sentenced her to wear the tracker.

The man in the pin-striped suit strides over slowly, a grin pulling up his lips. I step in front of her.

"Move aside," Damien says calmly.

"No."

"Do it," Aunt Penny whispers.

Damien stares at me, his face a mask of calm.

"Do it," Aunt Penny repeats.

I grunt, then reluctantly step aside.

Damien crosses over to her. For a long moment, he just looks at my aunt. And then he reaches up and tenderly brushes her matted hair away from her eyes. I bite my lip hard to keep from screaming out, but Aunt Penny remains very still.

"Penny, Penny, Penny," he clucks. "Why couldn't you just follow the rules? You knew we'd track you here." He sighs. "What am I going to do with you?"

"She violated the AMO!" a witch yells out. "Burn her!"

A cheer of support goes through the witches. My stomach gives a violent heave.

"It seems your witch family doesn't think very highly of you," Damien says, a mock-sad look on his face. But I see something beneath his act—the way he looks at her, it's almost like he loves her. In a flash, I remember what Aunt Penny told me before about Damien—that she was his pet, his favorite. He could have had her tossed in Los Demonios for having a relationship with their enemy, and yet he fitted her with a tracker instead.

Damien runs his finger along her trembling jaw. "You really leave me no choice—"

"She did it for you," I announce loudly.

Damien looks up at me, like he's just remembering I exist.

"She did it for all of us," I add. There's a loud sob behind me, but I refuse to look back, to see the scared looks on the teenagers' faces. Or maybe I don't want them to see that I'm just as frightened as they are.

I swallow. "The Chief was trying to open a portal out of this place. He was kidnapping teenagers and mind-wiping them so he could use them as sacrifices for the spell. When they got out, they planned to overthrow you. Aunt Penny came here to help me stop him."

The hillside is quiet for a long moment, save for the cracking and popping of fires burning and the quiet tears from behind me.

"Is that true?" Damien finally asks Aunt Penny. She gives a tiny nod. His face breaks into a wan smile, and he utters a soft chuckle. "Well then, you're either very brave or very stupid."

"So you'll let her go?" I ask.

He considers. "I suppose it's the right thing to do," he says after a moment. Then he gives me that same false sad look. "It's just a shame she doesn't look like she'll survive much longer."

I look at Aunt Penny and know he's right. It could be hours before we get shot back to Los Angeles, and we'll be all the way in Venice Beach, far from any hospitals. Aunt Penny doesn't have that long. She needs help now. And even then, she might not make it.

"Next order of business," Damien says. "Bring forth the traitor."

I don't know whom they're talking about, and I'm not sure anyone else does either. And then she speaks.

"I'm right here."

Jezebel stands with her chin held high, her mask tipped back on her head. Her brown robe is ripped and torn, but her curls still hang in perfect loose ringlets down her back.

"Kill her!" someone shouts. The crowd goes into a frenzy. A dozen witches spring forward and grab Jezebel, tearing at her from all angles, their eyes burning with intense hatred. She flinches as they pull her in every direction, but she doesn't cry, just keeps eye contact with Damien.

"Well, Jezebel. Do you have anything to say for yourself? Any heroic story to share?"

She shakes her head.

Damien raises his eyebrows. "So it's concluded, then. You'll burn at the stake."

I think I see Jezebel shudder, but when she speaks, her voice is loud and confident. "I ask only one thing," she says.

"Oh?" Damien holds up a hand, and the witches pulling at her clothing let go. "And pray tell, why should we do anything for you?"

"I'm not asking for much. All I want is one minute to speak with Penny Blackwood, and then I'll go with you willingly."

My spine goes ramrod straight. "No!"

"I won't hurt her," she says. "I just need a word."

"Absolutely not," I say.

"I'm afraid that's not your decision," Damien says. He turns to Aunt Penny. She looks between Jezebel and me through drooped eyelids. If it's possible, she looks worse than just minutes before.

"Okay," she whispers.

I exhale, unable to believe what's happening.

"Go ahead," Damien says, gesturing to Aunt Penny. "Hurry up."

"In private," she says.

"What? No! She's going to kill her!" I shout.

"And what would that accomplish?" Jezebel says.

I open and close my mouth, searching for an answer.

Damien gestures toward the tree cover. "I'm looking forward to burning a witch today, so make sure she doesn't get away."

Jezabel turns to Bishop. Her eyes are pained, and for a moment, I think she's going to say something. Apologize, or profess her undying love for him. But then Aunt Penny is carried toward the trees, and Jezebel turns to follow. The man who'd been carrying her emerges a second later, alone.

I watch the woods, my stomach clenched in a tight knot. Every second that passes seems like an eternity. My heart feels like it will give out at any minute, but still I keep watching the trees, waiting for Aunt Penny and Jezebel to emerge again. But minutes pass, and no one does. I look desperately to Damien, but his face is impassive.

Finally, I burst into flight toward the trees. Others follow me, but I touch down first and let out a primal wail when I discover them.

Aunt Penny and Jezebel are lying a few feet from each other, and neither of them is moving. Behind the dense tree cover, it's too dark to know for sure what the black pools are all over the forest floor, but the metallic smell gives it away as blood. I take a feeble step forward, and my boots make a sickening slurping sound as I step in some. Vomit rises up my throat.

Jezebel lies facedown in a puddle of blackened leaves, a wet knife held loosely in her hands. Aunt Penny is on her back, staring unblinkingly at the tree canopy above her.

Oh God. I fall to my knees at Aunt Penny's side and pull her to my chest. Her body is heavy and slack in my arms.

"No, no, I can't lose you," I cry into her hair. Tears blur my vision. I can feel the eyes of dozens of people on me as I cry. "Come back, please, come back. You can't die. You're all I have."

I didn't even get a chance to say goodbye. The thought makes me cry harder.

I feel a tiny flutter of movement against my chest. I gasp, then hesitantly lay Aunt Penny down on the leaves again. My eyes rove over her body. Her chest moves up and down, and it almost looks as though her arms are no longer ravaged with burns.

It's impossible.

That's when I notice the glint of metal on Aunt Penny's hand. I lift her palm up and find a heavy metal ring on her index finger. Etched into the ring is the Roman numeral one.

It's just like Bishop's ring.

I look over at Jezebel's prone body just as someone flips her over. There's a stab wound in her gut; blood has seeped through layers of thick robes.

I suck in a breath, realization slamming into me so hard it takes my breath away. Jezebel used the same spell that Bishop's mom used on her deathbed—the spell that gave him extra lives. Jezebel transferred her magic to Aunt Penny, sacrificed herself to give my aunt another chance.

"She saved her," I whisper.

Aunt Penny's eyes flutter open.

"Well, it looks like your luck has improved." Damien stands over us, considering my aunt. "How brave of the traitor to give her life only after it became clear she was going to be killed."

"Aunt Penny, are you okay?" I run my hands along her body, checking for injuries.

"Well, as nice as this has been," Damien says, "I think we'll be heading back now."

"Wait!" I say, turning on him. "What about the humans?"

"What about the humans?" he repeats.

"We can't just leave them here," I say.

"And why not? Like you said, they've been mind-wiped. Taking back a couple dozen teens with memory loss would only raise questions that we can't answer. I'm afraid this is a sacrifice we'll have to make, my dear."

My heart beats hard.

"But what about the witches back home?" I ask.

He raises his eyebrows.

"You think everyone doesn't know about what you did to us on prom night? How you used your own people as bait and threw us to our enemies to get slaughtered? You can say it was for the greater good, but no one trusts you anymore. But if you returned all these teens, if you did something good, imagine what that could do for your image. I know you have a door into this place—let us take them out."

"I'm a smart man," he says. "I can tell when I'm being manipulated."

"They're going to hate you," I say. "When they find out you let all these kids get dumped into Los Demonios, there *will* be a revolt. Mark my words."

His jaw twitches. I leap on his moment of hesitation.

"Take them back. Wipe them again if you have to, feed them some bullshit story. It'll all blow over soon enough and people will trust you all the more for doing something kind and good."

"She's pulling one over on you," someone says.

"Please," Aunt Penny pleads, speaking for the first time. "Do the right thing, Damien."

He clenches his jaw.

"Fine," he says finally. He turns and walks away.

Relief floods through me. But it's not over yet.

I haul myself up and run down to Bishop, who remained to guard Paige and the rest of the humans in the stone formation. I'm scared that if given a moment to think, Damien will change his mind.

"What happened?" Bishop asks, his tense eyes searching my face.

"Aunt Penny's okay," I say. His jaw relaxes. I hesitate before adding, "But Jezebel's not." I drop my gaze before I say my next words. "She . . . she's dead."

He doesn't speak in the wake of my news. I work up the nerve to look into his eyes. His throat works, but he nods at me. Maybe sometime later he'll break down, but not right now.

My eyes drift behind Bishop. The aftermath of the war makes bile burn up my throat. Bodies lie in heaps all over the crumbled remains of the Hollywood Bowl, blood everywhere. Smoke curls into the sky from small fires littered across the mountaintop.

Paige stands away from the others, her arms hugged around her trembling body. Her eyes are red and puffy behind her glasses, and even though she's not crying anymore, I don't think I've ever seen her more upset in my life. It rips my heart open.

She spots me nearing and recoils. That stings like a slap across the face, but I swallow the lump in my throat, telling myself that it's normal, that she doesn't remember me, that she just witnessed me kill many people and it's natural to be scared.

I don't get any closer.

"We're going home," I say.

She eyes me warily. I look out over the rest of the teens, at the pile of bodies of those who won't be coming with us. Who will never go home. For a moment I consider begging Damien to let us take them home so they can at least have a proper burial, so their families can get some closure, but I know that pushing him will only put the rest of the teens at risk. We have to leave them behind.

I hesitate a moment before turning to Paige. "Wait here a sec."

Her eyes go wide.

"I'll be right back," I assure her. "You're safe now. No one is going to hurt you. Okay?"

I look at the rest of the teens crowded around, making sure they've heard me. I don't know what I expected—shouts of hurrah? high fives?—but my announcement just makes them cry harder.

I leave Paige and cross the battlefield, toward the bodies heaped at the altar. It doesn't take long to spot Samantha in the pile of fallen kids. Her unblinking eyes stare up at the sky.

I rack my brain for some prayer I can say for them, but in the end I don't know a single one. I bite my lip as a sob chokes my chest. So many parents who will never get to see their kids again. Never get to say goodbye. The unfairness of it throbs like a living thing in my gut.

"I'm sorry," I whisper.

I reach around my neck and unclasp the braided-leather protection amulet Aunt Penny gave me, and then I drape it around Samantha's neck, letting the little wooden box settle in the hollow of her neck.

"Be safe," I whisper.

And then I turn around.

That's when I see him. My dad, lying on his side at an unnatural angle, his mouth hanging open as if in a silent scream. His singed ox mask has been crushed from a stampede of witches, sorcerers, and kids.

I feel like I should go over and make sure that he's really dead, but one look at him and I know I don't need to take his pulse to get my answer—he's gone. And I killed him.

I turn my back on him for the final time.

"Come on," I say to the teens. "Let's get out of here."

Despite their hesitation, they follow me up the hill to where Damien impatiently waits for us.

I got exactly what I wanted. We're getting out of this place, and we're taking the teens with us—most of them, anyway. The Family will wipe their memories, make up some story to cover their tracks so that the teens will never really know what happened to them, but they'll get to go home to their parents. Live normal lives.

The nightmare is over.

I should get the hell out of here, but I can't leave yet. I tug Bishop's shirt, and he stops.

"Will you make sure they all get back okay?" I ask. "Make sure Paige is okay?"

"What?" He shakes his head, his eyes full of confusion.

"Just promise me you'll make sure they get home safe."

"And where are you going to be?"

"Here," I answer. "There's something I have to do first."

* * *

The door to the headquarters swings in a breeze, and the headlights of the car shine into the darkened tunnels. The mountain looks more like a tomb than a place people lived. Which, I guess, it is. My heart gives a sickening twist.

I take tentative steps toward the door, gripping the

flashlight I found in the console of the car in my sweaty hand. Just before I enter, I spot a clump of flowers in the underbrush hanging over the door. I reach up and yank them down. Daisies.

I step inside.

My footsteps echo in the empty tunnels. I walk for so long that I worry I won't be able to find the basement. And then I worry that he won't be there when I do.

But I find it. And he is there.

I beam the flashlight inside the tiny alcove. Cruz's hands are shackled over his head and bolted to the stone wall. His body hangs without any tension at all, his normally tan skin unnaturally pale.

He's been gone for a while.

I drop the flashlight and fall to my knees at his side. And then I tentatively reach up to touch his cheek. His skin is ice cold.

"I'm sorry," I whisper, tears falling fast down my cheeks. "I'm so sorry."

I kiss his cheek, letting my lips linger on his skin. He'll never leave this place.

I know it's morbid. I know I should let him go, but it's because of me that he's here. I stay with him until the pain flashes in my temples and I know I'm going home.

"Goodbye," I whisper.

Before the world goes black, I make sure the flowers are at his feet.

30

With her hair mussed up on the pillow and her mouth slackened in sleep, I can almost imagine that Aunt Penny is just nursing one of her epic hangovers on our couch, instead of resting after a battle that nearly killed her.

Almost.

I don't know if I'll ever be able to look at Aunt Penny the same way again. She saved me—she risked her life for the barest of chances that she could help me, because she cares about me that much. My chest feels tight, and I can't help the sniffle that escapes me.

Aunt Penny's eyes flutter open.

"Sorry, I didn't mean to wake you," I whisper, pulling the blanket up to her chin. "Go back to sleep."

She swallows as her eyes move across my face, taking in the tears streaked down my cheeks. "You're crying," she says. Her voice is harsh and thick with sleep.

"Happy tears." But when I try to force a smile, I just end up crying again.

"Indie . . ." Aunt Penny tries to sit up, but I gently push her back down.

"It's okay. I'm just emotional, that's all. You need to rest."

She falls back against her pillow, too weak to fight. She clasps her hand over mine. "Talk to me. What's wrong?"

What isn't?

There's so much going through my head right now—guilt over Jezebel giving her life for my aunt when all we ever did was fight. Guilt over Cruz. Guilt over Bishop. Guilt over Mom and Paige and even the Chief. Over all the people I killed. And maybe I shouldn't feel anything about them at all, but still, I can't help the heart-crushing feeling that comes over me when I realize I was the instrument of their deaths, can't stop the fear that comes when I realize I have something so black inside me that I could take a life.

I focus on what's bothering me this very second.

"You risked your life to save mine," I finally say. "And after I was so hard on you before. You tried to apologize and I wouldn't even listen—"

"Indie," she interrupts. Her voice is so unexpectedly stern that I look up through the blur of tears. She regards me without blinking.

"You have *nothing* to be sorry for."

"But—"

"Nothing."

I start to speak again, but she holds up a hand.

"Please," she begs.

I drop my gaze into my lap. Her shoulders relax, her tone going soft again.

"We didn't get off to a good start, did we?"

I give a brittle laugh, fingering the edges of the blanket in my hands. That's the understatement of the century.

"I wish I could turn back time somehow and do things over," she says. "Help you when I thought something was wrong. Bring Gwen back . . ." She sighs. "But since I can't do that, all I ask is that we start fresh now." She looks at me full on, watery eyes pleading.

I give her a weak smile as tears slip down my cheeks. "That sounds good."

She squeezes my hand, and I squeeze back. I can't imagine a time where I'll be able to think of Mom and have it not hurt in a physical way, but with Aunt Penny by my side, at least I won't have to do it alone. And who knows, maybe one day that ragged hole in my chest will go away. I'll think of Mom and I'll smile, like Bishop does when he talks about his mom. Maybe I'll think about the piles of dead bodies in Los Demonios and not shudder. Maybe I'll sleep at night.

"You did what you had to do," she says. "You were great."

It's like she can read my mind. I give her a grateful smile, my heart filling with so much warmth that it feels like the sun has been plucked out of the sky and put right into my chest.

It gets me to wondering. Maybe I'm not such a bad person after all. I've done things I'm not proud of, hurt people I care about deeply, but I've done good too. I saved Paige, put myself in danger and faced down my own dad to bring those teens home. Would someone made of evil do that? There's something black inside me, but maybe there's something black inside everyone. Maybe we all have to consciously turn away from it and try to be better—not just us teenage half witch/half sorcerers.

A knock sounds on the door before it cracks open.

"Hello!" Paige pokes her head inside, then stops short when she sees us on the couch. "Oh, sorry. I'll—"

"No, come in!" I call, wiping the tears off my face.

Paige edges inside cautiously, an uneasy smile on her face. We must not look too inviting, what with the tears and snot and everything.

"Are you feeling better?" she asks Aunt Penny.

"Much. I've had a great nurse." Penny looks at me, and we share a secret smile.

"Well, don't just stand there," Aunt Penny says. "Come in!"

Paige pads across the room and sits down in the big reclining chair across from us. A few awkward moments pass in silence.

It's been weird between us since we got back from Los Demonios. Paige didn't remember anything from before the Chief wiped her, but she remembered the headquarters and the ceremony. She remembered all of the deaths.

I wouldn't let them wipe her again.

I told her everything, about the Family and the Priory, about her old life before this whole crazy mess went down. I can't imagine how weird it must have been to be told her best friend is a witch and that it's a secret. Never mind—I can't imagine how weird it must have been to be told who your best friend is and not even recognize her. But she tries. *We* try.

I constantly worry that she doesn't like me. We met when we were kids, and without the endearing memory of our childhoods together, our moms forcing us to be friends, I worry she wonders how she ever liked me in the first place. From what she's told Aunt Penny, I know she worries too. That I'm disappointed with her—that she's not the best friend I remember. I try hard every day to show her that's not true. I think that might be part of the problem: we're both trying too hard.

But I tell myself I made the right choice. After everything

that happened to her, I couldn't bear the thought of another violation. I scour every spell book I can get my hands on for a way to reverse the mind wipe. I haven't found anything yet, but I won't stop until I do.

Together we decided on the story that she'd gotten homesick at music school. Her parents seemed hesitant, but they bought it—honestly, I think they were just happy to have her home.

The media have been having a field day with all the returned teens. They turned up the other night outside of Cedars-Sinai hospital in West Hollywood, their only memory of some underground rave. Doctors are calling it a "drug-induced amnesia." The families are calling it the answer to their prayers. The answer to the mysterious blackouts that have been ripping through Los Angeles ever since the Priory descended on our town. As for Mrs. Hornby, her daughter is still one of the "missing." It breaks my heart to know she's probably holding out hope that her daughter will stumble into a hospital in the middle of the night.

"Everyone seems so dour," Paige finally says. "Anyone up for a snack? I can make us some tea, and I think I saw some cream puffs in the pantry yesterday."

Hope flutters its wings inside my chest.

Paige goes to the kitchen, and returns moments later with a steaming platter of tea and cookies. We spread out across the couches, flicking between bad reality TV shows. It's so completely normal that it doesn't feel like my life. But it is.

Monday, I'll go to school. I'll do my homework in the evenings, and work shifts at the Black Cat, and I'll mourn my mom and everything I've lost.

I'll bring flowers to her grave.

And if more curveballs get sent my way, I'll just keep picking myself up. It's all I can do.

"Hey, haven't you got a date to get to?" Paige finally says.

I'd completely forgotten.

I flick my eyes to Aunt Penny. "I don't know, I should probably stick around here. . . ."

"Oh please." She rolls her eyes. "We'll be just fine without you. Besides, Jessie's coming over with that new friend of hers—Brooke or whatever."

"They are? Do they . . . Has Jessie . . ."

We ended up telling Jessie everything. I mean, we figured we at least owed her that much—if it weren't for her, we might not have figured out about the spell happening on All Hallows' Eve. I keep waiting for her to have a mental breakdown or *something*, but so far, she's been handling it remarkably well. But with Brooke coming over I have to wonder if she's finally spilled the beans.

"Oh, relax, Brooke doesn't know anything," Aunt Penny says, guessing my thoughts. "Jessie is trustworthy. Go see your man. And have fun!"

"But use protection," Paige adds. I chuck a pillow at her head. She dodges it easily, laughing.

I can't help smiling as I trudge upstairs to get ready.

I check out my reflection in the bathroom mirror, turning to see myself from all angles. Bishop wouldn't tell me where we were going for our date, no matter how much I begged, pleaded, and insisted that it was imperative so I could dress appropriately. So I settled on a simple pink flutter-sleeve blouse paired with a short black skirt and wedge sandals. I was tempted to slick on my trademark red MAC lipstick but decided against it at the last minute for reasons that have nothing to do with kissing, settling instead for a clear gloss. My hair falls in loose, springy curls around my face. I have to admit I look pretty great. (Well, if you discount the fading purple bruises faintly visible under my makeup, and the ugly pink battle scars zigzagging across my right elbow.)

An engine rumbles up the street.

"He's here!" Paige calls up the stairs.

Nerves flutter inside my stomach.

I haven't seen Bishop since I came back. I told him I needed to focus on taking care of Aunt Penny, on building a new relationship with Paige. And all of that was true. But if I'm being honest, I was also confused. I know I love Bishop, and so I don't know why or how I could have let myself have feelings for Cruz—there, I admitted it. I had feelings for him. I used to look down on the girls in movies who fell for two boys at once, until it happened to me.

I grab my bag off the counter and go downstairs.

"You look ah-mazing," Aunt Penny says. She's propped up on the couch, eating cream puffs.

"Total babe," Paige agrees.

All at once I'm reminded of homecoming night when the two of them ushered me off on my date with Devon. My chest gets tight. I wonder when the memories will quit hitting me so hard. When they'll quit making it hard to breathe.

"Well, I better go," I say, forcing a smile.

"Have fun," Aunt Penny says. She waggles her eyebrows suggestively. I roll my eyes as laughter follows me outside.

Bishop leans against the door of his Mustang, a single red rose held up under his nose. The setting sun makes copper highlights shine in the dark hair that falls in perfect, messy waves around his jaw. He's wearing his usual worn leather jacket, but underneath it is a button-down and tie. He gives me a crooked grin that makes adorable laugh lines sprout up around his eyes. My heart gives a thump.

I cross the road to him, and he holds out the flower. My first thought is that it's so unlike Bishop to get me flowers, but then I realize that he's never been given the occasion. We've never been on a real date.

"For the lady," he says, wiggling it in front of my face. "You look gorgeous." I give an embarrassed smile and take the stem from him, holding the bloom up under my nose.

"Well, come on, we don't want to be late." He crosses to the passenger door and holds it open for me.

"Late for what?" I ask.

"Nice try. Get in."

I fall into the seat. When he starts the car, the radio blares a song I recognize—the same song that we sang on our way to the Guadalupe sand dunes the day I tried to seduce him. He goes to turn the volume down, but I stop him.

"Don't. I love this song."

He smiles across at me before putting the car in drive.

It's so *normal* just driving around with Bishop that I'm sort of sad when he announces we're at our destination. He parks the car off the curb on Spring Street, right in front of the Last Bookstore. It's a grand building made out of light gray stone, with ornate carvings under the windows and a gilded placard across the door. The Open sign is switched off.

Bishop pulls a big canvas backpack out of the backseat.

"What's in there?" I ask, giving the bag a wary look as I recall the snake he'd brought along on our last excursion.

"You'll see." He climbs out of the car.

I trip after myself to catch up to him as he ducks into an alleyway. I find him tinkering with the lock of a metal door set at the side of the bookstore.

"So we're breaking and entering for our first real date? Nice."

"I have permission," he says.

I raise my eyebrows at him, a grin pulling up my lips. "And that's why you're using magic to unlock the doors?"

He smiles at me as the lock pops open and he throws the door wide. "After you."

The Last Bookstore is the epitome of old-fashioned charm. Cedar shelves stretch way over our heads so that a rolling ladder has to be used to access the books on the top. Velvety red carpeting covers the spiral staircase that twists up to a second floor, and the ceiling is painted in an elaborate fantasy mural. The scent of musty books and coffee beans linger in the air.

He takes my hand, his big and warm and callused around mine, and I feel the thrill of it like it's the first time I've ever had my hand held by a boy. Thoughts of Mom and Paige and Cruz and Aunt Penny push into my mind, but I push them right back out, because I need this right now. I need normal. As normal as breaking into a bookstore after closing time is.

He leads me upstairs, through the aisles, to a door set into a back wall. The door opens to a staircase. We climb up, and when we emerge through the door at the top, we're on the roof. I suck in a breath. Los Angeles unfolds before me, a city teaming with palm trees and vibrant-colored buildings and *life*. And beyond it all, set into a lush mountaintop, is the Hollywood sign.

"So we're not reading on our date," I say.

"Did I have you worried?"

I grin at him. "A little bit."

He reaches into his bag and pulls out a big red blanket, then fans it out in front of him.

"Have a seat, m'lady," he says. I smile coyly at him and duck into a spot on the blanket. He reaches back into his bag and pulls out a box of Pop-Tarts, followed by a package of juice boxes and some Fruit Roll-Ups.

"What is that, Mary Poppins's bag?" I ask.

"Nope, no magic on this date," he says. "It's a one hundred percent normal date. Or else I wouldn't be serving PB&Js for the main course." He produces a bag of smushed sandwiches.

"Oh, whoops," he says.

I can't help giggling.

I watch my boyfriend, his brow furrowed in childlike concentration as he arranges our ghetto picnic across the blanket, and all I can think is that I wouldn't be happier if he'd taken me to a five-star restaurant.

And God, there it is again, that guilt stamping down my happiness. Here's my boyfriend, doing all of this for me after every awful thing I put him through. After Cruz.

He catches my wrist suddenly, and I gasp.

"Don't," he says.

"What?" I ask, heat staining my cheeks.

"Don't think about it. Everything that happened is in the past."

"But, but there are things you should know. . . ." I force

myself to look up at him, letting the guilt show through in my eyes. His throat moves up and down as he swallows.

"It's okay," he says finally. His dark eyes burn into mine, and in this instant I know he knows. He knows I did something wrong—not exactly what—but he doesn't care. Or if he does, he forgives me. I nod, and he lets go of my wrist.

"Now turn that frown upside down," he says. "We're having fun tonight."

I force a smile and dig into a package of Pop-Tarts, cradling one in my lap as Bishop pulls the wrapper off the straw of his juice box with his teeth. He spits it out over his shoulder and punctures the top with the straw.

"So, what's your favorite color," he asks cheerily, like we didn't just have this intense moment.

I tilt my head, thinking, the setting sun warming my face. "I dunno. I guess I don't really have one."

"If you had to pick."

"I guess red," I say. "I like red lipstick and red nail polish."

"Red's a bangin' color," he says. "Mine's black."

"Black's not really a color."

"Depends who you ask. What's your favorite movie?"

"Easy. *She's the Man*."

"*She's the Man?*" he asks dubiously. "I've never heard of it."

I laugh. "It's this totally awesome comedy about this girl who dresses up like a boy so she can try out for their soccer team. There's this one scene where one of the boys on the team finds a tampon in her bag, and she sticks it up her nose and pretends she uses it for nosebleeds. . . ." I trail off at the look of horror on Bishop's face. We both burst into laughter. "It's much funnier in the movie."

"We have to watch it sometime."

I smile. "I'd love that." A beat passes in comfortable silence. "So," I say finally. "What's your favorite movie?"

"Don't have one," he answers.

"If you had to pick," I say.

He thinks for a moment. "Then it'd be a three-way tie between *The Goonies, Super Troopers,* and *I Love You, Man.*"

"*Super Troopers*? I love that movie! 'All right, meow, hand over your license and registration.'"

"'You boys like Mex-*i*-co?'" he adds. We both roar with laughter.

I can't believe we have the same taste in stupid one-star comedies.

"How 'bout books?" he asks.

"Hmm. That's hard. Maybe *Gone with the Wind*?"

"Really?" His eyebrows get lost in his hairline.

"Why is that so shocking?" I ask.

"Isn't that, like, three thousand pages?"

I slap his arm, and he laughs.

"So what are you going to do now? With me back at school and everything."

He shrugs. "I dunno. I guess drown my sorrows in booze and strippers."

I mock-scowl at him, and he laughs, but it dies quickly and unexpectedly turns into a sigh. He traces a pattern on the roof with a finger. "I have thought about it, actually. There's this boarding school . . . for witches and warlocks." He looks up at me from behind a twist of hair that's fallen in front of his face.

I sit up a bit straighter. "Yeah. Penny told me about that."

"I was thinking about applying there. Like, as a teacher."

My mouth drops open.

"Flies are going to get in there." He reaches over and closes my jaw.

I sputter for words. "Wh-where is that?"

"New York."

"New York!" I repeat.

"Is that a problem?" he asks.

"Problem? No." Well, besides the second heartbeat that's started in my stomach. But the more I think about it, I guess I can't expect him to just play with Lumpkins in his mansion all day until I get off school. I mean, he's this amazingly powerful warlock, and he has a life too. It strikes me then that if he were with someone closer to his own age, like, say, Irena from the Black Market, this wouldn't be a problem. They could just go together, travel the world. I still have another year and a half of high school.

"We'd still see each other," he says, as if reading my

thoughts. "I do have this nifty teleportation trick up my sleeve."

Well. That *is* a bit reassuring. I give him a ghost of a smile.

"Anyway, it was just something I was thinking about," he says. "Let's not talk about that now."

He smiles at me—a winking smile that makes my insides melt and all thoughts of boarding school fly out of my head. He's going to kiss me—he's going to do a lot more than kiss me. But I'm not going to wait for him to make a move.

I set down my Pop-Tart.

"What are you doing?" he asks.

Brushing the crumbs from my skirt, I step over the picnic until I'm standing over him, and he has to crane his neck to look up at me. He starts to get up too, but I push his shoulders down and straddle his lap. His eyes go wide at the way my skirt rumples up my thighs.

"First," I say, "I want you to know I'm not upset or vulnerable or anything else right now. Well, I am, but it's not clouding my judgment. I know what I'm doing, okay? So don't try to stop me. Unless, of course, you want me to stop, you know, for your own reasons, which would be totally okay—"

He takes my head in his hands and shuts me up with the barest of kisses. Soft and featherlight. A buzz of warmth travels down into my belly. I pull my fingers through the silk of his hair as he takes my mouth deeper and harder, his arms coming up around my body like he wants to devour me. When his fingers dig into my hips, my body turns to fire.

But then he stops suddenly and pulls back, looking intently into my eyes.

"Indie," he says.

"What?" I ask, out of breath. What could he possibly have to say right now that would make him interrupt the best kiss of my life?

"I love you."

My breath catches at the unexpected words, my heart fluttering like a bird trapped in a cage.

"I love you too," I say.

And I know it's true. Whatever happened with Cruz was messed up and wrong and inexcusable, but it doesn't change the fact that I love Bishop. And I'm going to spend the rest of my life proving it to him.

"I love you," I repeat.

Saying the words, I can't help but think of our odds. Some new band of sorcerers could attack us again. Bishop could go to New York and love it so much he decides never to come back. He could meet someone else, someone his own age. There are a thousand reasons it wouldn't work between us, way more reasons than it ever would. But sitting here, with Bishop's arms solidly around me, our odds don't scare me.

I'll take my chances.

Acknowledgments

This book exists because of the support I received from a host of amazing people.

Sincere thank-yous to:

Adriann Ranta, for her incredible business savvy and endless patience, but most of all, for "getting it." (Hopefully she knows what I mean.)

Wendy Loggia, for her kindness, sharp insight, and unswerving enthusiasm. I'm forever grateful to be under her wing.

Beverly Horowitz and the entire team at Delacorte Press, for making this book and its predecessor a reality. Particular thanks to Alison Impey, for creating not one but two covers I fell in love with; Nicole Banholzer and Sadie Trambetta, for handling publicity for my books; the copyediting department, for saving me from my own embarrassing mistakes; Stephanie O'Cain and the marketing team, for getting my book out there; and everyone who I've never spoken with but who have undoubtedly done more than their fair share for my books (Krista Vitola, I'm looking at you!). Thanks also to Amy Black, Pamela Osti, and the rest of the team at Double-day Canada for helping my book reach Canadian readers.

Brandy Allard, for putting up with years of conversation monopoly and always believing in me even when I didn't. (It's your turn. And yes, you *can* do it.)

Ruth Lauren Steven, for reading everything—sometimes two, three, and four times—giving me critical insight that manages to make me laugh, and letting me know when I'm being a miserable cow.

Amy Plum, for giving me a stellar blurb for *Hexed*. I'm honored to have her name on my books.

Amy Tintera, for not missing a beat when I said, "So say Los Angeles was a prison city for the paranormal divided into two rival gang territories—how would you split that up?" Thanks also for the very kind blurb for *Hexed*.

Everyone in Gunning for Awesome—Natalie C. Parker, Stephanie Winkelhake, Gemma Cooper, Deborah Hewitt, Amy Christine Parker, Lori M. Lee, Corinne Duyvis, Kim Welchons, and again, Ruth Lauren Steven and Amy Tintera—for the long emails filled with wisdom, insight, and belly laughs. Thanks also for brainstorming a title for this book, even though we eventually went in another direction. (It's a crying shame *Hex Pot 2: Bound and Waxed* didn't make the final cut.)

My blog, Twitter, Tumblr, and Facebook followers, for making this whole process fun.

The authors of OneFour KidLit, for being such amazing supports during the debut process (and for the bourbon and donuts).

Amanda Pedulla from Chapters in Thunder Bay, for hawking my book to everyone who walks into the store. (You're the best!)

My coworkers in the NICU at the TBRHSC, for eagerly asking about my books, even when it embarrassed me to no end.

The entire Krys and Couture families, of which there are too many members to name individually, for always being so supportive and excited about my writing. Thanks especially to my sister, Crystal Couture, and my mom, Phylis Kaukanen, for the plot ideas and the dinners in sweatpants, which is really the only way to have dinner. Thanks also to Barb Hemsworth, for being the best beta reader a friend could ask for, and for always suggesting a girls' recon trip for "book research."

My long-suffering husband, Logan, for letting me disappear for hours on end while I wrote this book and for hashing out plot points when witches and sorcerers aren't exactly his thing. My books wouldn't be possible without his commitment to letting me follow my dreams. And Benjamin, for being the kind of boy moms dream of—all the success in the world wouldn't be worth it without him. (I love you to the moooon!)

Finally, a heartfelt thank-you to my readers. You're the reason I do this. Much love.

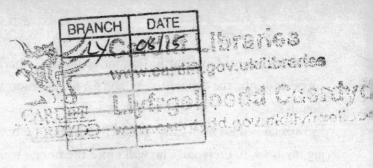

About the Author

MICHELLE KRYS is the author of *Hexed*. She lives with her husband and son in Northwestern Ontario, Canada. She works part-time as a NICU nurse and spends her free time writing books for teens. Michelle is probably not a witch, though she did belong to a witchcraft club in the fifth grade and "levitated" people in her bedroom, so that may be up for debate.

Visit Michelle online at
michellekrys.com

Follow Michelle Krys on